AFTER OIL

After Oil

SF Visions Of A Post-Petroleum World

Edited By

John Michael Greer

FOUNDERS HOUSE PUBLISHING
2012

These short stories are works of fiction. All of the characters, organizations, and events portrayed in these stories are either products of the authors' imaginations or are used factiously.

Published by Founders House Publishing, LLC
Cover design by Shaun Kilgore

www.foundershousepublishing.com

Printed in the United States of America

ISBN: 978-0-9843764-5-2

Contents

Introduction: *Facing A Different Future*
John Michael Greer
i

The Great Clean-Up
Avery Morrow
1

Autumn Night
Randall S. Ellis
7

The Urgent, The Necessary
J.D. Smith
15

The Lore Keepers
E. A. Freeman
25

Bicycleman Sakhile and the Cell Tower
Kieran O'Neill
53

Small Town Justice
David Trammel
73

Traveling Show
Philip Steiner
103

Maestra y Aprendiz
Susan Harelson
125

Caravan of Hopes
Harry J. Lerwill
141

The Going
Catherine McGuire
169

Think Like A Tinkerer
Thijs Goverde
193

Winter's Tales
John Michael Greer
221

After Oil

SF Visions Of A Post-Petroleum World

Introduction
Facing A Different Future

By John Michael Greer

S cience fiction, that fractured but often insightful mirror of the human future, has had a complicated relationship all through its history with the way the future has actually unfolded. That relationship and its complexity go straight back to the day when Mary Shelley, watching the rain ruin a Swiss vacation in the summer of 1816 as her husband's literary friends toyed with ghost stories, penned the rough draft of what most historians of the genre consider the first science fiction story.

That initial draft turned into *Frankenstein,* which became a bestseller precisely because it was believable in terms of the science of the time. Recent advances, in particular Alessandro Volta's eerie experiment with electricity that caused a frog's amputated leg to kick, made it seem entirely plausible just then that some researcher might take the next step and bring a dead body to life. That sort of extrapolation from contemporary science has been central to the genre ever since; so, equally, was the risk that the extrapolation would fail— for life, of course, turned out to be quite a bit more complex than the researchers of Shelley's time guessed, and reanimating corpses is still well out of reach of science nearly two centuries later.

That misfire did nothing to dent the enduring popularity of *Frankenstein*, or to slow the rise of the newborn genre founded on that soggy Alpine day. Take some recent innovation in science or technology, push it further in the direction it seems to be going, and see what happens—all through the 19th century, and well into the 20th, that's what science fiction (or "scientifiction," as it was often called) most often meant. Jules Verne and H.G. Wells, the two great masters of the early genre, rang just about every change on that theme that the science and technology of the age would justify. Both of them wrote voyages to the Moon, but it was just one of the many lively improbabilities they and other authors explored in their stories.

The wild card, of course, was that a good many of their ideas didn't stay improbable for long. In the first decades of the twentieth century, a generation that had grown up on Verne and Wells started putting scientifiction's dreams into practice. Captain Nemo's *Nautilus* quickly took on an uncomfortable reality as the first U-boats slid down the ways. Wells' "The Land Ironclads" provided the conceptual blueprint for the first generation of tanks, just as his *The War in the Air* got military minds around the world thinking of the possibilities of aerial bombardment. Many of the other technological notions that filled science fiction at the turn of the century got tried out by somebody or other during those

Introduction

years, and those that worked found ready acceptance among audiences that had plenty of fictional models in the back of their minds.

Meanwhile, the fictional models were shifting focus. It was in the 1920s and 1930s that science fiction stopped focusing on single scientific and technological advances, and became the vehicle for a much more grandiose vision—a mythology of limitless progress that would sweep humanity outward from Earth toward a glorious future among the stars. By the late 1940s, many science fiction writers set their stories in a common future history that began with the first voyages to the Moon and then went soaring onwards from there, colonizing the solar system, then leaping the gap that separated our solar system from others and beginning the settlement of the galaxy. Nor was this merely a setting for adventure tales; a great many of the writers and readers in the genre by then expected to see the first steps of that future history become realities in their own time.

It's a useful exercise to revisit the nonfiction written by leading SF authors in the 20th century's middle decades, and take in what they had to say about the coming Space Age. The conquest of space wasn't something they felt any need to promote or argue for; they were convinced that it was simply going to happen. Inevitably, they believed, there would be the first tentative flights into space, followed by the first Moon landing, and somewhere in there the first of many space stations would go into orbit, perhaps as a way station to the Moon. Mars and Venus were next on the agenda: first the landings, then the bases, then the colonies, growing as naturally as Jamestown or Plymouth into booming new frontier societies. The asteroids and the moons of Jupiter and Saturn would follow in due order, followed by the outer planets, and then would come the challenge of the stars. The only alternative seriously considered was apocalypse, nuclear or otherwise, and even there the more hopeful authors saw this as nothing more than a temporary delay to the great onward march to the heavens.

It's all the more remarkable that this grand vision emerged at a time when science fiction was still considered the last word in lowbrow reading. Until the paperback revolution of the late 1950s, most SF appeared in pulp magazines—so called because of the wretched paper they were printed on—with trashy covers on the front and ads for X-ray spectacles and Charles Atlas strength lessons in the back. The cheap mass-marketed paperbacks that picked up from the pulps dropped the ads but by and large kept the tacky cover art. ("There has been a great deal of talk over the years about the 'big questions' of science fiction," SF author L. Sprague de Camp said at a science fiction convention I attended many years ago. "The one truly big question of science fiction is 'What is that woman in a brass brassiere doing on the cover of my novel?'") As for the stories themselves—well, there were a handful of very good authors, de Camp among them, and some very good short stories and novels, but there was much, much more that was really, astonishingly bad.

Still, just as the young engineers and military officers of 1910 grew up reading Jules Verne and H.G. Wells, and acted on that reading, when America stumbled into its age of empire after the Second World War, a very large number of its young men (and a smaller but still significant fraction of its young women) grew up daydreaming of rockets to Mars and adventures with the Space Patrol. All that was required to make those daydreams a powerful force in the American psyche was a well-aimed shock, and that was supplied in 1957 when a small group of Soviet scientists and military officers talked their superiors into letting them strap a 22-inch steel sphere on top of a big new ICBM and launch it into Earth orbit.

Sputnik I sent the United States into something halfway between a tantrum and a nervous breakdown. Suddenly it became essential, in the minds of a great many Americans, for the US to beat "godless Russia" in the Space Race. For their part, delighted to have found an effective way to goad the United States, Soviet leaders started putting real money into their space program, scoring one achievement after another while Americans played what was at first a feeble game of catch-up. Before long, smarting from the string of Soviet triumphs, a new US president proclaimed a project to put men on the moon, the first rockets were blasting off from Cape Canaveral, and a nation already fascinated by outer space, and alternately amused and intrigued by the space-centered folk mythology of the UFO phenomenon, signed on to the opening stages of the grand future history sketched out for them by decades of pulp science fiction.

For the next decade and a half or so, the extraordinary dream of a future among the stars shaped the decisions of politicians and the public alike. By the time the Apollo program was well underway, staff at NASA were already sketching out the next generation of manned spacecraft that would follow the Moon landing, and cutting blueprints and contracts for the probes that would begin the exploration of the solar system. That's when things started to run off the rails to the stars, because the solar system revealed by those

Introduction

probes turned out to have very little in common with the "New Worlds for Man" that the fantasies required.

It takes some reading in old books on the prospects of space travel to grasp just how wide a gap those first planetary probes opened up. Respected scientists were claiming as late as the 1960s that the Moon was a world of romantic vistas with needle-pointed mountains glinting under starlight; it turned out to be gray, largely featureless, and stunningly dull. Venus was supposed to be warmer than Earth but still probably inhabitable, and C.S. Lewis' classic *Perelandra* was only one of hundreds of novels that portrayed it as a jungle world; the first Venus probes revealed instead a searing furnace of a world with surface temperatures hot enough to melt metal.

Since 19th century astronomers mistook optical effects of telescopes pushed to their limit for markings on the Martian surface, Mars had been the great anchor for dreams of alien life and offworld adventure; when the first Viking lander touched down in 1976, the ancient canals and four-armed swordsmen of Edgar Rice Burroughs' Barsoom went wherever dreams go to die, and were duly replaced by what looked for all of either world like an unusually boring corner of Nevada, minus water, air, and life. As gorgeous photos of one uninhabitable world after another found their way into lavish *National Geographic* articles, you could all but hear the air leaking out of the dream of space.

There was another factor, too, that emerged right about the same time that the hothouse visions of Barsoom and Perelandra dissolved into barren rocks spinning through hard vacuum. The vision of limitless progress central not only to science fiction, but to the entire ideology of industrial civilization, ran into the unwelcome reality of limits to growth. In

Introduction

the 1970s, as US petroleum production peaked and began its irreversible decline, the first round of energy shortages hobbled the developed world, and the feckless optimism that insisted that pollution couldn't be a problem found itself confronted by a rising spiral of financial and human costs driven by industrial humanity's unwillingness to clean up after itself.

In the decades that followed, ignoring the implications of those twin encounters became a major growth industry. Ronald Reagan swept into office insisting "It's morning in America," and pundits, politicians, and ordinary citizens alike did their level best to ignore the awkward details that contradicted that breezy promise—the unraveling of America's infrastructure, the sacrifice of its industrial economy and its working class, the repeated Ponzi schemes that heaped up hallucinatory wealth to absurd heights, and of course the slow and shamefaced abandonment of the space program and the dream that drove it. As predicted decades before, "peak oil"—that is, the peak of global production of conventional petroleum—arrived right after the beginning of the new millennium; as predicted decades before, none of the alternatives turned out to be viable without immense and unsustainable government subsidies; soaring energy costs accordingly percolated through the world's economies, tipping nation after nation into financial and political crisis, and the aging dream of perpetual progress came slowly and silently apart.

And science fiction? It fragmented and faded. The early successes of the space program gave science fiction a larger and more critical market, and this midwifed some of the greatest works of the genre; a series of loudly ballyhooed literary movements, none of them long-lived, zoomed off in assorted directions and, as avant-garde movements generally do, left most of their audience behind; efforts at crass commercial exploitation, of which the *Star Wars* franchise was the most lucrative example, came swooping in for their share of the kill. While other media boomed—visual media are always a couple of decades behind print—sales of science fiction novels peaked in the late 1970s and early 1980s and then began a decline that still continues, and a genre that had once exercised potent gravitational effects on the collective psyche turned into just another option in the smorgasbord of mass-produced popular entertainment.

There were plenty of reasons for that transformation, but one of them, it seems to me, was central. Science fiction spent most of its formative years, and produced a good many of its major classics, at a time when it was basically a collection of wish-fulfillment fantasies for teenage boys. (And that, Mr. de Camp, is what the woman in the brass brassiere was doing on the cover of your novel.) Even the most lurid fantasy, though, depends for effect on what has been called "the willing suspension of disbelief." If the absurdities pile up too far, as J.R.R. Tolkien commented in a characteristically acerbic passage, disbelief has not so much to be suspended as hanged, drawn, and quartered.

Thus there was always pressure on SF authors to check their facts and make the details consistent. As SF fandom became a significant force on the evolution of the genre, the sort of geeky obsessiveness you find in teenage fans of anything became a badge of honor, and pushed the process further. Before long, it was no longer enough to tell a rousing tale about square-jawed space captains and nubile females on a distant planet; no matter how hackneyed the plot and two-dimensional the characters might be, the planet had to make some kind of sense in terms of current scientific knowledge, and so did the hero's laser pistol, the tentacled horrors that menaced the heroine, and the rest of it. Even when authors made things up out of whole cloth, as of course they did constantly, they had to figure out some way to graft the invention onto existing knowledge so that the seam didn't show too clearly.

Even before science fiction hit the big time in the wake of Sputnik I, the demand for believability had become one of the essential elements of the genre. The dismissal of legendary SF editor Raymond Palmer from the senior position at *Amazing Stories* in 1948 was arguably the turning point in the process. Palmer had made the Ziff-Davis pulp chain an astronomical amount of money with a mix of trashy science fiction, popular occultism, and highly dubious alternative science, but the higher-ups at Ziff-Davis sensed the way the market was moving. Palmer ended up at the helm of a new magazine, *Fate*, that for all practical purposes created the New Age movement, while SF took a different path.

Unexpectedly, science fiction's unscientific twin, fantasy fiction—which had a similar prehistory in the pulp magazines and broke through into respectability roughly a decade after SF did—followed much the same trajectory. To some extent this was driven by the overlapping readership of the two genres, but of course there was another factor as well: the force of nature already mentioned that went by the name of J.R.R. Tolkien. There was plenty of fantasy fiction before *The Lord of the Rings*, to be sure, but none that succeeded so stunningly in evoking the presence of another world with its own history, languages, cultures and conflicts. In Tolkien's wake, fantasy authors who hoped to get away with the casual disregard for plausibility that ran riot through Robert Howard's Conan stories, among many others, started getting rejection slips in place of contracts. Expectations had changed, and the genre changed with it.

By and large—with important exceptions, to be sure—those expectations remained glued in place in both genres for a good long time, and when a book failed to live up to them, you could count on a raucous response from the fans. Sometimes this went to remarkable lengths. Among others, *Analog Science Fiction*—under its original title, *Astounding*, the great rival of Palmer's *Amazing*—for many decades had an abundance of retired engineers among its loyal readership. Get a story published in *Analog*, and you had thousands of pairs of beady and remarkably well-informed eyes scanning every scientific detail. If you got something wrong, in turn, you could expect to hear about it at length, complete with calculations hot off the slide rule, in the letters to the editor column two issues down the road.

While this may seem extreme—and it often was—it reflects the extraordinary feature of science fiction already mentioned: those who were passionate about the genre didn't expect it to stay fictional for long. Getting the details right was important, to a great many fans and no small number of writers, because the fans and the writers alike believed that the stories were tracing out, in a very real sense, the future trajectory of our species.

That, I've come to think, is the conviction that trickled away as science fiction peaked in the 1970s and 1980s and began its own decline. Human nature being what it is, one of the first signs of its faltering was an effort to close ranks

Introduction

around the failing belief. Support for the space program took on a nearly religious intensity, and so did crusades to purify science fiction, and society as a whole, of the legacy of the Raymond Palmer era—the popular occultism and folk science that formed so important a part of late 20th century American alternative culture, in and out of science fiction, and provided believers in the dream of progress with a convenient scapegoat on which the waning of the dream could be blamed. All these efforts failed, as they had to, because what stood in the way of infinite progress wasn't a lack of zeal or the spread of intellectual heresies; it was the simple and immovable fact that the universe hadn't gotten around to supplying humanity with energy resources limitless enough to make the dream come true.

Just as the conviction that science fiction traced the future's trajectory in advance gave the genre its power, in turn, the loss of that conviction has left it floundering, spinning tales in stereotyped futures that nobody quite believes any more. One consequence is a curious atrophy of the imagination that makes it remarkably difficult for writers to envision any future that isn't simply a continuation of the present. There are plenty of traces of that in the SF of an earlier era, to be sure; read such classics of the genre as Isaac Asimov's *Foundation* trilogy, for example, and the social customs of the decade when the stories were written stick out on every page. Still, the atrophy has become much more evident in recent years. Consider the recent bestseller *Anathem* by Neal Stephenson. This is not only set on another world but takes place at a point in its history more than 3400 years past the equivalent of our own time, but characters wear T-shirts, eat energy bars, and use cell phones to call each other or access the equivalent of the internet.

It shouldn't even need to be pointed out that even if we get through the crises of our age the way the people of Stephenson's world got through the period they call the Terrible Events, and create a technological society on the far side of it, our descendants won't be wearing T-shirts or calling people on cell phones in the year 5400 AD, any more than we wear togas or take notes on wax tablets the way the ancient Romans did. They'll wear other clothing and communicate with other tools—and with any luck they'll snack on something less repellent than energy bars. Back in the day, science fiction fairly often caught wind of such shifts; sometimes it succeeded in guessing them in advance; tolerably often, for that matter, what started out as imagery from science fiction became the inspiration for design in the real world—I trust nobody thinks that it's accidental that most early cell phones looked remarkably like the communicators from the original version of *Star Trek*.

That capacity for sensing the possible shape of the future, and even influencing it now and then, is something the world badly needs right now. The concerted effort to ignore the limits to growth—an effort that's been a massive social force in the industrial world for three decades now—has had many effects, but making those limits go away isn't one of them. We thus stand on the brink of a cascade of social and technological changes at least as dramatic as those that followed Sputnik I, but this time there isn't a body of colorful and thoughtful fiction exploring the meanings and possibilities of the approaching era. The literature of the future we have instead still fixates on the twin mirages of technological progress and technological apocalypse—both of them, please note, narratives of human omnipotence, playing off either end of the old paradox that asks whether man can create a crisis so big not even he can get it out of his way—at a time when we need to be talking instead about technological decline, about the difficult process of downshifting from a way of life that demands more energy and more raw materials than the future can offer us, and about the challenges and triumphs that people will face in that future.

We need, in other words, a literature willing to discuss how humanity might deal with peak oil and the limits to growth—deal with them, not evade them. It's all very well to insist that petroleum and other fossil fuels can be replaced by some other equally cheap and abundant energy resource, or that we can still have an industrial system churning out plenty of consumer products in the absence of cheap abundant energy, but those claims have been retailed endlessly in fiction and public relations for decades now, and the future is showing no signs of cooperating. Nor is there much point, it seems to me, in another rehash of the notion that friendly aliens will land in flying saucers to solve all humanity's problems, or of some equivalent *deus ex machina* that are supposed to bail us out of the consequences of our own decisions—conveniently timed leaps in consciousness, divine interventions, divine interventions in cybernetic drag such as Ray Kurzweil's Singularity mythology, and the rest of it. All of that has been done to death in and out of science fiction, and here again, the future shows no signs of cooperating.

In the most likely futures ahead of us, rather, people in the currently industrial world are going to have to learn to get by with much less energy, and far fewer of the products of

Introduction

energy, than their equivalents have to hand today. They will have to cope with the complex legacies of the industrial age, and with the lingering social, political, and ecological consequences of any number of past and present mistakes. Like people in every age, nonetheless, a fair number of them are going to live challenging, interesting, and even appealing lives, and confront the challenges of their own time with some hope of success.

This last, to my mind, is the most crucial point. There's nothing easier, in fiction or out of it, than wallowing in the pornography of despair—insisting that life isn't worth living in the absence of cheap energy and its comforts and conveniences, say, or in the presence of widespread poverty, illness and warfare. The vast majority of humanity's existence on this planet has been spent in exactly the conditions so many people nowadays find unthinkable, though, and somehow our ancestors found life worth living in spite of it all. There's nothing to be gained by sugarcoating the deindustrial future, to be sure; there are good reason to think that we've got plenty of hard times ahead; but it's only in the imaginations of the overprivileged that such times have to consist of unrelieved wretchedness. Nor, of course, are such troubled times empty of possibilities for the storyteller.

It was with all this in mind that my weekly blog, *The Archdruid Report*, threw down a gauntlet in the fall of 2011. I asked readers to try their hand at science fiction short stories set in a world when today's abundant energy have become a thing of the past, and the limits to growth have become an unavoidable presence in everyday life. The twelve stories that follow are among the very best of the many responses I received. They offer diverse glimpses of future

Introduction

worlds in which the old certainties of the age of space have long since faded, leaving new challenges to be faced alongside the enduring problems and possibilities of human existence.

All science fiction deals in some way with technology, but these stories ask us to rethink what counts as high technology in an age of decline—a collection of books, a new use for bicycles, a surviving laptop computer, a slide rule handed down across generations. In the process, they challenge us to face a future that differs drastically from the one that science fiction used to offer, but shares several crucial factors with that older vision: an orientation toward unexpected possibilities; an attentiveness to the directions in which our societies and our species might be headed over the long term; and, improbable as it may seem to those whose minds have been jaded by the last century's parade of technological marvels, a sense of wonder and hope.

—Cumberland, Maryland
4 February 2012

The Great Clean-Up

By Avery Morrow

A cathedral built of garbage, standing on a dump—sublime, sublime! A lotus flower growing from our own shit! Even from afar, the eye waters at the sight; around us, women and men alike are falling prostrate to the ground, overcome with—what? Gratitude? Justice? Awe? Or the sense that this is what the world needs, what should have happened so long ago? The tongue struggles to find the right word, but the image is before us. The mountains of crushed video game consoles, the valleys of food waste and maggots, the rivers of running mercury and arsenic—in the midst of it, could there be any triumph more human, more victorious over our baser nature, than the windows and towers of Her Holiness St. Acharya of the Landfill?

The scene at the cathedral should be chaos, for people are pressing in for a glimpse of the saint. There are too many to reasonably fit inside the cathedral walls, and the crowds overflow from every door, but the atmosphere is one of com-

1

plete peace and acceptance. We have come from cities that are falling apart, friends and families pressed uncomfortably close by sorrow and disease and ruin, warnings all around us that all is lost and there is no way out. But here, in the desolate place the system had found the least useful, the place where we put the things we have given up on, here in Gehenna springs hope.

Twenty years ago, driven far from Los Angeles by brownouts and food shortages, an unemployed management consultant wandered by herself through the Frank R. Bowerman Landfill, hungry and tired and beset with agony at the uselessness of the human struggle. Then, at 2:33 PM (or some time; it had to happen at some point) she caught a glimpse of something in the corner of her eye; slowly she began to scan the trash piles, stack empty paint cans, drag the husks of cars across the rubbish. It was futile, it was ugly, it wasn't helping anything, it didn't even look like anything. Why was she doing it? Could the explanation be found in art history, Marxist theory, psychological investigation, teleological inspiration? She couldn't have told you herself. Does the answer even matter? All we know is that a week later, a cell phone salesman looking for unspoiled food saw the base of the temple and gasped. The next day, her friend the tech support representative came to the site and could not believe his eyes. After that there were five visitors, a dozen, a hundred. "This is it," someone said. "I want to stay here," said someone else. "This is where we belong." Now the saint (for she was a saint already in the eyes of the pilgrims) had a posse of volunteers. Now there was food flowing into the church, green vegetables in the black rubbish, when no food could be found outside. Now the Dalai Lama is visiting; now the

Pope; now the President, and now that's the story the parents are telling their children as they walk across the 50 million tons of waste to the Pure Land at the end.

It's not in the news anymore, of course. It was a human interest story for a few weeks, Millions Flock To Landfill, and then things moved along to starvation in India, North Pole disappearing, Internet infrastructure at risk of failure. But few have the ability to watch the news anymore. The cheery, well-fed fellows who enjoy that privilege are uninterested in the strange new habits of the teeming masses. Let us leave those relics of the past behind, for the vast majority clamors for a cosmic redemption of the human species, and that hunger that seems to penetrate every aspect of life is satisfied by witnessing the creation of Her Holiness. Perhaps more monuments are not far behind; perhaps a new means of communicating with oneself and the universe is being found, and a new world will spring from the ashes of the old. At this point we only know the truths within ourselves; we know that all the unspeakable, crushing depression we could not understand has been transformed into a brilliant light, and we feel as if we are all newborns.

And look; we have talked too long; the saint is emerging! She is old, and she wears the excess output of an online T-shirt peddler, and she carries in her hands a vase that holds a weakly flower from her personal garden. The crowd rises to its feet, not to see the tricks of a magician or applaud the platitudes of a glorified con artist, but to comprehend. They are still. They do not fear, for Saint Acharya has never disappointed. But their excitement does not overwhelm their thoughts; the crowd listens with all its might.

Sitting on a plastic lawn chair, setting down the flower beside her, Her Holiness speaks:

"This is the Great Clean-Up.

"We built our home, and our home collapsed. It was an accident. There is no time to feel guilt, or regret, or anger. We must build again and take more care than we ever have before.

"All our striving in the past was for a false heaven where we pushed out everything we disliked. But as long as the world is finite and changing there can be no permanent heaven. We must always remember the consequences of our actions. We must always remember that when we tried to impose this heaven in our minds, our doubts and sufferings were pushed to forgotten corners, a hell within ourselves. We must always remember that when we tried to impose this heaven in our cities and towns, we produced with our thoughtlessness countless hells on Earth where we left unneeded things to rot forever.

"There will be no more heavens in this impermanent world and there will be no more hells. Now there will only be human beings, full of virtues and flaws and a little wiser for our history. Now there will only be the one undivided Earth, the real ground where life must grow, no matter how much we abused it in the past.

"Too long we have neglected our trash. Too long we have taken, and taken and always disposed of what we took. But now there is nothing left to take, and there is nothing else to build with but trash. Trash could have been beauty all along; now it must be beauty; now it is our duty to make it beautiful. We must build monuments with our trash to forever remember what happened when we threw the world away.

4

The Great Clean-Up

"I did not build for myself a place of worship. I have no special honors to offer to that which we should honor at all times. I have no desire to plead for forgiveness, or to make an apology. I built this house for us so that we might understand. This is a place of hope. I built it when I saw the hope in my mind's eye. Now, if you see what I saw, there is no need for me to tell you what to do."

Her Holiness recedes, and the crowd is still. We stare at the plastic lawn chair and wonder if we have been frozen on the spot and might never move again. But eventually, one by one, in silence, we file away. Not to return to what we were doing before, because our past lives were unconscious, only glimpsing the truth through a glass darkly. No, we are not going back. We are marching forward.

Autumn Night

By Randall S. Ellis

> *The world is as unstable as the pools and shallows of Asuka River. Times change and things disappear: joy and sorrow come and go; a place that once thrived turns into an uninhabited moor; a house may remain unaltered but its occupants will have changed. The peach and the damson tree in the garden say nothing—with whom is one to reminisce about the past?*
>
> –Kenko

Arthur walked through the pale autumn moonlight, occasionally scattering the brittle leaves that covered the surface of what had once been a prosperous suburban street. It never ceased to amaze him, even after ten years, how rapidly things had changed. How the sanguine middle-class world of backyard barbecues, soporific evenings of television, and the religion of ever-increasing prosperity had dissolved before his eyes. On quiet residential streets like this one, middle-class fathers would putter about on Saturday mornings with power mowers cropping small patches of

grass; and later perhaps would drive car loads of small ur-
chins to crowded theaters suffused with the odors of popcorn
and chocolate.

Now the cars stood derelict, their rusting hulks in evidence everywhere. The cinemas had now become palaces of
worship: crowds of ragged, cold and hungry souls huddled
before the flickering screen, upon which altar visions of Ma-
terialism Past alluringly danced before them. Hungers whet-
ted by scenes of abundance groaned with pleasure and pain in
the darkness.

Arthur had been lucky. His bookish temperament had
spared him from the delusions of the frantic consumer culture
into which he had been born. The siren call of ever greater
consumption had never held sway over a soul given to a mild
asceticism.

It was Arthur's very indifference to this spirit of the age
that had in the end saved him. While others had gone mad
through despair and frustrated longing at even the thought of
the gilded-sty running dry; he had quietly sat amongst his
books drinking coffee (of which he was inordinately fond),
and taking the nightly walks which he greatly relished. Em-
bracing a life of voluntary poverty had meant that he had
changed little while an entire world had convulsed about him.

An autumn wind rustled the elm leaves and he drew his
scarf more tightly about him. He hesitated briefly, stared at
the leaden October sky as a waft of smoke passed over the
autumn moon, then breathed deeply of the scent of mulching
leaves and walked on.

He looked about him at the tract houses that lined the
street; their yards were denuded of trees, which had long ago
been cut for fuel, and the grass had given way to vegetable

8

gardens. The picture windows were boarded over to conserve heat and the paint was peeling from bare walls.

He approached a long familiar house of weathered gray brick. Weeds laden with autumn frost surrounded it, giving it a forlorn appearance. Arthur was greeted at the door by the aged Professor Hardisty, dressed in his usual baggy trousers and shabby jacket. He looked all of his sixty-five years with his gray hair and beard.

The interior was dimly lit by a small coal fire that cast a pale glow over a room filled to the bursting with books. Books lined the walls and were piled on the floor in tumbling heaps. What few articles of furniture there were, a couch and a table, were also repositories of books. There was that mellow odor of old books mingled with that of brewing coffee: a heady combination for any book lover.

Animated conversation greeted them as they entered the kitchen. Five men in threadbare attire were seated about an old kitchen table. Friday evenings for years they had met at their various lodgings to discuss books and the past. Antiquarians and bibliophiles, they chattered endlessly over books and ideas that had long ceased to matter to anyone but themselves.

"I remember the secondhand bookshops," said Larkin, "row upon row of books crammed indiscriminately from floor to ceiling, and all of them begging to be purchased...and for so little, really. How many afternoons I have spent rummaging amongst the stacks, oblivious to all the world! I would purchase a few chosen volumes, and with the exhilarating euphoria that comes from finding a long-sought book return to my lodgings. I had something of a ritual that went along with getting new books. I would put some coffee on to brew, then settle myself in a snug overstuffed chair before the fire and contemplate each volume, longingly wiping the dust of neglect from their covers. Then later, between sips of coffee, I would lovingly turn their pages dreaming of the ever greater enjoyment that would come from reading them."

There was a general sigh of assent from around the table. The others had spent many such evenings.

Books were now things of the past. Paper shortages had dwindled the torrent of publications to a mere trickle, and that mainly of government publications, massive volumes of statistics and law. Old books had suffered an even worse fate. They were now sold on street corners by ragged hawkers to heat the ramshackle homes of suburbia.

Professor Hardisty shuffled about the table filling mugs with hot coffee, which sent spirals of steam into the kitchen air. Homes were now impossible to heat properly because of shoddy construction and the scarcity of fuel.

"I shall have to make more coffee," said Professor Hardisty, as he picked up a small plastic bucket and walked to the back door. He stopped briefly at the threshold and peered into the darkness trying to discern if muggers were lurking near the community well.

"Professor Hardisty will outlast us all," said Saunders as he watched the aged figure slowly make his way along a well-trodden dirt path.

Professor Hardisty was a superannuated professor of literature, who had formerly taught at a state college. When the Great Decline had begun he was retired on a small pension. He had spent the last ten years reading books and writing unpublished essays.

Autumn Night

Arthur had been a clerk in a secondhand bookshop, one of the few remaining even then. It was housed in a large Victorian brownstone, weathered with that patina of age that complements so well a bookshop. Arthur made little money but it had been the happiest time of his life. Days spent rummaging about searching for obscure volumes to satisfy a patron's needs. Even the mundane tasks which others might have found objectionable such as dusting books and shelving new acquisitions, he took a real pleasure in performing. Autumn afternoons with the pale sunlight filtering through the book filled windows fronting the shop, and he behind the counter reading a book. Later, after closing, he would make his way through the leaf strewn streets with a pleasant autumn wind biting at his face, to a room above an old clothing store. Here he would make a frugal but satisfying repast of buttered bread and coffee. They were fond memories.

It was here at the bookshop that Arthur had met the men seated about the table. Professor Hardisty on hands and knees scouring the bottom shelves for old Victorian novels. Saunders complaining in his timid and ineffectual way about the dearth of good books to be had, and then going off into the stacks mumbling to himself to emerge an hour later with three or four books in hand. These were memories now faded into the past.

Arthur silently gained their attention by placing a large package wrapped in tattered brown paper on the table. There was no mistaking its content: it was a book, and as such became the immediate object of curiosity. Gingerly Arthur unwrapped it, laying aside the brown paper for reuse.

It was a large book enclosed in a frayed slipcase. Arthur turned the spine toward those seated that they might read the title on it: *The People of the Abyss* by Jack London.

"I've not seen a copy of that in years," said Larkin, "not since the libraries closed. It was difficult to find even then, I remember."

The book was passed around the table as delicate and loving hands admired its cream-colored, acid-free paper and beautiful jet-black typography.

"How ironic in a way," said Larkin, "that the living conditions Jack London found so appalling are now those of the majority of mankind."

Arthur glanced about the ragged figures huddled at the table and thought to himself how true the statement was. In the sputtering glow of the candle he looked deeply into the hardened, unshaved faces, creased and worn by years of worry over food and warmth: the plight of modern man. It was the face of the present; it was the face of the future.

The hour grew late and one by one they went into the darkness of the autumn night to return to cold lodgings with shabby furnishings. But Arthur knew they were the fortunate ones with their books and dreams of the past.

As he walked from the house Arthur could just see Larkin on his bicycle receding into the distance; the autumn leaves in clouds swirling around his worn gray overcoat. Once Larkin had been a librarian, long ago, when there were libraries. It must have been six years ago, reminisced Arthur, when the last library had shut its doors, the books having long since gone to stoke the heating stoves of the city. Larkin now worked at odd jobs, as did all of them, picking up small change here and there. Then, too, he scavenged about the deserted parts of the city as did everybody else. But this, necessarily, was becoming less fruitful as the years wore on.

He walked on in the moonlight, his eyes surveying the cracks in the buckled sidewalk where the weeds had begun to force their way through. He must be careful here, for several times the loose soles of his shoes had been torn irreparably on the jagged cracks; and shoes were becoming impossible to find. The new shoes, made of an artificial leather cardboard-like substance, wore out within a month, and anyway, only the rich could afford them. Yet Arthur didn't worry greatly about this, for the Friday evenings always put him in a good mood. It was nice even for a mere hour or two to be around others who spoke of books and things past; it made the dreary monotony of the present more bearable.

It had been an especially good evening, really. The ersatz coffee tasted good and the conversation was memorable. And then he had the weekend before him, always pleasant to contemplate. It was true that he must devote most of Saturday morning to searching for wood to burn in the heating stove. Yet, even this pastime was enjoyable mostly. He would return to his rooms with its books and overstuffed chair. There he would sit before the fire reading Lamb's *Essays of Elia* or Grossmith's *Diary of a Nobody*.

Yes, life was not bad now, not as it had been at first during the famines and strikes. Then there were riots and all the world seemed crumbling before his eyes. Now people like himself and Larkin lived relatively well. He drew the tattered overcoat more closely about him and walked on into the autumn night.

The Urgent, The Necessary

By J.D. Smith

The waiting is over. Whatever they contain, the quarterly performance reviews have been distributed. Besides the relief of no longer waiting, there's a certain entertainment value in the distribution ritual. Like any number of other rituals, it is aggressively outdated, drawing on the paraphernalia of earlier times. At the end of the appointed work day, the Director himself, like his predecessors stooped and gone gray in a handful of years, oscillates among our workstations in alphabetical order rather than seniority, passing out envelopes signed across the left half of the seal and sealed again with wax on the right. The specifications for this procedure must be guarded among files at a higher level of access, or successive directors have come to believe that they are, and do not question them.

While the Director's ritual is a public performance, each of us greets the envelope with a private counterpart. Some tuck it into a pocket, or lay it slowly in a briefcase. A few crumple their envelopes, violating the folds, or grasp them by one end, like a knife handle, and hold them that way as they walk out the door. Analyst Perez sets his unopened envelope face-up on the desk and takes out a bottle of something brown and strong to toast the contents, as if he were propitiating an unknown god. On more than one occasion others have helped him continue the ceremony after work. Analyst Barton tucks the envelope into her brassiere.

Because our actions vary no more than the Director's, there is no apparently no correlation between the handling of the reports and what the handlers expect to read. "Apparently" is all that can be said, because we never discuss our reviews. There are too many other topics. On the way out this evening, or tomorrow morning, we will discuss the weather, as a matter of course, and as a factor in our work. We discuss family, sports, love lives or lack thereof, and even money. All of our small talk circles around a larger silence.

My ritual before not discussing my review—such as it is—consists of setting the envelope under a paperweight and waiting for my colleagues to leave. Then I slide it out from under the paperweight with my left hand, the one I could live without if the contents burned or shredded it, a less painful outcome than losing my position and descending from subject to object of energy calculations. I let the chunk of crystal resist, even turn over as the envelope comes free at the usual thirty-degree angle. It is long past time to think of imitating a magician pulling a tablecloth from under place settings. The bones that already are revealing themselves, precocious fossils emerging from the erosion of flesh, tell me as much. Such talents as I possess lie elsewhere.

16

The Urgent, The Necessary

At this point, when the envelope is cantilevered like a fishing pole, a diving board, a future over uncertainty, I tear open a corner and insert my right index finger. A letter opener seems too impersonal for the text that will extend my tenure for another three months or end it forever. Though I might be difficult to replace, leaving my successor with a steep learning curve, I am by no means indispensable. Analyst Montrose came to believe that he was, with predictable results, and he was widely acknowledged as the most brilliant of us all. Six years ago, on a hangover day when he merely skimmed his data sheets rather than read them cell by cell, he missed a sudden dip in projected supply and did not activate the protocol for issuing a shortage alert. The official explanation is hidden in thickets of polysyllables, saving face for the rest of us, but everyone knows the results as the Atlanta Gas Riot. When last I heard he was shining shoes near the ruins of the St. Louis Arch.

I raggedly open the flap and let the contents fall onto the desktop. At this time of day the landing is audible.

I withdraw the review and unfold it in two steady motions. Perhaps something of this magnitude in my life, if no one else's, should blossom like a paper flower in water, or perhaps it should be unveiled like a statue. It doesn't; it isn't. Instead, my recent past and near future disclose themselves as marks on a page. This time, though, the review runs to two pages: along with the usual quantitative section and its twenty items, the optional qualitative section continues at great length. The comments are handwritten in the Director's poor script, learned when almost everyone had a computer. Yet, like the rest of this ceremony, these comments are hallowed by obsolescence. All that remains for me is to sign the review

17

and indicate my agreement, or at least my acquiescence, a final antiquated touch.

Deciding whether to sign seems to call for no less care than any other part of my work, for the habits of analysis do not end with the turn of a clock's hand as the workday closes. In the last few hours terawatts of energy have in effect flowed through my synapses as I've allocated them according to source and destination. No thought, no drop, should be wasted.

That was the goal, the theoretical ideal or omega point toward which our training was directed. No shortages, no complaints, no surpluses that produced regional disparities in allowed energy use. Whither gas and gasoline? Where could brownouts settle and blackouts roll with the smallest losses of life and property?

Our performance could never attain perfection, as our instructors were the first to admit, but we were charged all day, every day with reducing the distance between the real and the ideal: the asymptotic null, better known as Zeno's arrow, forever approaching but never reaching its target.

But arrows reach their targets as we never can. The archer aims at what lies before his eyes, and only an instant separates his intent and his action. The target can only move or be moved so far in that time. We have fewer options. As the image of a star conveys only how that star appeared light years ago, the data at our disposal summarize a state of affairs that has already changed. Populations shift, firms expand and contract, or they arise and vanish like bubbles.

We could only hope to minimize the damage, like goalkeepers. Also like goalkeepers, we were given equipment, and our pay was based on performance. We've always paid for our gasoline and electricity like everyone else, but it took little from our sizeable salaries. In my first years, when cars were still common, I took drives in the country with no destination in mind. I would be lying if I said I didn't enjoy the speed and freedom, or the illusion of it, and the envious looks. Those were youthful indiscretions. That's what I keep telling myself, anyway. Whatever they were, at some point in life a man has to stop working at cross-purposes with himself. I returned to doing a good job instead of having one.

All things old are new again: I circled back to the ethos of our charter class of employees at the Energy Distribution Agency. Once the climate warmed unto volatility, floods competed with droughts and stable conditions disappeared. Even rented experts would no longer testify that these were only cyclical variations of Earth and Sun, or that we had the fuel to make and run machines that would rescue us, fetishes engineered to the tightest tolerances. At that point things were not as they had been; science began to shape policy. We were recruited from the best universities, and our pictures appeared in magazines and on websites. A newspaper called us "Stars of an age of limits," and a business journal feature story on us bore the headline "Scouts on the Pareto Frontier." We were celebrities, or as close to it as a person could get without singing or acting, and for people who didn't act or sing we were paid very well.

In spite of our means, though, many of us did not marry, as I didn't. This used to seem like coincidence, a small random cluster, but over time the pattern continued as our numbers grew, and as vacancies were filled. What started out as a prestigious job turned into a vocation, and some of us even spoke of it as a calling. Something larger than our private happiness was at stake.

This sense of vocation, or a penumbra of it, forces me to read and reread the evaluation like a sacred text. As with parsing data, I believe reading the comments hard and long enough should allow significations and shades of meaning to emerge and guide my next quarter's work, as others have discerned courses in tossed sticks, tea leaves or the entrails of a bird. Evidence for this belief waxes and wanes, or slips just beyond the horizon. Whatever I believe, it is certain that much of Arizona and New Mexico, and large portions of Texas, depend on me. All there are strangers I have made a point of not meeting or corresponding with. Personal acquaintance would cloud my judgment.

Evaluating the evaluation, I find that the quantitative section neither pleases nor surprises me. Shortages and complaints are up. So, too, are temporary surpluses, though they are resolved quickly enough; later records usually show that populations have declined as some leave for land to farm, or a place closer to work. But there is no getting around the fact that my overall efficiency ratings are down. No business has closed, no hospital blacked out without warning, no one left without supplies and turned to leather in the Western air. (I've seen pictures of what happened in Laughlin, and read several accounts. Analyst Martin hanged himself before he could be dismissed.)

The incident report section is filled with numbered entries, and incidents are never good. The larger events are accompanied by citizen complaints and bad press. Mine include browning out parts of the Phoenix area, which people don't call the Valley of the Sun that much anymore, to keep electricity going to Tucson. I sacrificed retail in favor of homes both times, but next time my decision could come down to homes versus homes. Or hospital versus hospital. The existing backup generators are aging, and replacements are slow to come online. But that's another day's set of calculations.

From the ink thickets of the comments section arise a few phrases I haven't seen since my grade school report cards, such as "seems distracted," "a slowing of response time," "appears to be engaging in non-work activities." The latter go unspecified.

Signing off on these comments, on the report as a whole, would take only a stroke of the pen. Everyone goes through peaks and valleys of productivity, and in our training we were told to expect as much. It is only necessary to acknowledge the troughs, consent to a refresher course or two, and commit to improving performance. Then all is forgiven.

Yet this time I will not seek forgiveness, as there is nothing to be forgiven. At this point in my career it is not a matter of pride: analysts either outgrow their enfant terrible stage or move into the private sector. All that prevents me from signing my signature is a regard for the facts. This, too, might amount to a flaw, but it is less self-indulgence than an occupational hazard. We are all deformed by our occupations, and perhaps our greatest choice is how to be deformed. Rightly or wrongly, I have chosen to be deformed by paying attention, and by holding fast to what I see.

The facts behind the evaluation apparently do not fit in its boxes. The largest reported incidents occurred on days when I most strictly applied the Southwest Distribution Equation. On days with smaller incidents, or none, I went to the edge of my discretionary range and sometimes beyond it. Too many factors lie outside the equation, or the available statistics are out of date. Households are growing larger near the main roads and power lines; a glance at yards and sidewalks on a mild day shows as much. The gas and electricity have to follow them.

There is only so much we can do for the subdivision hold-outs. As if this weren't enough, the tappers have found ways around the pipelines' sensors, and hijackers more often than not outgun the armed guards on tanker trucks. After drugs were legalized the cartels had to diversify. What this means to me is that on any given day gas and supplies are overstated by five to ten percent. One day last year the difference reached twenty percent, and the Director took the next week off on the advice of his physician, in the sense of the word meaning press office.

My memos have covered my reservations, and confessed my furthest detours into discretion. When there is a reply, in eleven to twelve percent of the instances, my proposals are categorized as denied, taken under consideration, or presently unfeasible. A fourth category, adopted, exists exclusively in theory. I once wrote a memo inquiring as to the ultimate purpose of the equation, if it might involve something other than the allocation of energy, such as the appearance of allocating energy to prevent panic. Eighteen months later, this memo received no reply. Such replies as came noted that the issues I mentioned fell under the jurisdiction of the Review Committee, whose mandate was to review from time to time the regional equations. From time to time they did, those times lengthening, before being de-funded. Left behind are the formulae, templates set over conditions that fit them less and less.

With all due respect to the facts, I may initial some of the Director's comments. I am distracted, and move slower than I should. I can lose much or all of a night's sleep to examining news and other reports for trends, or modeling the outcomes of alternative equations.

Consulting my findings during the day is what must be meant by "non-work activity," a point on which I will not sign off. This will require an explanation, and I will provide one, placed under a request for extra time to discuss my review.

There is no choice but to prepare the materials now, while there is no noise to distract me save the low buzz of electric current and the blood coursing past my eardrums. Tonight I will need to rest, if I can rest while knowing that what I don't learn could change lives and fortunes, or end them. Depending on what happens, even more lives and fortunes could be in play, such as my own. The appearance of allocation might be served by a firing, an investigation, perhaps some other burnt offering to the public.

In any event, I have no children to provide for, and my own needs are few. There may be work in St. Louis.

The Lore Keepers

By E. A. Freeman

.

The summer heat on the metal roof created a visible shimmer. The west-facing window in Julie's room was hot to the touch. A bead of sweat trailed down her cheek, but still she shivered under a heavy quilt. The smell of mint and honey hung in the unmoving air.

Julie reached for her laptop. It wasn't there. *Ugh*. Had it slid between the bed and the nightstand? She leaned toward the edge, and nearly toppled over from dizziness.

She laid her head back and tried to stop the room from rocking. She felt old. How old was she anyway? That seemed like something a person should know about herself.

The bed, too, felt old. It made creaking and thrumming sounds when she moved. Her body seemed to constantly migrate to the depression in the center of the mattress. Just how long had she been sitting here?

The muscles of her back and shoulders cried out for a long massage, but her skin flinched at the thought of anybody touching it. She could feel her heartbeat hammering away at every part of her body.

She desperately wanted something to occupy herself. Where was that computer? Was it downstairs? Did this house even have a downstairs? Her mind felt so muddled.

"Hello?" Julie called. "Anybody here?"

"Yes, ma'am," came a high, crisp voice. "I'll be right there!"

Moments later, a girl of about fifteen walked in. She was smallish, but she seemed old for her age. She had a pale complexion, and she was thin – almost gaunt – with short-cropped brown hair and blue-gray eyes, and a look of concern on her face.

"Is everything okay, Grandma?" the girl asked.

Grandma? Julie hadn't expect that. Her expression must have showed it too, because the girl almost immediately said, "It's me, Callie. Can I get you anything? I put some hot tea on the night stand if you want it."

"I was just looking for my laptop," Julie said, after a short pause. "I thought it was right here."

This time it was Callie's turn to look momentarily flustered. "Oh… we had to send it out for repairs," she lied. "Broken."

The pounding inside Julie's brain intensified. She felt lost. Shaky. Disoriented. She just wanted to look up symptoms, compare contagions, search outbreak information, read health bulletins…

She felt profoundly tired. She couldn't even begin to unravel the thoughts tangled up in her mind. Callie was clearly sweating, yet Julie couldn't wrap the blankets tight enough around herself.

"Oh," she said finally, not even trying to mask her disappointment, or her fatigue. "Well… never mind. I guess I'd better try getting some more rest then," she said. "Thank you, Caledonia, dear."

Caledonia? She *did* remember. At least a little. Baby Callie, beaming up at her. Toddler Callie, running round and round her kitchen table. Callie's father—Parker? Mason? Declan? It was some name she never liked…

"Yell if you need anything, Grandma," said Callie, halting the flow of memories. "I'm heading out in about an hour, but Ellis will be here before then."

Julie gingerly rolled over onto her side, drew in a deep breath, and tried not to think about anything at all.

* * *

Callie sat in the living room, feeling guilty. Not for lying about the laptop – she had moved beyond beating herself up about arranging their lives to minimize stress and frustration.

Her grandmother's mind was clearly starting to go. The fever was making it worse, but even when she was healthy, she was struggling with words and thoughts. Callie figured she was probably in the early stages of Alzheimer's disease. Another slow-moving crisis to deal with.

No internet connection meant most of what Julie wanted to do with the computer wasn't going to work anyway. That would lead to the same round of questions, the same confusion, the same frustration. Callie hadn't even realized her grandmother still had a computer until early in the fever, when she'd gotten it out from some unknown storage place and started trying to use it.

Caring for somebody with dementia had always been

difficult. But in many ways it was even more difficult now – ever since Everything Changed. No, the computer had to go, for everyone's sake.

Besides, she and her crew needed it. Desperately.

Callie knew the justification was legitimate, but the thought brought forth another surge of guilt. Had she done the right thing? Of course. This was critical stuff. The answer was obvious. That didn't make it feel any less wrong.

But then, nobody ever said being a Lore Keeper was going to be easy.

* * *

Callie removed the laptop from her backpack and set it on the workbench. A pair of practiced hands scooped it up and turned it around and over, inspecting it quickly but thoroughly. The owner of the hands, a young man in his early twenties, with dark hair and a neatly trimmed beard, looked up at her.

"You *stole* this from your grandmother?" he asked.

"Not now, Kasim," said Callie. "It's been a long day."

"That's Nick to you, remember?" he said. "After the latest fiasco, I'm not Kasim any more. Not any time soon at least."

"You really think you can pass for Greek?" Callie asked, looking doubtful.

"Second generation, born and raised in Watertown, Mass.," he said with a grin. "My dad, Nikos, was an electrician. My mother Connie was a high school history teacher."

Callie looked at him, still skeptical. "What letter comes after epsilon in the Greek alphabet?"

"Zeta."

"Really? Zeta?"

"Yes really," he said, trying to contain a look of triumph. "Now can we get back to the part where you stole this beautiful old pre-cloud laptop computer from your poor ailing granny?"

"Speaking of which, I've got to get back to her," Callie said. "Sorry to drop and run, but it'll almost be dusk by the time I get home."

"Go," he replied. "Take some good notes from her. She's a gold mine." *While you still can*, he added, internally.

"Of course," said Callie. "See you Thursday... *Nick*."

"Don't forget to tell Ellis to bring more paper!" he yelled as she hurried out the door.

* * *

Callie stood up on her bike to pedal harder up the hill. Whenever she traveled solo, she tried to look, act, and carry herself like a boy. She was less likely to be bothered by strangers that way. It wasn't as easy to pull off as when she was younger, but with a wrap beneath her shirt, and her short hair under a baseball cap, she could still pass pretty well. But riding in this heat and humidity, she wondered if the extra layers were worth the risk tradeoff.

By the time she reached the halfway point, she was drenched in sweat, and her legs ached. But like the chickens her older brother Daniel had raised years ago, she had an instinctive need to be in a safe place by sundown.

She missed Daniel terribly. He was lost during combat operations in Nigeria almost five years ago. So many didn't come back near the end. The official status was "Missing in

Action," but Callie suspected there was just no money left to round them up and bring them home. Those years were some of the worst. Not just for her, but for everybody.

She felt her throat starting to constrict and her eyes get a little watery. He'd be twenty-three by now. Kasim had been in boot camp with Daniel.

She refocused her attention on the road. The trees seemed to loom on either side of her. She wasn't fond of this part of the ride. She didn't know the families who lived along this stretch, their dwellings tucked away among the trees. She pedaled on. Despite her efforts, her thoughts drifted back to her family.

Callie's parents were gone too. Her mother had lost a brief battle with cancer when Callie was just seven. Her father had left town for a three-month contract job almost a year and a half ago, and they hadn't heard from him since. Was he dead? Had he abandoned them? Would they ever see or hear from him again? Or Daniel, for that matter?

Her stomach tightened. Tears spilled over her eyelids. She tried, but failed, to hold back a convulsive sob.

Suddenly, the handlebars of the bike jerked violently sideways. Callie saw ground and sky and treetop and road in a disordered blur as her mind flailed wildly to process what had happened. Images and sounds and sensations replayed in quick succession: the momentary feeling of disoriented weightlessness. Her body, sliding across gravel onto the berm. The bike scraping and clattering to a stop. The acrid smell and the heat coming off the asphalt. The one wheel of the bike spinning after everything was over.

There had been a brief notion that someone had knocked her off the bike, or maybe shot her or something. But no. A simple pothole. A nasty one, but a pothole nonetheless.

Why, why, *why* had she not stayed focused on the road? She was furious with herself. Riding at dusk was not the time or place for self pity.

Or for anger, she realized. She looked up at the tall trees on either side, their branches almost touching in some places. A blue jay cawed from some unseen branch. The leaves high in the treetops danced a bit, and she felt the slightest waft of a breeze. She silently wished for wind, and for rain.

The breeze rustled the tall, weedy grass in the berm of the road. She briefly imagined the noise as a person, or possibly an animal, stalking her from the undergrowth. Of course she knew it was just the breeze. She figured it was probably just her frayed mind's way of telling her to get moving.

Was the bike damaged? A punctured tire or a bent rim would be disastrous right now. Stinging pain in her hands and along her left forearm reminded her to assess her own state. Was she bleeding? Was anything broken?

She wiped her eyes and got up gingerly. Road rash on her arm. No glass, thankfully. No bleeding from her palms, but some shredded skin on the heel of her hand. A sore wrist and shoulder. Nothing seemed broken or severe. After assessing the bike, it appeared to be in a similar condition – scraped, bruised, battered, but still very functional. She took a breath and mounted the bike. The fading light and lengthening shadows were already making it harder to navigate.

She could not afford to grieve for her losses right now. Besides, she tried to reassure herself, she still had her grandmother, and her brother Ellis. Ellis was thirteen. The two of them, along with their father, had moved in with Grandma Julie several years ago. Julie had been taking care of them as well as she could, ever since he'd gone.

But now, the roles were reversing. Callie and Ellis were going to be their grandmother's guardians. That was becoming clear. Ellis seemed unfazed by this turnaround, but Callie was scared to death. She was determined not to let Ellis know, but she wasn't sure how they were going to manage.

Their only source of income at this point was whatever Ellis could earn selling and trading things at the Gringo Market.

For years, there had been a sort of impromptu farmer's market beside a local tire shop, where Latino growers would congregate, socialize, buy, sell, and barter with each other. But as things went from bad to worse, more and more non-Latinos started showing up, at first to buy things—the market was stocked better than most grocery stores at that point—and later to try to sell things as well. Between limited space, culture clashes, and rising tensions in so many aspects of life, the atmosphere at the tire shop market deteriorated. Fights were becoming more frequent and more violent, and a full scale riot seemed almost inevitable. Only fast-talking diplomacy by some of the vendors kept it from turning really ugly.

Some enterprising (and desperate) minds managed to get permission from the local authorities, such as they were, to start using the old "big box" electronics store as an all-purpose market. The new Gringo Market was an instant success, and the old tire shop settled back to its cultural roots.

The new market had been a favorite haunt of Ellis ever since it had opened, and he began working there right after their dad left. It helped that Ellis was such a natural scavenger. He had a rare gift for finding discarded items and convincing people they had value. He knew where to look, what to keep, and above all, how to talk to people. And that, though Callie, was as good as gold. They had access to items through his bartering and salesmanship that many people in their situation could only dream about.

* * *

"Hey," said Callie as she walked in the front door, breathing hard. Fatigue, but also relief, made her double over with her hands on her knees.

"What happened to you?" asked Ellis, slightly alarmed at her bloody, dirty, disheveled appearance.

"I'm fine," she gasped. "Just took a dive into a pothole."

"Wow, are you okay?" he asked.

"It looks worse than it is," she said, still breathing a bit hard. "Really, I'm fine."

"The bike?"

"Fine too. Might need a little work, but definitely rideable," she said as she walked into her bedroom to change.

A moment later, a shriek came from her room, followed shortly thereafter, by a fluffy, lavender projectile.

"I am going to *kill* you for that Ellis," she said. But her words were lost among the peals of laughter coming from her brother.

He leaned over and retrieved the plush purple pachyderm. He pointed the stuffed elephant's oversized head toward her and said, "Aw, come on! How can you be afwaid of dis widdle guy? Wook at his cute widdle face. Wook at his beady widdle eyes…"

She turned away with a look approaching disgust, which

only made Ellis laugh harder.

Callie had always hated stuffed animals. *Hated* them. Even as a baby, having a teddy bear in her crib made her cry. They looked unnatural, she said. The proportions were always wrong. And the faces were always creepy.

"I'll get you back," she muttered from her room. "You just wait."

"Whatever," said Ellis, finally gaining some composure. "It was totally worth it."

Ellis decided a change of subject might be better than letting her plot in silence. "So, how's things down at the workshop?"

"Things is good," she said, mimicking his improper grammar. "It's coming along."

"Was Kasim able to use those chip drives?" he asked, trying to sound nonchalant, but always eager for praise.

"I forgot to ask," she said, walking back into the room. "But he told me to tell you he needs more paper." She was dabbing at her scraped arm and hands with a damp cloth.

"Oh, and we're supposed to call him 'Nick' now," she added. "He wants to pass as the son of Greek immigrants or something. He's got a whole back story worked out and everything."

"Nick it is then," Ellis said, with conviction. "I don't blame him. Besides, it's not like anybody but his neighbors even knows him yet, so it shouldn't be too hard to make that happen."

"Yeah, I s'pose so," said Callie. She was busy spreading a thin layer of honey onto her wound, as a salve, and as an adhesive for the scrap of cloth she had chosen for a bandage.

"So how's Grandma?" she asked.

"Not great. She was hallucinating or something earlier – babbling something about docked wages and a mustard sandwich. But she's got the quilt off now, so maybe the fever broke? I don't even know how these things work. Is that a good sign?"

"It's probably not a bad sign. But she may be up and down for a while yet."

A pause followed. Then Ellis blurted out, "What if she dies?"

He felt a little embarrassed for sounding scared, but he couldn't help himself. "I mean, will those Wellness people make us move or something? Go into Service? I am *not* living in some creepy old lady's house with a pack of tiny dogs and a weird smell. And I'll live in the woods by myself eating grubs before I get sent to a shanty."

"I guess we *are* kind of orphans," said Callie somberly.

She paused. "They'd probably place you with the Mattlensons," she said, stifling a smile.

Ellis heaved a fake sigh. "I'll go start digging for grubs."

The reference to the neighbors they both disliked had hit the mark. Callie just couldn't have that discussion right now, because she had no answers. Ever since Grandma Julie had started getting sick, Callie had spent many of her waking hours worrying about that very problem: How could they get by with no adults? How would they keep themselves out of any number of bad situations if their last available parental figure was gone? She hoped that in time, answers would present themselves, because right now, she was at a loss.

"No," said Callie. "If you're a good boy, then maybe you can have a bowl of grubs at bedtime. Right now, we need to get the washing done."

"Aw, man!" cried Ellis. But after few moments of looking sullen and rebellious, he did get up.

* * *

Julie sat up slowly in bed. She felt awful. Sweaty. Clammy. Achy. And tremendously hungry.

"Hello?" she called. "Is anybody here?"

"Yes, ma'am," said a voice. A boy appeared in her doorway. "It's me, Ellis," said the boy. Callie had coached him on saying his name when he entered. He forgot to end with "grandma," so she'd know the context of the relationship.

"Is your mom around, Ellis? Or your dad?"

"Um… no," he said. "Not right now. Is there anything I can do for you, grandma?"

"No, that's okay. I was just starting to feel a little hungry, but I can wait."

"I made some potato leek soup," said Ellis. "There's still some left. It's not bad."

"You made it?" said Julie with an affectionate smile. "Well, I'll have to try some then."

"It probably needs to be warmed up a little – I'll be back in a bit," he said, and disappeared before she could tell him not to bother. Like most people stuck in bed, she hated the thought of being a bother.

Of course, Ellis didn't want to give her the chance to turn him down, even if it did mean lighting a small fire on a hot day. Not only was he eager to share his budding culinary skills, but he also wanted an excuse to try out the new little stove he'd built out of some old metal cans.

The design was something Kasim had showed him—

something *Nick* had showed him, Ellis corrected himself. Nick said it was called a rocket stove, though Ellis had seen something similar called a twig stove over near the shanty village.

The stove was made from one large coffee can, and three smaller soup cans. Ellis fashioned an "L" shaped chimney out of the three soup cans by using just a can opener, a pair of tin snips, and some pliers. The chimney fit down into the larger can, which had a round hole cut into the side of it, so the base of the "L" stuck out the side. He filled in the gap around the chimney with sand and mud. At the base of the "L", where it stuck out the side, he used some leftover scraps of metal to create a little shelf or platform inside the chimney.

Ellis put some small dry sticks onto the platform, and stuck some scraps of paper in the space underneath. The gap underneath was for air to flow in and up through the chimney. The beauty of the design was that you could use it to start a fire quickly without a lot of tinder, and without wasting precious matches. And you could boil water with it in just a few minutes using only sticks. At least that's what Kasim had told him.

The stove needed some work. He considered this one practice—a prototype. It simultaneously leaked both smoke and sand, but even this slapdash version was working better than he expected. He'd have to start collecting cans to see if he could make some to sell or trade.

After a few minutes, he headed back inside with the warm soup, wishing it was meant for himself. He grabbed a biscuit that he hoped wasn't too stale, and headed for Grandma Julie's room.

She wasn't there.

"Grandma?" he called. No answer.

"Hello?" he called again, looking around.

"Julie?"

The bathroom. He took a breath, glad she hadn't gone for a walk or something. She seemed a bit unpredictable, and she was in no shape to be wandering the streets at this point.

She opened the bathroom door and said to Ellis, "There's something wrong with the toilet. It's not flushing. Do you have the super's phone number?"

"No, uh…"

How to explain? "He's out of town," Ellis said at last. "But there's a bucket of water in the tub. You can wash up and then flush with that water," said Ellis. "Just set the bucket in the hall and I'll fill it up in a few minutes."

"Thank you," said Julie when she came into the bedroom. "You're so young to be working in a place like this. And so helpful. I bet your mom and dad are very proud of you."

He said, "thanks," in a barely audible voice, and looked down at the floor. He usually basked in a compliment, but for some reason, this last mention of his parents caught him off guard. A complex swirl of emotions filled his chest: grief, sadness, anger, affection, pride, regret…

Sometimes he just wanted to be a kid again. He wanted to go on vacations, play with toys, and goof off all day. He wanted to go to school and Cub Scouts and baseball practice. He wanted to complain to his mom about how bored he was, and complain to his dad about how there was nothing *fun* to do.

He wanted *them* to tell him how proud they were. He wanted *them* to tell him what chores he had to do, or what fun things they had planned, or what they'd be having for dinner. He even wanted them to yell at him for not cleaning up his room.

Most of all, he wanted to hear their voices again.

Would he always remember their voices?

Would he always remember what they looked like?

He wanted to keep every last detail fresh in his mind forever. What memories would fade? His mother's infectious laugh, or that crinkle in her brow when she was on the verge of blowing her top? His dad's bristly face, or his slight New England accent....

"This soup is really delicious," said Julie. "Is this from the cafeteria?"

"No, it's, uh, homemade," said Ellis, suddenly feeling a bit shy. "I just made it this morning."

"Well, my compliments to the chef. The texture and the flavor of the potatoes are so distinctive."

"Yeah, my sister just pulled them out the other morning," said Ellis. "The leeks too."

"Sounds like you and your sister are a great team," she said, tipping the bowl to get the last of the soup in her spoon.

"Sometimes," said Ellis. "Other times we want to strangle each other."

"That's how I was with my sister growing up," Julie said with a smile and a distant gaze. "I'll never forget when she pulled out all my strawberry plants that I had saved my allowance for *weeks* to buy. She said she thought they were weeds. But she had never pulled any weeds in the garden before! I was so mad I think my face was as red as a strawberry," she said, her smile widening.

Ellis grinned too. "One time Callie 'accidentally' stepped on my Lego battleship that I'd spent *days* constructing," he

39

said, "even though it was in the far corner of my bedroom. She never went in my bedroom any other time. She hated all that mess."

"Why do they do stuff like that anyway?" asked Ellis after a pause.

"I don't know," said Julie. "I guess siblings have always been like that, from the dawn of time. My sister," she said, pausing. "I… I'm blanking on her name for some reason… um… gosh… Anyway, do you know, my sister didn't even like strawberries! I mean who doesn't like strawberries?"

"That is weird," said Ellis. "Callie doesn't like Legos, which is a little strange, but strawberries?"

"I know!" exclaimed Julie. "But that's okay, I tore off her doll's head and threw it in the trash to get even."

Ellis laughed at the thought of his grandma and his great aunt Amy fighting. And at his own revenge on his sister. "I spread out a bunch of Lego bricks on the floor next to Callie's bed so she'd step on them when she woke up," he said.

Julie laughed, which led to some raspy coughing. Recovering her breath, she said, "Thanks for the delicious soup. It was just the thing for my poor old stomach. But now, I'd better try to rest some more. I'm a little shaky sitting up this long."

"Holler if you need anything," said Ellis.

"Good night Amy," said Julie.

"Err… Good night, Julie," said Ellis uncertainly.

* * *

Callie woke with a start.

She'd been sleeping on the couch. The first thing she was

aware of was her swollen and painful right wrist. The second thing was that someone was standing outside the front door.

Her heart started pounding. Break-ins while they were gone were bad enough. Her mind fumbled over what to do.

Maybe it was somebody who thought the house was vacant. Maybe it was somebody lost or confused. Maybe it was an armed home invader. A hundred scenarios flicked through her mind in an instant, and few of them were good. She thought about what could happen, *what could happen to her*, and the pit in her stomach grew.

Slowly but silently, she moved the few feet from the couch to the side of the door, grabbing an iron fireplace poker in her right hand. It quivered from the pain and swelling in her wrist. She'd have to brandish it left-handed.

What time was it? Dusk? She tried to re-orient herself.

The last she remembered, she had dozed off on the couch after dinner. It must be morning already. She'd been so tired she must have slept right through all of the evening tasks. Why hadn't Ellis woken her up?

Something wasn't right.

Who was at the door? Was it more than one person? And why were they just standing there? Should she call out? Was Ellis home? Could it be her grandmother out there?

A sudden knock made her flinch, causing her to bang the wall with the poker.

Ellis appeared abruptly from the hallway, and exchanged a glance with Callie.

"Who's there?" he called out, in his best tough guy voice.

"Nick," said Kasim's disembodied voice from the other side of the door.

Callie flung it open, and said, "Man, Nick. You scared me

41

to death. What were you doing standing there?"

"Oh wow, sorry about that," he said. "The strap on my satchel tore loose coming up the steps. Everything was in the process of dumping out."

"You're lucky," said Callie, "I was about to make a kabob out of you."

She motioned for him to come in, and turned to her brother. "And *you*," she said to Ellis. "Why did you let me sleep through chores last night? I was so confused when I woke up."

"You were so tired, and banged up," said Ellis. "I just took care of everything myself."

Callie's intense look dissolved.

"Thank you," she said. "You didn't have to do that." She looked down at the floor. "But next time, at least send me to bed. Waking up on the couch made me feel... exposed."

"Got it," said Ellis. "So Niko, what brings you all the way out here? I thought you were a city mouse?"

"I know I don't get out much," said Nick, "but does Saxapahaw count as a city now?"

"Compared to here, yes," replied Callie.

"You two are riding all the way up to Graham all the time," said Nick. "I'd just rather stay close to places I know and people I trust."

"Do you trust them already?" asked Callie. "And more importantly, do they trust you?"

"We trust each other enough," Nick replied. "A long way to go yet, but I've been upgraded from 'stranger' to 'outsider.'"

"Enough pointless jabber," said Ellis. "I'm dying to know: *Why are you here?*"

Nick set his bag down on the counter. "I need help with this," he said, pulling out Julie's laptop.

"Ohhh, now I see why you were so worried about dumping your bag," said Callie.

"Yeah," said Nick. "These old hard drives don't always appreciate gravity. Anyway, I managed to get the battery charged up, but I can't get in. If this were an old movie, I'd have cracked the password by now, but sadly, it's not. I have no idea what the login credentials are."

"Oh right," said Callie. "That would be a problem."

She turned back to Ellis. "Do you think Grandma Julie can help us?"

"Only one way to find out," he said. Turning to Nick, he added, "but let's wait a while, if you can. She's asleep right now, and if we wake her, she'll be confused and disoriented. She's usually at her best around mid-afternoon. Can you stick around?"

"As long as I need to," Nick said. "I can stay overnight if you've got a place for me."

"Aren't you worried about exposure to Julie's fever?" she asked.

"I'll be fine," he said. "I'm strong, like bull."

"Yeah, like bull alright," said Ellis, grinning. "You're built like a loblolly pine. A stiff breeze could take you out."

Nick laughed. "Yeah kid, have you ever noticed that it's never the pines that go down in a storm? Bend but don't break, baby."

"How are we going to explain all this to Grandma Julie?" asked Callie. "What are we going to tell her?"

"The truth?" said Ellis. "And then hope she remembers the password."

43

"Oh boy," said Callie, rolling her eyes upward. "Let's hope."

* * *

Nick and Callie sat in the kitchen, discussing exactly what to say to Julie when she woke up. Ellis had just headed out back to get some things for the market, when there was a loud knock on the door.

Callie walked to the main room and peeked out the window at a convex mirror that Ellis had rigged up on the porch just an hour earlier. He'd had the mirror for weeks, but hadn't found the time to set it up. It allowed her to see, if not who was at the door, then at least whether somebody was there. And how many somebodies.

In this case though, the distorted figure with copper-colored hair was unmistakable. It was Mrs. Mattlenson. Callie sighed, realized there was no escape, and opened the door.

"Is everything alright?" asked Mrs. Mattlenson. "I thought I saw a suspicious man creeping around here earlier." She came toward Callie, nearly pushing her way through the door and into the house.

Really, thought Callie. *She's going to play the nosy neighbor card?* "Everything's fine, ma'am," she replied, trying to sound polite. "It was just a friend of ours."

"Well, you know how I worry about you two since… well… " her voice trailed off.

If you were really worried, thought Callie, *you would not have come alone.*

Callie wondered if her husband had sent her over on a reconnaissance mission, or if she had come over on her own.

The Lore Keepers

"Are you sure you should be letting people in your house?" she asked. "I mean, considering the whole… " her voice trailed off again.

Ellis stepped from the hallway and gave a non-committal wave. He stayed at the far side of the room, with his hands behind his back—a spectator to the neighborly train wreck.

"Don't worry, Mrs. Mattlenson," Callie said. "It was just Nick. He's a friend of Daniel's, from the Army."

"Oh well, uh, I see…" she said.

Could she be any more awkward? thought Callie.

"How is Daniel?" Mrs. Mattlenson asked. A mortified look came over her face when she realized what she'd asked.

"Well, that answers that," Callie thought.

"Haven't heard from him lately," said Callie. "I'm sure he's fine." Callie was willing to say anything at this point to bring this visit to a close.

"I brought you some clothes," blurted the neighbor suddenly, as if struck by a revelation. She held out a bag filled with what looked to be the contents of a ten-year-old girl's closet. "My niece outgrew them."

"Thank you so much," said Callie, hoping against hope that it sounded at least half sincere.

"And there's this too," said Mrs. Mattlenson, reaching deep into the bag and grinning for the first time since she had arrived. She pulled out a stuffed orangutan, with preposterously long limbs. She wrapped the fuzzy arms around Callie in a plush embrace. The hands secured together with Velcro behind Callie's neck. "Isn't it *adorable*?"

Callie looked down at the orange, fuzzy face staring up at her from a few inches away. She gave an involuntary shudder.

45

"What's that noise?" asked Mrs. Mattlenson. Ellis had disappeared from the room. A rhythmic snorting sound was coming from down the hall.

"Nothing," said Callie, detaching the pseudo-simian offering, and trying her best to casually hold it at arm's length. "I think our cat just has a hairball."

"Cats'll bring fleas," said Mrs. Mattlenson.

"She's an indoor cat," said Callie flatly.

"What do you do about the, uh, you know, the poo?" The snorting from the hallway was joined by wheezing.

"Thank you for reminding me," said Callie, without missing a beat. "I need to go change Grandma's bedpan."

"Oh, well… I'd better let you go," stammered Mrs. Mattlenson, backing into the door, her hand scrabbling for the knob.

"Thank you so much for everything! We'll see you later!"

As soon as the door was shut, Callie turned and threw the stuffed primate toward the hallway. Ellis and Nick tumbled into the room, both doubled over and red-faced from suppressed mirth. Callie put her hand to her mouth, and made a snorking noise. The triple burst of laughter that followed was more than enough to wake Julie in the back room.

* * *

"Explain it to me again," said Julie. "The whole thing. My mind's not what it used to be, it seems." She mopped her forehead and temple with a damp cloth. She didn't entirely trust these two people in her bedroom.

Julie seemed fairly lucid, for her at least. But Callie could see that it was going to be tricky penetrating the fog in Julie's mind.

"Things aren't like they used to be," said Callie, who sat on the edge of her bed. "Modern society kind of crumpled under it's own weight."

"And this happened when?"

"Well, I guess it kind of started before I was even born, but it really started getting bad about seven or eight years ago."

"I have a few friends who always love to make my flesh creep, talking about collapse. You're saying they were right? The day finally came?"

"It's not like we woke up one day and everything was different," said Nick. He took a seat on the wooden chair in the corner. "It just sort of happened in fits and starts. Everybody had their own personal 'D-Day.'"

"How can I not know this?" asked Julie. She leaned forward to scratch her lower back. "Why can't I resolve this in my mind?"

"You've been ill," said Callie. She wanted to reassure her by saying something like, "it'll come back to you." But would it?

"And now you want me to give you my computer password?" Julie asked, still skeptical. "I don't understand."

"We're with a group that is trying to make things better," said Nick. "To rebuild. No — to build something new. We're a subset of the larger group that, well, let's leave that for some other time. Anyway, our goal is to collect and preserve knowledge, wisdom, and information of value. We've been calling ourselves the Lore Keepers."

"Catchy," said Julie.

"It sounded better than The Librarians," deadpanned Nick. A smile spread across Julie's haggard face.

"The reason we want to use your laptop is that we want to build a sort of archive, or library of whatever we can collect. We're looking for anything that seems useful, now or in the future – from formal writing to passing comments that might contain a key piece of information."

Julie tried to process his words. "And you want my computer so you can go online and…"

"No," interrupted Nick. "There is no 'online.' At least not from our standpoint. Internet connectivity is expensive, and nearly useless for our purposes."

"What are you talking about?" said Julie incredulously. "I use it every day! There's all the knowledge you could ever want out there. Granted it's a lot to sift through, and you have to watch for inaccuracies, but…." Julie's voice faltered as she saw Callie shake her head a little.

"It's not like that now," said Nick. "The money ran out, just like everywhere else. People held on as long as they could, but useful sites disappeared, one by one. Now it's just another place where rich people can go to feel better about themselves. Escapism and status is not useful to us."

"So what, then? You want to use my laptop to store all your information, like a database?" asked Julie, a look of concentration on her face. She rubbed her foot against the opposite ankle, trying in vain to satisfy another itch.

"No, not that either," replied Nick. *Though it is tempting,* he thought. An actual hard drive could be so useful… But for how long? These components were well past their intended lifespan. He opened his mouth to go on, but Callie gave him a significant look.

Julie looked tired and lost. She longed for things to make sense.

"I'm sorry, Grandma," said Callie, pressing her hand on Julie's shin. "I know it's a lot to take in, especially in your condition."

Callie regretted the phrase as soon as it was out. She withdrew her hand, cringing at how condescending she sounded. *Why hadn't she had Ellis talk to her instead?*

She took a breath before starting again.

"There are two things we want to do," she said, deciding to just stick to the basics. "First, we want to just look through your computer and see if there's any useful information on there – documents that were downloaded, garden journal entries, news clips, even chat logs about the weather. You've lived here all your life, and we might find some valuable local information. I know it seems invasive to rifle through your personal records, and if you don't want us to, we won't. But the information could really help some people."

Julie sat, wordlessly contemplating for a moment.

"Did you say two reasons?" she asked.

"We have a working printer. We want to connect it to the laptop, and print pamphlets," said Nick. "We want to spread the word about what we are doing. Most of what we do is hand-written and hand-copied. But if we can print a handful of flyers and distribute them to key places, we think we can collect a lot of books, papers, articles, notes, and equipment into one place. Printed materials might give us a measure of credibility – of legitimacy.

"From there we'll turn to printing and distributing the most useful or valuable information, so it can be circulated. At least until the printer ink runs out. Working printers and ink are hard to come by. But we'll do what we can with what we have."

Callie pondered an unspoken third reason: if they ran into another money problem, Ellis could probably get a pretty penny for it at the market. A drop-dead gorgeous penny in fact.

She hoped it didn't come to that… or at least not before they could squeeze a little bit of usefulness out of it.

"Why do you think people will go along with this?" asked Julie. "Give up their books and other materials to you, I mean."

"Because if they give us one book, we'll loan them two in return," said Nick. "The more they bring, the more they'll have access to. People are dying for want of information. Literally, in some cases.

"We grew up thinking we lived in the Information Age," he went on. "People came to rely on easy access to almost any information at almost any time of day or night. So they stopped worrying about remembering every little detail. It was all stored in the cloud."

"It's not like people forgot everything, but deep knowledge has become scattered and sparse, and hard to come by," Nick added. "And some of the knowledge we need now is stuff we never even learned – stuff our great-great-grandparents knew by heart, but that we thought we had no use for."

He ran the back of his fingers across his beard, along his jawline. He wondered whether this was getting through. Not sure what else to do, he kept talking.

"Experts still exist, of course," he said. "It's just that at one time we were all experts on everything. Now, without that electronic brain capacity available, people can't tell an oak tree from a poplar, just to name one. It may not seem like

50

much, but come wintertime, we'd notice a huge difference in the heat."

"This is a bit overwhelming," said Julie. She was slumping against her pillows now. "I can't even remember what you said at the beginning now."

"I know, grandma," said Callie. "I know."

Seeing the look on her face, and fearing they were losing her, Nick said, "Are you comfortable with giving us your password at this point, ma'am? You can supervise us, if you'd like."

"No… no," she said.

Nick's heart skipped a beat. Which part was she saying no to?

Julie stared out the window. Neither Nick nor Callie were sure what to say, if anything.

"I can't remember the password," Julie said at last. She looked blank. "I used the same one for ages… It's just not coming to me."

Callie and Nick felt the hope draining from them. How could a flu-addled Alzheimer's mind be expected to remember a password that hadn't been used in years?

They'd been foolish to get their hopes up.

"What now?" thought Callie. An uncertain silence settled on the room.

Suddenly, Nick grabbed the laptop and powered it on. He set it on her lap. "See if your hands remember," he said.

Julie placed her fingers on the home row of the keyboard. After a moment's hesitation, they began to move. Mechanically, but surprisingly quickly, her hands typed what seemed to be a random series of numbers and letters. She hit the Enter key.

They all sat, expectantly. Had it worked?

Some ambiguously melodious startup music played. Callie gasped, and Nick beamed.

"Can you write it down?" Nick asked Julie. Callie quickly produced a pencil and a small scrap of paper. Julie put her fingers back on the keyboard and pantomimed typing the password again. She wrote it on the slip of paper. Callie and Nick both thanked her profusely.

"Now," she said, "I need to rest. This has been exhausting. Don't go stealing my credit card numbers now." She handed the laptop to Nick. Callie stood up, grabbed her pen and paper, ready to take notes while Nick searched the computer.

"One more thing," Julie called after them as they left the room. "In exchange for that password, there had better be some damn fine trashy romance novels on my nightstand when I wake up."

Bicycleman Sahkile And The Cell Tower

By Kieran O'Neill

Gather around, prentices, and hear the story of Sakhile, first Bicycleman of Siphongweni.

The midday sun glinted off the cell tower's PV panels far above him as Sakhile rode towards the face of Siphongweni, the ridge from which our region takes its name. He climbed steadily, carrying his bicycle where the path was too rocky or too steep, racing against the coming storm. Most he would have ridden through, depending only on his rain gear, but the towering storm clouds and sudden chill in the air told him that this was no ordinary summer afternoon shower. He had no desire to be out when it struck, and the tower keeper's house was the nearest shelter. Besides, he and Nomvula the tower keeper had been making eyes at each other whenever she was in the town below, and she brought her bicycle in for him to be repaired far more often than she needed to.

Sakhile had sent a text message ahead to Nomvula from his cell, and she welcomed him with a wave. She wasted no time, however, in putting him to work securing the tower for the storm, for then, as now, the equipment was too precious to risk losing to lightning. Like Sakhile, she knew that this storm would be worse than most she had seen, although she had found out from a weather information service which she had accessed through the internet, for that was still available at the time. Together they tied down and lowered antennae, disconnected systems from each other, and covered the PV panels in case of hail.

Just as they were about to secure the last of the equipment, and shut the system down, Nomvula was called on her cell. It was Londisizwe, the inDuna of that time, and he was not pleased.

"Nomvu, my child, I have seen the messages saying that the system will be going down. What is the meaning of this?"

"Londisizwe, with all respect, this is what I do every time there is a great storm. We cannot risk losing the equipment. I am already using the backups—it could take months to get replacements."

"This is unacceptable. I will tell you when there will be a great storm, and this is one is not. Besides, I have very important business that requires that I have internet."

"Londisizwe, the weather service has said this may be the worst storm in ten years. And I know what kind of 'business' you use your internet for. Watching naked women on the other side of the world does not justify me risking our whole region's connectivity."

"You dare! You will keep my connection running through this storm, or you will answer to me!"

And with that, he ended their conversation.

This left her little choice, for then as now, it was best to obey your inDuna, both out of respect, and because his henchmen were some of the most dangerous you will find. So, in the last minutes before the storm struck, Nomvula reconnected enough of the systems to give Londisizwe his internet.

The wind had already died by then, and the sky had darkened. It was not long before a howling gale brought the first rain lashing against the tower. The storm was one such as you may see maybe once or twice in a lifetime; hail the size of your fist, wind strong enough to snap trees, and thunder to make the earth shake. And, of course, all around lightning flickered like the tongue of a giant snake. Sakhile and Nomvula held each other as they shook in fear inside her tiny house, not touching the equipment for fear of their lives.

As the storm passed and the sun broke through, they emerged into damp, crisp air to assess the damage. Nomvula inspected each piece of equipment in turn, using tools much like those of the Radiomen and women today. Lightning had struck close several times, and the damage was severe.

"Well, what am I supposed to do now? My whole system is down, and I cannot repair it without parts from Pietermaritzburg, if they even have them."

"We will need to go into town. Old Londi will have to call an ibandla to decide what to do. You will have to be there."

Nomvula made a face.

"Leave my tower unguarded? And you know how they feel about women participating in those things."

"I am sure Londisizwe will send someone out here to safeguard it before long. And you are the only one who knows how all this stuff works."

"Yes, you are right. We will just have to hope they will not lynch me."

Leaving a paper note at the tower, Sakhile and Nomvula descended through the long shadows of the afternoon to the gathering of buildings that marks the centre of Siphongweni. They stopped at Londisizwe's mansion, where he greeted them calmly, and informed them that yes, there was indeed to be an ibandla the next day to discuss the matter, and yes, they should ensure that they both attend as guests. They could tell that underneath his calm, he had been raging, and suspected that they were not his first, or last, visitors that evening.

Finally they made their way to Sakhile's family kraal, where Nomvula stayed with Sakhile's older sister. Although they were courting, Sakhile's brothers and sisters were very traditional, and forbade them to sleep under the same roof until they were married. Unfazed by the situation, as he had used his cell only rarely, Sakhile rested well, but Nomvula slept fitfully.

They arose early, and attended the great gathering of family heads and Londisizwe's councilors. It was rare, even in those days, for a woman to be allowed to take part, but Nomvula's expertise was needed, and Sakhile was a witness to the events. As is the tradition, each in turn spoke their part uninterrupted, and the ibandla did not end until all agreed.

On hearing Sakhile and Nomvula's story, even told as cautiously as they told it, there was much muttering, and several of the speakers after strongly voiced their criticism of

Londisizwe's pride. Finally, the issue of what to do next arose. Nomvula explained:

"Critical parts of the tower's electronics have been destroyed. Normally, I would have a backup, but I was already running on the backup, and am still waiting for the replacement for that. I would need to send for the parts by post. Since the post wagon only arrives once per month, and we have no other way of getting a message back to Pietermaritzburg, it would take two months at least. I cannot see what else we can do."

This prompted lively discussion, full of imaginative yet impractical solutions.

"Hah—Londisizwe could go in his motor car. It would be quick, problem solved."

"You forget that, even if we knew that Londisizwe's car worked, which we do not, there is no petrol anywhere in Siphongweni to run it on."

"What about a bicycle? Young Sakhile is always out and about in the countryside. It would only be a few days' travel."

"Yes, and Sakhile could repair the bicycle, in case of trouble along the way."

"Nomvula would also have to go, to deal with the cell company."

Sakhile, given his turn, responded, "I am honored that you would entrust me with such a task. But I worry that I would be leaving my shop unattended. Many people are waiting for me to repair their bicycles, and that is lost money for me too."

"Perhaps some compensation could be arranged."

Eventually, with the sun low in the sky, the talking subsided, and Londisizwe summarized the agreed course of action: "It is essential that we have cellular and internet. People have savings in bank accounts which they cannot access, and relatives in other parts of the country they cannot speak to. Nomvula and Sakhile will travel to Pietermaritzburg by bicycle and return with the parts. I shall provide some funds to aid them in their journey, and will pay for their time. They should leave as soon as they have made adequate preparations."

The next day was one of preparation. Sakhile and Nomvula put on their church clothes, and attended a special service at the big Zion Christian Church in town. There they were sprinkled with holy water, blessed and prayed for by the congregation, and granted a special audience with the prophet, who gifted them with holy tea for the journey.

Later, Sakhile made his way quietly to the huts of gogo Msizi, a sangoma and old friend of his late grandmother. In her beads and white feathers, Msizi cast bones and consulted with her amatongo, then gathered the necessary items to make muthi.

"Your family is of the time of AIDS, when the men who should have led families were weak, and when grandmothers were the heads of families. It is your grandmother we shall call upon."

"She was a great woman. We care for her itongo as best we can."

"You have visited the Church, and they have given you tea blessed by God?"

"Yes, Gogo."

"That is well. Your grandmother was very fond of tea, so it will also keep you in alignment with her."

"Are you taking any other medicine, such as from the clinic?"

"No, Gogo."

"Very well. Drink the tea as the prophet has directed you. Here is muthi that will compliment the tea. Wait until the sun has travelled one quarter of its path after drinking the tea before you take the muthi. Here, also, are herbs to burn each evening with your cooking fire.

"Your ancestors will guide you, Sakhile. Go well."

Strengthened and confident that both God and ancestors were with him, Sakhile returned home to prepare the bicycles and pack.

On the day of departure, Sakhile and Nomvula made everything ready so that they could leave as soon as the cows' horns became visible through the mist. To save time and firewood, Sakhile boiled dried samp and beans, and placed them in a plastic thermos flask, one of his most prized possessions, where they would cook and be ready by evening. They loaded the bicycles, and set out into the cool morning air.

On the first day, they left Siphongweni and passed great pine plantations from the days when the paper companies used giant machines to plant and tear down forests. At one point, in the distance, they could hear the saws and axes of a felling crew, the days of great machines being already long past, just as the days of vast pine plantations are in the past now. The day went by without event; they camped, ate their samp and beans, and proceeded again the next day.

Rounding a corner as the road took them up along a hill, they were stopped by a large yellow dog standing in the road. In those days, feral dogs were not uncommon to find in between towns, though they always worked in packs. Most dogs would content themselves with wild animals, but some would go so far as to eat humans. The growling that suddenly emerged from the bushes all around them left no doubt that they were surrounded, and in great danger.

Sakhile turned to Nomvula, and said quietly,

"We can outrun them on the bikes, but only downhill. We turn around, leave the road at the bend, and make for those trees at the bottom of the valley. It will be dangerous, but we have little choice."

Carefully, they turned, watchful of the dogs slowly advancing around them, and prepared to take flight.

"Now, Nomvu! Ride!"

Down the hill, they rode like the wind. Sakhile almost fell as a dog wrapped its teeth around his rear spokes. But as its head struck his stays, it fell and he was away. Across rocks and grass they raced, praying they would not fall, the dogs just meters behind them. After what seemed an eternity, they were at and up the trees, their bicycles dropped upon the ground.

Scraped, bruised, and with their hearts pounding, they watched, helplessly, as the pack savaged their supplies. With each ripping and tearing of their jaws, they were painfully aware that it could well have been their insides, and not their food supplies, being torn to pieces. Finished with their bags and the bicycles, the dogs waited patiently under the tree until the sun was low. Finally, a passing duiker provided them with the prospect of easier prey, and they left to give chase. Sakhile and Nomvula climbed down to inspect the damage.

Their bicycles were chewed upon, but intact, as were their clothes and camping equipment. Their food, however was scattered, and anything immediately edible had been devoured. They salvaged what they could of the food, scooping together a pile of cornmeal out of the dirt, and left that place as quickly as they could. That night, they made a barrier of thorn branches and collapsed into sleep, exhausted, against a cliff.

They awoke to stiffness and aches from the narrow escape. Only half-full from a meager breakfast of the last of their gritty maize meal, they pushed aside the thorns and guided their bicycles carefully down the narrow trail to the road. It was not long before their stomachs were growling.

"Sakhi, we have no food, and you say it will be at least another day until we reach Pietermaritzburg", moaned Nomvula, "I'm sick of this. Let's turn back."

"Nomvu, we have been charged with a duty. We must continue. As for food, we will do as our ancestors did, and gather imifino."

Sakhile foraged for the leafy greens while Nomvula gathered firewood. With a little salt, they made a thin soup.

"It may not fill us for long, but at least it will keep our eyes and skin healthy," joked Sakhile.

"If you believe that old witch at the clinic, that is," replied Nomvula, sourly. "I am not happy."

"I know. But we must go on."

The road wound on, past farmers fields and an old railway track. They were tempted by the fields, but farmers of those days were suspicious of thieves, and well armed.

Sakhile wondered as they rode the path beside the tracks—trains seemed like such a good idea, but he had heard about them only in books.

Just as even Sakhile was becoming so hungry that he was beginning to seriously consider giving up, they rounded a hill to see at the bottom of a valley a laager of ox wagons, of the kind preferred by Boerevolk.

"See, Nomvu, we are guided!" Sakhile announced, triumphantly.

"I don't know, Sakhi. Boerevolk don't like outsiders. Some of them shoot strangers, especially those less pale than them..."

"No, I recognize these wagons. They are traders who come to the Siphongweni. Baba Jakes and I send for parts with them sometimes."

"You had better be right."

As they drew nearer, a man on a horse, in Boerevolk dress and carrying a rifle, rode up to them, and from a cautious distance called out,

"Oi! Where do you two think you're going?"

"Come now, Koos, I know you. It's me Sakhile, from Siphongweni," replied Sakhile.

"Sakhile? Jakes' assistant? What on earth are you doing all the way out here?"

"That is a long story. But right now we need to buy food. Do you think we can negotiate something?"

Koos brought them to the Johan, unmistakable in his long grey beard and hat as the leader of the caravan. He sat in the centre of the laager watching a large, three-legged iron pot bubbling on a bed of coals. Jets of steam escaped the lid, filling the air with the smell of cooking, and clenching Sakhile and Nomvula's stomachs like a clawed hand.

"So, let's hear your story, then," said Johan, and Sakhile related to him the fall of the tower, their quest to Pietermaritzburg, and their misfortune at encountering the dogs.

Johan thought for a while, and responded in the rich, deep voice of a Boerevolk leader, "Ja, the cell network is becoming spotty everywhere. And dogs, dogs all over the countryside. Once upon a time it was lions, now dogs.

"Anyway you are in luck," he said, "Electronic parts we cannot help you with, but we're particularly well stocked for food right now, and as you can see last night's potjie is just coming to a boil. I'm sure we can arrange a reasonable price."

He paused, and his face softened.

"You guys have been through a lot these past days, and Jakes is a good customer. I tell you what, my lightie has taken it upon himself to own a bicycle. I don't know why he can't just use a horse like the rest of us, but kids are kids. He is constantly bothering me about his brakes not working right. Fix them up, and the food is free."

Seeing they were starving, Johan served them up thick stew from the pot, with the hard, dry bread the Boerevolk like to dip in it, and they ate their fill. Later, under electrical lamps charged from PV panels on the wagons' rooves, Sakhile corrected the brakes on the bicycle, which were cantilevers requiring only minor adjustment, and explained to the caravan leader's son how to adjust them himself the next time. They then sat with the Boerevolk around the fire, told stories and shared songs over peach brandy. At one stage, Sakhile, ever curious, inquired whether the "4 x 4" painted on one of the wagons referred to the eight oxen drawing it. This was greeted with laughter, and then a long and nostalgic lecture about the mechanics of motor cars, to which Sakhile only half listened. That night they slept in the safety of the laager.

Before they set out, Johan came to wish them well, and with a warning,

"Nomvula may know this, since she went to technikon there, but, things are even worse now. In parts of Pietermaritzburg there are people who are poor in ways you have never thought people can be poor. Out there in the countryside, you can grow your own food, but down there people are packed together as close as they can be. When they don't have money, they starve. It hasn't been helped by all the refugees from up North either. These are desperate people. Some would kill you just for your bicycle. If you give me your map, I will show you the places where you never want to go."

With this advice in mind, they set out.

The road became tarred as they neared the city, allowing them to ride faster when they weren't dodging potholes. They passed fields of sugar cane, making Sakhile wonder why, with people starving, they were not growing a more useful crop like corn or beans. He supposed, and we know, that it was to make fuel for the last motor cars.

Soon Nomvula found that her cell was responding to the city's tower, though she seemed perplexed at its behavior. Several times she attempted to use it to contact the company, but got no response. All her attempts to use the internet left her frustrated. They decided that they had no choice but to go to the cell company directly, and find out what was going on.

Bicyleman Sakhile And The Cell Tower

Despite their weariness, they followed Johan's advice and took the long route into town. In the lengthening shadows they could see in the distance large stretches of tin shacks, and these areas they avoided. At this stage they also began to encounter motor cars, for in those days the very rich could still afford them. This was dangerous, for they had never cycled on a road with cars, and as you know this was once a great threat to cyclists. Guided by Sakhile's faint memories of a book at the school about the rules for riding in the city, they made their way into the city centre. But even when they seemed to be getting the rules right, few if any of the drivers of cars seemed to, and several times they narrowly escaped being killed. Finally, they came near to their destination, and Nomvula grew excited at the prospect of showing Sakhile where she had studied.

The cell company building was a towering block of concrete and steel, made in the old way when iron was cheap and diesel made building easy. It stood in a square of tarred gravel where motor cars had parked, now cracked and growing weeds, and surrounded by a rusted barbed wire fence. At the locked gates stood a small house in which sat a guard. Nomvula was perplexed, but approached the guard.

"I am here to speak with the director of rural maintenance. I've tried on the phone, but had no response—" began Nomvula

"That isn't too surprising," said the guard, "since the company no longer exists."

Nomvula had difficulty believing what she was hearing.

"What do you mean it doesn't exist?"

"I mean that it went bankrupt, and the bank took the building away, " replied the guard. "I am left here to keep skebengas and the homeless out, but there is nobody inside."

While Nomvula remonstrated with the guard, Sakhile studied the building. It was covered in dirt, and no furniture was visible through the glass windows, many of which were broken. Saddened, he studied the guard's bicycle instead. It was very much like something he would have built, matching the better parts of old throw-aways into a whole that would last for years. On the top tube, a small sticker read "I like Amabike".

"But, but I still have reception," whined Nomvula, by which she meant that her cell appeared to be working.

"Yes, we will see how long they have the parts and the persistence to keep that going," said the guard.

"They? Who do you mean?"

"These crazy kids with their co-op. They've been fiddling around with the towers, and have them running, somewhat. Actually, you look like their kind of people. Perhaps they could help you. They're set up in some old houses down Jabu Ndlovu Street. Good people. I got my bike from them."

With no better ideas, and the daylight fading, Sakhile and Nomvula went in search of the co-op. As empty concrete buildings gave way to older houses, they came upon a cluster that could be none other than the co-op. The fencing between them had been taken down, and the space was a maze of sheds filled with surplus bicycle parts and lush, dense vegetable gardens. On one house hung a sign saying "Amabike". Another, its roof sprouting aerials like some strange tree, was marked "FreeGeek". And on the ground, spelled out in growing vegetables, "the co-op".

Bicyleman Sakhile And The Cell Tower

Nomvula headed straight for the house with the aerials, but Sakhile could not resist venturing into Amabike. Inside, he found rows of bicycles, bins full of parts, and all of the tools of his trade, including many he had only read about in books. Studying the tool rack, he quickly lost his composure.

"You have a tubing straightener! And a bottom bracket thread chaser! And a headset remover – I had to make mine out of old tubing, but that is the real thing!"

A young, long-haired man standing at a bicycle clamped into a stand put down his tools, looked up, and said, "Well, I see I'm talking to a fellow mechanic, though from your clothes you don't look like you live around here. My name's Michael. Welcome to Amabike. What brings you here?"

Sakhile recounted their quest, spoke of his bicycle shop on the side of Baba Jakes' Spaza, and about cycling through the countryside around Siphongweni. Michael showed him the workshop, introduced him to the other mechanics, and began explaining the co-op.

"We're really just a bunch of people working on solutions to the world's problems, in our own little way. Here at Amabike, we build bikes out of scrap and fix people's bikes for them, like you do with Baba Jakes. But we also let people use the tools themselves, and teach them in the process. Then there's the growers coop. They work on food – you might have noticed their demo garden out front and back. And last, there are the FreeGeeks..."

At that moment, Nomvula burst in, and making straight for Sakhile, bubbled, "Sakhi, it's amazing! They do things with old computers and cell equipment, crazy new things, like you with your bikes. And radios. Old style radios, from before computers."

67

"Well that," said Michael, "would be the FreeGeeks. I take it you are Nomvula. Welcome!"

"Michael, this has been enlightening, and I thank you for your time," began Sakhile, "but we must be finding somewhere to spend the night, and to buy food, before it gets dark."

"Hang on—I think I can help you with that. We'll need to clear it with the others, but for now you can stay here as my guest."

"Oh, we would not want to impose."

"That's okay—you can both help out, and learn a bit more about what we're doing at the same time. I have the beginnings of an idea to help you with your problem back home, too. We'll need to bring it up at the pan co-op meeting on Thursday, but you can stay here until then."

That night they dined with Michael and a group of co-op members, some of whom lived on site. The ground maize was nothing new, but the fresh vegetables and grilled fish that accompanied it amazed the two. The vegetables were all colors and shapes, and while fish alone was a luxury, fish outside of a can was something they had never seen before.

"Oh we work with some pretty diverse heirloom varieties," explained a grower, "it keeps things interesting, and helps with disease resistance. I can hook you up with some seeds to take home for next season if you like. And the fish are tilapia. We have an aquaculture setup. We could live solely on vegetables, but the fish are nice for a change, and they provide fertilizer for the plants."

Sakhile debated the merits of bicycle components with Michael and the other mechanics, while Nomvula did the same with the FreeGeeks, late into the night. In the excitement, their quest to repair the cell tower was almost forgotten.

The days flew by, as Sakhile learned more formal techniques of bicycle repair from the Amabike mechanics, and in turn taught them what he could of the art of using improvised or minimal tools. Nomvula, meanwhile, was breaking free of her rigid education in cell repair, and learning to create and invent new solutions herself. During this time, Michael began to outline his plan. They would go in a group, and set up a co-op in Siphongweni. The tower could be made to work with some minimal parts and inventive workarounds. At the same time, knowing that the cell network's days were numbered, they would outfit the tower with simpler but more robust radio equipment. It would need to be discussed with the rest of the co-op, and agreed to, but Michael did not feel this would be a problem, as expansion into rural areas had long been on their agenda. Soon, the day of the meeting came around.

The pan-co-op meeting reminded Sakhile of nothing more than Londisizwe's ibandla. Each would talk in their turn, and every issue was talked out until all were in agreement. The difference was that here nearly all the participants were young, in their early twenties or thirties, and often far less polite, interrupting and talking over one another. This left Sakhile and Nomvula feeling too intimidated to contribute much, and they could see that the less outgoing of the meeting's participants felt the same.

Sakhile noticed, however, that Michael presided over the meeting in much the way that Londisizwe had, gently steering discussion on hotly debated issues towards compromise, and ensuring that the quieter board members were heard.

When it came around to the issue of Siphongweni, Sakhile was glad that Michael was on their side.

"Mike, some of us need to work for a living. We can't just leave the workshop to go jaunting through the country-side for a few weeks."

"We can put aside some money from the special projects fund to cover living expenses. And perhaps the people of Siphongweni could help out."

Mike glanced at Sakhi, seeming to indicate that he should speak.

"For a time, some would be welcome to stay as guests of my family. Nomvula could probably house some in her house by the tower. The harvest has been good this year, so it will be easier to arrange food. I also have a great many bicycles awaiting repair, and this will only have grown while I've been gone. I am sure we could find work for an assistant or two. And come to think of it, the Mandlekhosis' pedal mill is broken down and needs a few parts which I do not have. If we could repair it, I am sure their gratitude would keep us going for some time."

This improved the mood greatly.

"It would be a chance to properly test out the PPT," said one of the mechanics.

This, too, produced many nods, and a few smiles. Sakhile wondered what a PPT was.

By the end, it was clear that the co-op membership was in favor. Pete concluded the discussion:

"Okay, so who's up for this? Come on, it'll be an adventure!"

Several members put up their hands.

"Joe, can we cover the workshop in our absence?"

"Yeah, a few of us can take some extra shifts. A little extra pay wouldn't hurt anyone."

"Excellent! Sooner is better. How does the day after tomorrow sound for everyone?"

More nods, and it was decided.

As the day arrived, Sakhile and Nomvula set out once more, this time with a pack of riders, and a load of parts and tools to help in founding fledgling coops in Siphongweni. Sakhile had asked Michael several times about the PPT, but he had remained mysterious, saying simply that they would find out soon enough. Near the outskirts of Pietermaritzburg, as they reached an old railway in an area Sakhile and Nomvula might have avoided coming in, they found out. Michael began to explain the contraption sitting on the tracks, but Sakhile already grasped what it was.

"PPT – pedal powered train. The trains stopped running a long time ago, and nobody has yet come to steal the rails, so it seemed like the logical thing to do."

"And the stands are set up to interface to bicycles, so you can take them with you!" exclaimed Sakhile "It's genius!"

"It won't take us all the way there, since the rails turn away about 15 kilometers outside Siphongweni, but it'll easily cut out half the travel time. We've been itching to try this out on a real journey."

In the early morning light, with mist still wrapped around them, they set out, gliding along the rails like a bird through the air.

That, prentices, is how the Bicycle Guild and the Radio Guild both came to be established in Siphongweni. It is also why in Siphongweni, and in the surrounding towns, Radiomen and women often work closely with Bicyclemen and women, although elsewhere in the land this is rare. Sometimes, you may even see ubabamkhulu Sakhile tinkering on some project in a corner of the workshop. If you have the chance, listen to him, for he has seen and learned much in his time. Now be off with you! I see Master Shembe waiting, and it is time for your wheel building class. Go well, and remember what you have heard today.

Small Town Justice

By David Trammel

So that just leaves the South two acres to seed for winter," Zeddie said, taking a sip of his chicory coffee. "We should be able to start on that tomorrow once the ground dries out a bit."

Alex Patterson nodded. The early October storm had come up suddenly late yesterday afternoon, with heavy rain and wind. While it only lasted a few hours, it had soaked the new plowed field well enough to make it impossible to plant that day.

It was a little after 7 a.m. and while the Sun was busy chasing the clouds from the sky, the air still had a chilly nip to it. The two men were sitting on the main house's porch going over the day's chores. Alex found it a comforting ritual. At 67, it took him more and more time to get going anymore. They had been up for a couple of hours now, getting breakfast before first light. The farm's old solar electric system, installed that first year Alex and Mary had moved to the country, ran well enough to let them run a few lights in the main rooms. With days growing shorter as winter came, they needed to get as much done as they could.

Alex could hear his wife, Mary, in the kitchen finishing up. She'd mentioned before bed last night that she wanted to do some canning this morning. He needed to tell Zeddie to get a load of wood to the outside kitchen for later.

"Where's everyone at?" he asked.

"Manuel and Hector are in the big barn, feeding the livestock and seeing to the milking. John said he had some tack which needed to be repaired."

This was the two brothers' third year working for the farm. Their family had been farmers in southern Mexico before the worsening climate had forced them to move north. Alex knew they could do their work without supervision.

John was new but Alex liked the man. He had a good way with the horses, which spoke well to his character, and he knew quite a bit about engines and farm equipment. That was part of the reason Alex had taken him in the Spring Lottery, when the migrants, the temps from the cities showed up looking for work on the farms.

With their small tractor on its last leg, he'd been resigned to hiring Luftjen's plow team to get the fields ready. John had not only managed to get the tractor running again, but it sounded so good, Alex expected to get a few more years out of it, barring something breaking that they couldn't get parts for, or repair themselves. They'd changed their plans and planted quite a bit more corn this year, expecting to increase their share of the local ethanol production so they could fuel the tractor next year. Alex had already told John he was welcome back next spring, and hinted at more, but that was something Alex needed to discuss with the other permanent members of the farm.

"I've got all of the rest of the temps checking the apple trees for damage and collecting any fruit blown down." Zeddie continued. "We need to decide who to send to town tomorrow for community duty..."

A young man's voice suddenly rang out.

"Hello in the house!"

* * *

"Morning, Zack," Mary said. "Would you like some chicory?"

The visitor turned out to be one of the deputies from Ashburn. It was the closest town, about three miles south of their farm. Mary had joined them on the porch while the young man had ridden up.

"Sorry, I don't think I have time, Ma'am," Zack nodded from atop his horse. "Sheriff Gelb sent me to get your husband."

"What's the problem?" she asked.

"Not sure, Ma'am. The Sheriff just said it was important that the Judge come to town." He touched his hip where a small ham radio sat. "Sorry, the battery is low but I think he said someone's been shot."

"Let me grab some things and I'll be right with you." Alex said, standing.

"I'll saddle you a horse," Zeddie said.

* * *

Ashburn was a little more than a hundred miles north of Saint Louis, on the Missouri side of the Mississippi river and twenty miles south of Hannibal, the nearest town with a bridge across the river since Louisiana's Highway 54 bridge became too dangerous to cross a few years back. The words that best summed the town up were sleepy and dull, and the residents seemed to like it that way. It had about two thousand people if you counted the surrounding area, and then perhaps another thousand from across the Mississippi from neighboring Illinois by way of the informal ferry a mile south.

As they came within sight of the field that served as the town square, Zack brought his horse to a stop. "Look at that! It's a balloon."

"It's not a balloon," Alex said. "It's a zeppelin."

The vehicle squatted like a pregnant sow, fat and happy. From the surrounding trees he could tell it was over three hundred feet long. Its dual gasbag set up took him a moment to recognize.

"That's one of the Arctic heavy lift vehicles," Alex stated.

The rush for Arctic shale oil had been both a godsend and a curse. It had tempered Peak Oil but the companies had oversold the length the fields would produce, and when the inevitable happened and the gas stopped, it all came crashing down on the world. Still in the early day of the Rush, as the permafrost melted and the roads turned to mush, companies had scrambled to get men and equipment to the drilling sites. An old technology had been resurrected, and a fleet of zeppelins had brought supplies north. Now they had other duties, but what one was doing in Ashburn was a mystery.

The airship wasn't the only thing new in town. As they got closer to the Town Square, where the Police Station and City Hall was, Alex started noticing the Visitors.

Ashburn had two general stores, as well as a variety of other merchants. The goods and clothing you found in those stores was practical and sturdy. Jeans and flannel shirts, sturdy leather coats, were the staple of the dress in the community. There were some fancy dresses for the women folk to wear at festivals, but Alex very much doubted he'd find what the Visitors were wearing on the local racks.

Alex led their horses at a walk up Second Street towards City Hall. They passed Jagger's General Store. Outside two of the Visitors were looking over the fall apples in bins against the wall of the store.

He recognized the style then, from classes he'd taken back in college: Victorian, with the long skirts and blouses tightly bound with corsets, but the old English had never seen such colors—neon yellows, oranges and blues, with trim of pinks and purples. The two ladies looking at the fruit both had frilly parasols on their shoulders. A man came out of the store and joined them. Alex swore he had a waist coat and tails. The short jacket he wore was a bright lime green with yellow cuffs. He had tall boots of polished leather almost to his knees. One of the ladies aimed a small device at her companion. The other laughed and held up an apple for display. It had been years since Alex had had a cell phone, and he didn't miss having one, but he guessed that was what she was using, though he didn't expect he would recognize it if she showed it to him.

The other thing that stood out to Alex was the Visitors' weight. The man had to be over 250, he estimated, and both ladies over 160. Alex grown up when obesity among his peers was common enough, but living here for decades now, eating food grown by hand and without the additives and hormones Big Agro used back then, being overweight wasn't something that happened much.

"They look like movie stars," Zack said.

Alex turned towards the deputy.

"Movie stars?" he asked.

"Yeah, they all look so well fed and healthy. Peter King swears he's never been better since hitting 225. I read it the other day in an e-zine at Julie Wilson's," Zack explained. "Her sister lives in Kansas City and mails her flash chip downloads of the media e-zines and sometimes new movies too. Julie's brother Michael rigged up a pedal generator to their old 3DTV so we can watch them. We all get together whenever she gets a new one in."

"Peter King?"

"He's only *the* number one action star now." Zack said. "You know, *Heavy Weapon* and *Heavy Weapon—Reloaded.* You have to have seen one of those?"

Alex gave him a blank look.

"Anyway, yeah, you know." Zack smiled. "Big is the new small."

They arrived turned off the street into the City Center. There were a couple of other horses tied up in front of the Police Station, along with Doc Gozio's little ethanol three wheeler.

"I'll take your horse around back and see she gets some water," Zack said as Alex slid from his horse. "Let Marsha know when you're ready to leave and I'll bring her around."

To the side of the building were about a dozen people with a wagon and team. That would be community service going out to gather firewood for the town offices and the coming winter. Ashburn, like most small towns, coppiced trees. Every household pitched in a couple of days each month. There was always something that needed to be repaired, replaced, or in this case, a long day of chopping wood and dropping a few trees.

There were two of the Visitors sitting outside the City Hall door, but both had different dress: a utilitarian uniform that Alex didn't recognize. Both were big, but in a muscular way. He gave them both a neighborly nod, which went unanswered, then entered the building.

* * *

"Thanks for coming, Your Honor." Sheriff Gelb stuck out his hand. "Sorry it was on such short notice."

Marsha, the City Clerk, had led Alex not to the Sheriff's office as he'd expected but to the Mayor's. Danny Waters, the Mayor, was there as were several of the City Council. They all looked nervous.

And there was one other.

"This is Grant Morris, captain of the airship."

Captain Morris was a short man, with close-cropped black hair. He wore a uniform like the two outside, but with outrageous edging and frills you would expect of someone who held command. He also had a few pounds on him, but nothing like the Visitors Alex had seen as he'd ridden in.

"My pleasure, Magistrate." Captain Morris held out his hand.

"What brings you to our small town?" Alex asked.

79

The man had a firm handshake, and his speech held a trace of accent that Alex associated with the French.

"The Canadian company I work for is starting up a new air travel service along the Mississippi River, from Duluth to New Orleans. We already have a route along the Great Lakes from Quebec to Duluth." Captain Morris explained. "The 'Josephine' was headed to Saint Louis to set up our base there, with equipment and personnel, as well as some of our investors and their families. This is our third day out."

Air travel, now that was something from before the Descent. The day when you could just board an airplane and fly across the world went the way of oil below $200 a barrel. Now with oil ten times that price, air travel was the kind of fairy tale you told to your grandchildren. Once or twice a year, you might see a white contrail, high in the sky, as some remnant technological marvel winged its way from point A to point B, taking who knows who, important enough to command scarce resources. For the rest of mankind, a long trip, if you could afford it, meant a hard bench on a slow train. Alex could see where the mega-rich, and there were still those out there, wouldn't appreciate rubbing shoulders with the great unwashed masses, even in a private train car.

"Someone got shot?" Alex asked, bringing the focus back to why he was here.

"The incident happened last night, around 11pm." Captain Morris began. "We had tied down and were secure for the night."

"You had landed?"

"Yes, with the high winds yesterday, I decided it was best to wait it out on the ground. We have an airbag landing system so we can set down just about anywhere there is open ground. We found a spot on the north side of the island a few miles upriver from here," Captain Morris explained. "The 'Josephine' is a hybrid airship. When she was retrofitted a few years back, the Chinese installed solar cells across her upper half. The engines can run on electricity or hydrogen gas. The panels' output is high enough to give us extra, once the batteries are fully charged, even with the engines running, so we have a small hydrogen cracker on board. We draw up fresh water and refine our own fuel."

"That's nice tech," Alex said.

"Yes, but our top speed is around 40 miles an hour, and when the winds get high it's usually better to wait them out than fight them. This is my first journey along this route, so with darkness and storm, I thought it best to play it safe."

"Probably a wise move." Alex nodded. "The shooting happened around 11pm?"

"I was having some coffee before bed, updating my logs on my laptop when I heard the gunshot. Think it was 11:05 or 11:06. I rushed down to see what was going on."

"What did you find?" Alex asked.

"Several of my crew had arrived before me. They were tending to Mister Ceriveire's wound after they secured the criminal. I had them lock him in one of the storage lockers."

"Did anyone see the shooting?"

"No, the two men were alone in the lounge," Captain Morris answered. "The 'Josephine' has a small sitting area off the dining room, and both of them have a nice view of the ground as we travel. Many of the passengers like to sit there as we fly."

"You know the two men?" Alex asked.

81

"Jacques Ceriveire is the son of the company's owner. I've met the younger Ceriveire a few times but don't know him well. He is going down to Saint Louis with us to help with the operations there. His father wanted him to have some experience in the field."

"The other man?"

"I do not know him. He is one of the small groups of passengers we picked up in Minneapolis."

"Kevin Schow, by his identifications." Sheriff Gelb added. "Though he has a second ID that names him Louis Maselus. Says he's from Chicago and that he was on vacation."

Vacation, Alex thought, and chuckled. He tried to remember when the last time was that he went on a vacation. Working a farm you depended on to feed you during the long winter wasn't conductive to a vacation.

"Our cook was the first there," Captain Morris continued. "He found Schow standing over Mister Ceriveire, holding the gun. Mister Ceriveire said that Schow was the one who shot him, while trying to rob him. He said Schow had been playing cards and lost badly, then came back to get the money by force. Schow had Mister Ceriveire's wallet on him when we secured him."

"Seems pretty open and shut," Mayor Waters said.

"Most regrettable, I assure you. All this trouble." Captain Morris replied. "I have told everyone here that we would be taking the criminal on to Saint Louis for the authorities to deal with there."

Alex never liked 'open and shut' when referred to crime. He'd spent six years on the Bench, including a year during the "Summer of Rage" back in 2024, and he knew there was always something more to it. Still he'd also learned not to go asking for trouble.

"So what is the problem then?" Alex asked.

"Well, your Honor," Sheriff Gelb answered. "Seems Mister Schow is demanding his right to trial here."

* * *

Someone was laughing as the sheriff unlocked the door to the jail cells.

"Damn," said a voice Alex recognized. "Never saw anyone with such bad luck!"

The jail only had three cells. Most of the time they sat empty, or had someone sleeping it off from a late night. At the moment only one had an occupant. Sitting in front of that cell was Brentley Little, deputy in charge of the cells today. He turned, seeing them enter.

"Hi Uncle Alex!" he waved, holding some playing cards.

Brentley was also his wife Mary's nephew, much to Alex's amusement. To say Brentley wasn't the sharpest knife in the rack was an insult to dull knives. From the look of things he had pulled up a couple of chairs next to the bars and was playing cards with the person in the cell.

"Deputy Little, what the hell are you doing?" Sheriff Gelb exclaimed. "Get over here!"

While the Sheriff read the Riot Act to his deputy, Alex took time to study the man in the cell. In his early thirties, Alex guessed. Brown curly hair to his shoulders, and a handsome face, though marred by what would soon be a world class black eye. He had dark red pants, knee high riding boots and a light blue shirt, which showed wear and a few stains. He shook his head, figuring that the man's treatment at the airship's crew had not been gentle. What surprised Alex was his build, he didn't have the weight common to the Visitors Alex had seen so far.

"Sheriff, can you give me a few minutes?" Alex asked. "I'd like to talk to the prisoner alone."

* * *

Sitting down in the chair, Alex picked up the cards: a standard deck, with a bit of wear. He shuffled them a couple of times in silence looking at Mister Schow. Alex had found that a man accused of a crime usually took one of several attitudes when first faced with a judge. Many were scared. Some were argumentative. A few were plain crazy. He wondered what this man would do.

The silence wore on, the sound of the cards the only thing in the cells for several minutes. There were few people Alex knew who handled stress very well, just sitting silently, and being in a jail cell accused of attempted murder was what he considered stress. Alex stopped his shuffling and dealt two hands of five card poker onto the chair being used as a table, then set the deck down and picked up the hand closest.

After a moment Schow reached through the bars slowly and took up the other hand. He studied them for a few seconds then discarded two. Alex looked his cards over and then discarded one of his own. He picked up the deck and dealt Schow his two and one for himself. Both men sat there for a minute in silence, studying their cards.

"Did you do it?" Alex asked, setting down a hand with three fives.

"Do what?" Schow asked, setting down a hand with a pair of tens.

Alex picked up the cards and reshuffled the deck, then dealt them both another hand.

"I think he shot himself," Schow said while he studied his cards, before discarding three. "It was a bit chaotic; we were both fighting over the gun."

"Why were you fighting?" Alex discarded three as well.

"He lost quite a bit of money to me yesterday," Schow laid down a hand with a pair of nines. "I think not all of it his. He wanted it back."

Alex laid down a hand with a pair of jacks. Picking up the cards and deck, he reshuffled it again slowly.

"You understand what it means to ask for a trial here?" Alex asked.

"Grew up in a dead end farm town in Kansas not half as big as this one." Schow chuckled dryly. "Yeah, I know."

Alex dealt them both another hand.

"Thing is, I'm a dead man if I get back on the airship." Schow said. "I overheard Ceriveire order a couple of the crew to see if I could fly later, while they were locking me up. They're planning on tossing me out a open door, once they get back to altitude. I think that the only reason I'm alive is they stopped here before they could do it."

"Maybe your luck is changing," Alex stood.

Schow picked up his hand and for the first time some expression showed on his face. Turning the cards over, he laid them on the chair. The hand was two pair, aces and eights: the Dead Man's hand.

"Or maybe not," Alex said.

* * *

A very chastised Brentley waited outside.

"Did you search him for weapons when they brought him over?" Alex asked.

"Of course, Uncle. I'm not a complete dunce."

"What about his boots?"

"No weapons, but he does have a sheath for a knife in the top of his right boot." Brentley looked past Alex into the cell block. "Think we need to search him more thoroughly?"

"You're fine, Brentley," Alex said. "No need for that. Go play some cards but just try not to let him cheat you as much."

"But I was winning, Uncle..."

* * *

"How's the patient?" Alex asked.

They had put Ceriveire in the City Council chamber. It was the one room in the old building with a wall of windows, only two boarded up now. The light from the morning sun streamed in. Would have been plenty of light if Dr. Gozio had had to work. While the City Hall had a Chinese solar system, just a decade old, no one wasted charge when sunlight would do.

"Pretty good," Hideko Gozio said. The doctor was putting his instruments away. "He was lucky the bullet went straight through his lower leg. Painful as hell but going down like it did, it didn't break anything. Even a little bullet like that can do some damage if it clips a bone."

He closed his bag up.

"He'll be on crutches for a while but I expect he'll fully recover. Leave him a scar he can use to impress the ladies, I expect."

"Can I talk with him?"

"Sure, he's got a local in him for the pain, but given the circumstances I didn't want to give him anything stronger." Hideko frowned. "Though he's still a bit hung over. He must have had a hell of a party on last night."

"Where did you get a local?" Alex asked. Drugs were hard to get nowadays.

"The medic on the airship had it. Gonna go over there right now and see about some horse trading. Latest batch of my tonic is ready." Hideko ran the town's only still. "Expect we can write off a lot of supplies because of this." The doctor grinned as he picked up his bag. "Daddy's boy over there only gets the best, from what the medic told me. No one wants to make him mad at them."

* * *

The young man sat in one of the Council's chairs, his leg propped up on a small table. Someone had cut the right leg of his trousers above the knee. The leg itself was bandaged from the knee down to the ankle. He was missing his boots, though he had a sock on his left foot. There was another man in the room, quite a bit older, who was on his knees, trying to put a sock on Ceriveire's bare right foot, without much success.

"Leave it be, Gordon, you oaf," Ceriveire ordered. "Get me a blanket instead."

The servant went over to where a stretcher lay, presumably from the airship, grabbing the blanket on it. He came quickly back and arranged it on the young man's lap.

"Mister Ceriveire, may I have a moment of your time?" Alex asked.

Ceriveire waved Alex over.

"You must be the local magistrate," he said, holding out his hand. "Captain Morris said you would be by."

Alex nodded.

"Is it true you plan on trying that scoundrel here?" Ceriveire asked. "I don't want to bother your town with my troubles. I'm sure we can handle it ourselves."

Taking his time to pull over a chair and sit, Alex took a moment to study the other man in the drama. Ceriveire was in his early twenties, with blond hair in a ponytail. He would weigh out at close to two hundred if Alex judged right, his stomach certainly stretched his shirt—and a fine shirt at that. His clothes spoke of his family's wealth.

"Yes, I've decided to grant Mister Schow's request." Alex answered. "I'd like you to tell me what happened."

"The man robbed me and shot me."

"Yes, Captain Morris mentioned that." Alex leaned back in his chair. "What I need to hear are the details, as complete as you can remember them. Are you and he friends?"

"No, I met the man for the first time yesterday at lunch. He came aboard at Minneapolis. Several people boarded there. He was sitting with Amber, and I asked to join them."

"Amber?"

"Miss Amber Flowers, she's on her way to visit her ailing mother in Saint Louis. She's a most delightful young woman. I gave her a tour of the airship after the meal and we had a wonderful afternoon. She agreed to have dinner with me."

"Do you know if she knew Mister Schow?"

"She said she did not."

"When did you next meet him?"

"That evening. Amber and I had enjoyed the duck; the chief on board is very good." Ceriveire smiled. "We were in the lounge sharing a bottle of champagne and toasting new friends when Schow came in. We had agreed to meet again in Saint Louis once she had seen to her mother and I was settled in. Amber asked him to join us, since most of the tables had other passengers."

"Whose idea was it to play cards?"

Ceriveire took a moment to think.

"Amber's, I believe. The lounge had thinned out a bit. There wasn't anything to see but trees and brush since we were on the ground. She had a deck of cards in her hand bag. I had just ordered us a third bottle as I remember."

"So everyone was drinking?"

"Yes, though Schow said he didn't care for champagne, so he was sipping from a flask he had. Scotch or bourbon, I'm not sure. We played for a bit, then a couple of the other passengers asked to join the game."

"What were you playing for?" Alex asked.

"Mostly coins. Amber told us she had to watch her budget."

"It didn't stay at coins, did it?"

"No, when the others joined us, Schow suggested we up the ante. Amber stopped playing but offered to deal the cards for us."

"How did you do?"

"Very well. She must have been my Lady Luck. I won about three thousand from them before the two decided to call it quits."

"And Schow?"

"I won about two hundred off of him by then. He stayed, saying he wanted a chance to win it back."

"So you continued to play?"

"Yes, after everyone had left and we had the lounge to ourselves, Amber took her leave." Ceriveire said. "She said the champagne had gone to her head and she was going to bed."

"So it was just the two of you then?"

"Yes. We played for about an hour and his luck didn't improve. I took him for about five thousand. He wasn't happy when he left."

"He left you alone in the lounge."

"Yes, I wanted to savor my win and finish the champagne."

"Then Schow came back?"

"It wasn't long. He must have gone back to his room to get his pistol. He claimed I had cheated him and demanded his money back." Ceriveire waved one hand around like a gun. "He was quite drunk, I think. I feared for my life so when he stepped close I went for the gun to get it away from him. While we struggled he shot me."

"That was brave of you."

"It was nothing my father wouldn't have done. We Ceriveires stand up for ourselves."

Alex stood and held his hand out.

"Thanks for your time; that was very enlightening," he said. "I'll want you to stay for the trial, which will be this afternoon, if you don't mind."

"So soon?"

"Yes, there's a few more people I need to interview but I believe we can get this wrapped up fairly quickly and see justice done."

* * *

Captain Morris was waiting for Alex outside of the Council chambers.

"I need to take a look at a few things on board the 'Josephine' if you don't mind, Captain?" Alex told him. "I want to take a look at where it happened, as well as that pistol if I may."

"Of course. Let me just speak with Mister Ceriveire for a minute and I'll take you over personally."

As the captain went past, Alex realized that a second person was waiting in the hall.

"Do you have a moment, Sir?" she asked.

"The delightful Miss Flowers?" he asked. "Here to see her new friend?"

She nodded.

"You should be able to go in to see him, as soon as the captain comes out."

"I hear you are going to have a trial today," she said.

Alex smiled his 'gravely concerned authority smile' and nodded his head. He could see where Cerivere had been so taken by her; she was probably a few years older than the young man, but still very attractive. Like Schow, she was thin and athletic. He bet when she turned up the heat, every man in the room noticed.

"Yes, shooting someone is a very grave offense," he said.

She was nervous as well, but whether that was from her concern for Cevireire and his injuries, or for something else, Alex wasn't sure.

"What will happen to Mister Schow if he's found guilty?" she asked.

The decades when liberals had protested the death penalty with signs outside of prisons were long gone. Too much violence up close, where you saw the results, had hardened people.

"Ma'am, robbery and attempted murder is a capital offense." Alex said flatly. "If he's found guilty, he'll be hanged."

* * *

"Well, sir, I'm a light sleeper, guess the yelling woke me."

Alex was sitting in the airship's dining room. Though it was almost lunch time, the room was empty except for him and Danny Ringer, the ship's cook. Captain Morris had gone to get some things for Alex, leaving him alone to ask his questions.

"I bunk out in the kitchen storeroom at night. Got a nice hammock," Danny said. "Guess it's an old habit. Hard for someone to rob the pantry if they gotta go past you to get it."

The cook was Alex's age, grey and wrinkled, thin but tall.

"And I'm signed for the wine we got," he pulled a key on a chain from his collar. "Some of those bottles cost more than my whole years pay."

"You heard yelling?" Alex asked.

"Yeah, so I got up and grabbed my best rolling pin. She's a beauty; you should see the way she has with a pie crust." Danny grinned. "Anyway, guess I was just about to open the door and see what was going on when I heard the shot."

"So you were over there?" Alex pointed to the door leading to the kitchen.

"Yeah."

"And then what?"

"After a moment I heard someone start yelling again, so I peeked out."

"What did you see?"

"Well that other fellow, he was standing over Mister Ceriveire, I guess. He had this little gun in his hand and was staring at it." Danny said. "Mister Ceriveire was on the floor clutching his leg and yelling."

"Do you remember anything of what he was saying?"

"Lots of curses. Calling the other man a 'cheat' and a 'thief'." Danny said, clearly embarrassed. "Said he was gonna kill him, I guess."

Captain Morris returned, holding a small box.

"Thank you, Danny," Alex said.

The cook got up.

"One last thing," Alex said. "When they finished playing cards and Mister Schow left, what was his mood?"

Danny looked a bit confused.

"It wasn't that other man who left, it was Mister Ceriveire." Danny answered. "And I guess he was pretty pissed."

Alex nodded as the cook left.

"That the pistol?" Alex asked.

"Yes, I bagged it up after we took it off Schow." Captain Morris said, handing it over. "Fingerprints are going to be useless, since a couple of the crew handled it."

"No problem," Alex said, opening the clear plastic bag and pulling the pistol out. "We don't have the budget for that kind of thing."

He didn't recognize the pistol, but the writing on the side was Asian, Chinese if he had to guess. It was also a small gun, with a single stacked magazine of something like .32

caliber. A 'hide-away' as the cops he had known would have said. He put it back into the bag.

"That the other things I asked for?" Alex said.

Captain Morris nodded.

"Damn, that's a lot of money!" he said once Alex had opened Schow's purse and pulled the contents out. "I would have locked it up if I'd known there was so much."

Alex counted over eight thousand in US new dollars and another fifteen thousand in Canadian sovereigns, mostly in one thousand notes: well worth shooting someone over.

"Yeah, there's motive aplenty." Alex said.

Ceriveire's wallet was there too, though it didn't yield as big a bounty, just two bills totaling fifteen sovereigns.

"Something's not right," Captain Morris stated.

Alex nodded.

"One last stop," he said. "And I think we can wrap this up."

* * *

"Those the boots?"

The airship's medic nodded.

The right one had been cut open to the ankle. Alex could clearly see where the bullet had entered by the powder burns. The barrel must have been mere inches away when it fired. The exit hole was a few inches above the ankle, a neat clean hole. The inside though was stained red from blood. The damage didn't interest Alex so much as the modification just below its top. A holster for a small gun.

"I'm going to need to take these," he said.

"Both of them?" the medic asked.

Alex looked at the man, then at the boots. The boots were probably worth a few hundred new dollars. The leather was top rate. He bet that the medic had plans to use that leather for something, or trade it for cash. Having been on the hard edge once or twice, he could sympathize with the man's motives.

"I only need the right one," he stated.

The medic smiled.

"Captain Morris, let's get back to City Hall." Alex said. "I'm done here."

* * *

"All rise," Marsha, the city clerk said loudly. "Court is now in session."

Alex wore his official robes of black. He mounted the raised platform of the judge's bench and set the papers he carried down on the desk. Zack, acting as court bailiff, walked to the front of the bench and set the box he carried down, before retiring to the side.

Schow as defendant sat at the right hand table before Alex's bench. Ceriveire had been carried over from the Council Chamber and now sat at the left. He had a companion. Above the top of the table floated an image of a man, just a foot tall, wearing Visitor style clothing, though a bit drab and dark.

He had introduced himself as Sebastian St. Germain, and was an attorney for Ceriveire's father, holocasted out of Ontario through the 'Josephine's' satellite uplink.

Mayor Waters and the City Council were there, along with Sheriff Gelb and his deputies, Captain Morris and several of his crew, a dozen curious local townspeople, and one more he hadn't expected, Miss Flowers.

"Thank you, everyone," Alex stated. "Please be seated."

He didn't need to, but he shuffled the papers he had brought a bit, letting everyone settle.

"Kevin Schow, do you accept the jurisdiction of this court in the matter of your actions yesterday pertaining to Jacques Ceriveire? You stand accused of attempted murder and robbery."

Schow stood.

"Yes, your Honor," he said. "I accept the court."

Alex nodded.

"Jacques Ceriveire, do you accept the jurisdiction of this court in the matter of your actions with Kevin Schows? You accuse him of attempted murder and robbery." Alex asked. "Given your injuries you don't need to stand, simply affirm your agreement."

Ceriveire clearly didn't quite understand what was going on, Alex saw. The image of St. Germain went translucent and a small sign popped up, "Private." Ceriveire clutched at his left ear and nodded several times before turning back.

"Are we not to have lawyers?" he asked. "People to testify? Detectives to present their findings?"

There was a soft chuckle among the attending crowd.

"What do you think we've been doing all morning?" Alex said. "Mister Ceriviere, I can say from my own experience, lawyers don't bring justice, they bring confusion. We did away with them years ago out here.

"Mister St. Germain, we are working under the 2025 Community Justice Initiative Act. I know you are Canadian but I expect you are familiar with it." Alex continued. "I can't enforce a ban on wi-fi communication between you and your client, given the state of this Court." Alex waved at the simple room. Exotic electronic communication disruption equipment wasn't something you'd find in a country court the size of Ashburn's. "Just remember if he begins spouting legal rulings or law citation, I will pull your plug, understand?" Alex stated. The small avatar bowed.

Alex looked across the room, settling his eyes on Miss Flowers.

"Mister Ceriveire, if I find Mister Schow guilty as you charge him, there will not be any appeals. Sheriff Gelb will march him out of this court room, throw a rope over a tree limb in back, and hang him today."

Alex watched Amber blanch at the prospect. It confirmed his conclusions.

"Then yes, your Honor," Ceriveire said, grinning. "I accept this court and await its verdict."

Alex nodded.

"Kevin Schow, please stand and approach the bench."

* * *

The young man stood and slowly walked forward, coming to a stop before the bench. Alex could see the sweat beading on his brow. He'd made his bet, and now it was time to see how the cards fell.

"As to the charge of attempted murder," Alex banged his gavel once. "I find you not guilty."

There was an explosion of emotion from the room. Ceriveire said a loud curse, while others talked among themselves. Alex banged his gavel a few times to quiet the room.

"The evidence is pretty clear," Alex continued. "Jacques Ceriviere, not you, returned with the gun, and in the struggle one of you shot him. There is not enough evidence to tell who. I find the shooting accidental and non-criminal."

Schow nodded, relieved. Ceriveire, though, was clearly angry, fighting Captain Morris' hand on his shoulder.

"However," Alex continued. "In the matter of robbery, I find you guilty."

That quieted the room.

"The evidence shows you conspired to put Mister Ceriveire into a situation where you could steal his money. That with an accomplice who will remain unnamed, you set him up to trick him out of his money." Alex grinned. "Put myself through law school dealing blackjack at the local casino, son. I can spot marked cards."

Alex saw Ceriveire turn and look Amber's way. The young man had finally connected the dots, Alex thought.

"I order your winnings to be returned to Mister Ceriveire," he said. "And I order you to serve 90 days in community service."

Schow nodded and sat back down.

His verdict clearly had been a surprise for those watching, and for Ceriveire and his people, a big one.

"There is a case yet unresolved before the Bench," Alex said. "Jacques Ceriveire, given your injury you may stay seated."

Looking across the small crowd, Alex shook his head.

"There is no stronger bond than a man's word. In a world turned upside down, and civilization in descent, when one person swears a thing to be true, it must be." Alex banged his gavel once. "For lying to a court of law, Jacques Ceriveire, I find you guilty and sentence you as well to 90 days community service. Deputy, take both men into custody."

That caused a commotion.

* * *

"May I approach the Bench?" St. Germain asked. Captain Morris was holding the holocaster and standing a few steps away.

Alex nodded.

"I have a proposal," the lawyer said. "Let us put up a bond. The boy is clearly unfit to do any work, what with his injures. Let us take him to Saint Louis so he can heal, then say, in a few months he'll return and serve out his sentence."

"And he would actually return?" Alex asked.

"If he doesn't you will get to keep the bond."

"I'm not going to let you buy us off," Alex stated.

"I know his father. He'll hire a bunch of mercs to come down here to get his boy out, whether he's guilty or not. Your people might fight back, but you're a hole in the wall dirt town, whose disappearance no one will miss. This way you get to punish him and still serve justice."

"How so?" Alex asked.

"I know that his father sent sixty thousand in Canadian sovereigns down as seed money, expecting a better exchange rate in St. Louis. I also know that the boy didn't bring any Canadian money of his own. Obvious that the money isn't his," St. Germain replied. "Set his bond at eight thousand new dollars, which will clean him out. His father will hear of this 'misjudgment' from me, I promise. He won't get off lightly."

The hologram flickered a couple of times and the words "Low Signal" appeared.

"There's another reason," the lawyer continued when the transmission firmed up. "I don't know how much news you follow down there, but there's going to be war. The Arctic oil fields, everyone wants them. There was another incident this past week, two naval ships collided. The newsies are all clamoring that it wasn't an accident but a deliberate..."

The hologram flickered again and froze. The words "Lost Signal" appeared.

"It's worse than that," Captain Morris said, when it was clear the lawyer wasn't returning. "Fuel prices, food, electricity, everything is going up. Unemployment is back up over 35%. There were three days of riots in Ontario last month over the cuts to the Basic Ration allocations." Captain Morris pocketed the holocaster. "A smart captain would know when to land and batten down," he said. "Eight thousand would make for a lot of battening down. This town could use it to buy some things now that would help see it through hard times."

Alex considered what had been said. He thought back to the chaos of 2024, and the way the violence had swept up everything in its path. He also considered what that kind of rainy day fund could do for Ashburn.

"Mr. Schow," Alex said.

"Yes, your Honor?"

"I'm going to modify my sentence in your case. You are hereby ordered to serve the time, or pay a fine of two thousand."

"I'll pay the fine, your Honor."

Alex nodded.

"In addition, I declare you a person of low moral standing, and give you until sunset to get out of the city limits." Alex smiled. "I doubt you want to continue on your present journey to St. Louis by air."

"No, I don't think so, your Honor."

"See the clerk then," Alex said.

* * *

"Did you see the fruit?" one said.

"Yes, you'd pay ten times at much home for them," the other replied.

The two Visitors headed back towards the airship, with Julie Wilson, one of the locals, trailing behind them, carrying two huge sacks of what looked like fall apples. The passengers of the zeppelin had been out in the township, and from the reports Alex had heard, buying everything in sight.

"We have to get them to stop here on the way back home," the first said.

"Oh of course!" said the second.

"Our town can profit from this," Mayor Waters said, standing next to Alex on the lawn of the City Hall. "Especially if they make it a regular stop here. I got Captain Morris' pac-mail address. Gonna send him the date of the Harvest Festival."

Across the street, Alex watched Netty Couvion and her older daughter, arms full of homemade blankets, follow two other Visitors towards the ship.

Schow and Amber were being escorted to the city limits. She'd chosen to join him, rather than stay on the airship. A few minutes ago, several crew men had carried Ceriveire to the zeppelin. Everyone seemed happy. Alex just shook his head.

"Someone once told me a very wise thing that I always try and keep in mind." Mayor Waters said. "Justice isn't about the rules; it's about doing the right thing when you know it, even if it breaks the rules."

Alex chuckled.

"The man who told you that was a young idealistic fool at the time," Alex replied. "And he's now an old fool as well, who needs to get back to his farm."

"Tell Mary I said hello," the mayor said, smiling. "See you later then, old fool."

Across from them, the 'Josephine' lifted off.

Traveling Show

By Philip Steiner

The leaves on the maples blazed red and orange along the roadside leading into Arlington that morning. The pair of docile draft horses plodded along, pulling the old Class C Winnebago along the rutted asphalt at a comfortable pace. Grampa reined the converted camper-van to the left, over the faded double yellow line, to avoid a pothole the size of a bathtub. "Annabeth, every time I pull us over into the oncoming lane, I feel like a truck's gonna come around the bend and smack us one."

"Ha ha, funny, Grampa. I don't think that's gonna happen today." They hadn't seen more than two other horse-drawn wagons on the road since setting out at dawn, both loaded high with hay. Every few miles, Grampa pointed out a distant gang of red-capped laborers, mowing a hay field or stooping over rows of potato plants, watched over by two or three constables cradling rifles in the crooks of their arms. Apart from the trees and the birds, they had the road to themselves.

Annabeth's Uncle Ray stuck his head through the hatchway in the wooden bulkhead fitted behind the seats. "Morning," he said, in a mock British falsetto.

"Morning," Grampa replied in an equally ridiculous falsetto.

"Whatcha got, then?" chimed in Annabeth, stifling a giggle.

"Well, there's egg and bacon; egg, sausage and bacon; egg and spam; egg, bacon and spam," said Grampa, rolling his eyes beneath his bushy eyebrows. Uncle Ray began chanting, "Spam, spam, spam, spam," as Grampa continued reciting the lines from Annabeth's favorite Monty Python sketch.

"Have you got anything without spam?" Ray complained. "Have you got anything without spam?" he repeated. By now Annabeth was laughing too hard to respond. Grampa and Ray carried on chanting "spam, spam, spam, spam," until Annabeth, scrubbing tears from her eyes, pleaded with them to stop. Uncle Ray gave her a friendly punch in the shoulder then disappeared back into the van.

As the road rose up to meet the bridge over the Stillaguamish River, Annabeth noticed three men slouching against the chipped concrete barrier that divided the roadway. Still wiping the tears from her cheeks, Annabeth felt her heart skip a beat as they approached the smallest of the trio, who wore a green checked shirt and a wide-brimmed straw hat tipped down over his face. "Tommy?" she said with a tentative wave at the young man. As the drew abreast of the group, the youth looked up, a crooked, toothless leer splitting the straggly whiskers sprouting under his flattened nose.

"No, darlin', the name's Buster, but I can be your Tommy

if you like," he cackled. She slouched down into the bucket seat, her cheeks blazing as bright as the leaves on the trees. Grampa glared back at the trio as they whooped and slapped each other's shoulders.

"Goddam, Annabeth, you don't go calling out to strangers like that," he huffed.

"I thought he was someone I met at the spring planting, he has the same shirt," said Annabeth between sobs, "please don't be mad at me, Gramps."

Uncle Ray stuck his head back through the hatchway curtains. "Everything alright up here?" he asked, reaching for the shotgun in the rack mounted above their heads.

"No trouble," said Grampa, "No need for that, yet."

Still slumped in her seat, Annabeth toyed with the bead bracelet around her right wrist. She raised the beads to her lips, thinking of the warm spring evening when Tommy had surprised her with it. No boy had ever given her a gift, never mind something so pretty as the bracelet. She had thrown her arms around him and kissed him square on the lips without thinking. Now she felt her breath shorten at the thought of seeing him again.

Grampa slowed the horses as they approached the high gate barricading the far end of the bridge. The guard standing atop the platform waved at them and called out, "Howdy, strangers."

"Yeah, howdy yourself, Stan," Grampa called back. "You gonna open that gate today, or do I have run it down?"

Stan chuckled as he pulled on the rope that slid the gate open. "With those two old nags? Thanks to Larkin, you got a fair bit less horsepower than your buggy once had."

"That's a fact, Stan," he replied, "but back in the good old days I couldn't find gasoline growing at the side of the road to make 'em go. Yeah, President Larkin had his strengths, but keeping the tar sands going and the Caliphate on our side wasn't among them."

Stan waved them through and started pulling the gate back into place. "Those boys out at the end of the bridge give you any trouble? I've seen them hanging around for a couple of days. Lieutenant over at the militia post says they're mostly harmless, but who knows."

"Naw, Annabeth thought she knew one of them. Mistaken identity. Well, we better get over to the school grounds and get set up. You'll let Mayor Chu know we're in town?"

Stan lifted up an antique candlestick phone from behind the barrier with a flourish. "We found a complete telephone switchboard in the basement of the post office. Been there in boxes for nearly a hundred and fifty years. Took a hell of a lot of scrounging to find enough three conductor wire. We got it hooked up over the summertime, now the guard stations, the militia post, the mayor's office and the town gates are all wired together." He rattled the hook then said, "Ellen? Put me through to the mayor, if you please."

* * *

On the way into town, they rolled past abandoned strip malls, supermarkets and gas stations gone to weed and rust. Young alder and cottonwood thrust up through the tall grass and bush encroaching on the cracked pavement of the deserted side streets. At the first intersection crossed by a connecting road, a gang of laborers in red caps shoveled gravel from a small wagon into pot holes. Trios of the laborers compacted the gravel fill by lifting and dropping six foot sections of old telephone pole, fitted with spike handles at waist height, singing a rhythmic dirge as they worked.

Not long after Grampa pulled the Larkin Limo into the empty school parking lot and turned out the horses to browse the overgrown weeds amid the drifting autumn leaves, townsfolk stopped by to ask about the show that evening. Annabeth worked hard, dragging out folding chairs from the old school auditorium and setting them up in neat rows before the long side of the Winnebago. She did her best to scrub the chairs clean, despite the blooms of rust and mildew around the seat cushions, stained by the winter rain leaking into the abandoned building.

Annabeth paused to take a drink of water, looking across the road at the store where she had first met Tommy. At some point in the past, an enterprising shopkeeper had replaced the plate glass windows with clapboard siding and constructed a wooden porch along the front of the shop, transforming it into an old-time general store. The aluminum shell of the backlit sign above the door and the once-rotating sign on the post at the corner remained in place, proclaiming "Kwik-Mart" in heavy black letters on a faded orange and yellow field.

Under the shade of the original aluminum canopy, a half-dozen elderly men sat on wooden chairs and crates, spitting sunflower shells into the road and sipping from tall brown bottles. A couple of teenaged boys came out of the shop carrying sacks of grain. Neither wore a green checked shirt.

"Annabeth, I need you to go down to Chesko's to see if he's got anything new for us," Uncle Ray called down from the roof of the camper-van. "Tell him I'm looking for any RNL connectors he can spare, doesn't matter male or female.

He'll know what I'm talking about." He tilted up another of the solar panels hinged to the top surface of the camper-van, angling it to catch the maximum sunlight.

"Don't worry, Uncle, I know what those are. Didn't I help you tinker that contraption together all last winter?" said Annabeth. She lifted a black and green coaster bike off the back of the van, the tires patterned in a quilt-work of the reused automobile seat belts from which they were fashioned.

She passed a farrier's workshop as she rolled down Union Street, a thread of grey smoke streaming from the chimney that poked through the roof of the former auto body shop. Remembering Grampa had muttered something about Alice's left shoe needing replacement, she stopped outside the open bay door. She banged on the door to get the farrier's attention over the rhythmic clanging of his hammer on the anvil.

"Well, if it isn't Miss Annabeth. That must mean it's show time tonight," exclaimed the farrier as he scrubbed his forehead with his sleeve.

"Yes, sir, Mr. Leeman," she replied.

"Oh, none of this 'sir', business, Annabeth. My Katie's been asking for weeks when you'd be back in town. It's nice for her to have another young lady her own age to gossip with, anyways."

"Yes, uh, you can tell her we're setting up for tonight, right at dusk. I'll look forward to seeing her, too," Annabeth said, "but I was also wondering if you can have a look at Alice, maybe tomorrow morning? She's losing a shoe, Grampa thinks."

Leeman scratched his head. "I s'pose I can try to nail it

back in place, but if the shoe's bust, I won't be able to replace it. I'm still waiting for a load of rebar."

"Alright, I'll let Grampa know he can bring Alice over in the morning," she said as she stepped onto the bike.

Further down the road, she skirted around a gang of red-capped workers loading lengths of steel I-beam onto a horse-drawn wagon. A constable outfitted in a dark blue uniform and high leather boots cradled a long rifle in his arms as he watched over the workers. One of the workers stooping down to lift a rusted steel bar, a gaunt man with a blond ponytail hanging down below his floppy red cap, looked up deliberately at Annabeth as she negotiated the corrugated surface of the pavement.

"Get your eyes back where they belong, stooker," barked the guard, who was not much older than his prisoner. The man's eyes held Annabeth's for a moment longer, then he heaved at the end of the steel beam with a congested grunt. Annabeth felt a wave of revulsion. Grampa hated the refugees from California, who raided fields, barnyards and orchards. Grampa explained they were called "stookers" because they often set fire to stooks, the stacked sheaves of grain lying out in the fields after the harvest.

She churned the pedals quickly the rest of the way up the dusty road, halting with a screech of brakes before a plain shopfront huddled in a row of boarded-up commercial workshops. A simple hand-carved wooden sign nailed over the door announced, "Chesko Industries".

"Hello, Parker," said Annabeth to the Chesko's scruffy assistant, who sat tipped back on a rusted metal chair beside the gated door. As he tipped forward to stand, she said, "I can get the door myself."

"Thank you, young lady," said Parker with a cough, "my old bones don't move as quick as they once did." He nodded toward Annabeth's bicycle and said, "I'll keep a good eye on your bike while you're inside with the boss."

Inside the musty shop, Chesko greeted Annabeth with a smile. "If it isn't my best customer," he said, setting down a carton on the counter.

"Hi, Mr. Chesko. Have you got anything for my Uncle Ray?" she asked. "Oh, and he also wants any RNL connectors you can spare."

Chesko nodded and ducked behind a curtain, leaving Annabeth alone with two tabby cats stretched out on a dingy carpet amid boxes and cartons of old magazines and books. She lifted a small magazine from a box, the pungent aroma of cheap ink and decaying pulp paper tickling her nose as she brushed away a layer of dust. On the front cover, a scantily clad woman cowered behind a heroic man, clad in silvery overalls and a clear bubble helmet, pointing an outlandish blaster at a furry green alien space bat. The gaudy text below the image promised "Dirk Steele Tames the Savage Beasts of Venus!" She flipped through the yellowed pages, wondering how her great-grandparents ever believed such fairy tales, then tossed it back in the box. She scratched the caramel tabby behind the ears until he purred.

The shelves along the one wall were lined with salvaged LED lamps, toasters and other small appliances that Chesko mended and resold to those folks who could still afford to buy solar PV panels or one of the generators Chesko built in the back of the shop. One of the ungainly generators stood in the middle of the floor, crafted from an old bicycle, a 12 volt automobile alternator and four high capacity batteries.

Chesko reappeared and handed a DVD, two Blu-Rays and a Holo-D remake of "Gone with the Wind" to Annabeth. She looked them over as Chesko rummaged in a bin under the counter.

"Hmm, the DVD looks interesting, but I think it's incompatible with Uncle Ray's equipment. I'll take it any way in case we come across a player." She flipped the Holo-D over and studied the notes. "Hey, this was engineered using Pixar's Realityscape Engine. Copyright, 2023. Let's see, stars Kira Knightley as Scarlett O'Hara, Clark Gable reprises his role as Rhett Butler, and Leo Seeves as Ashley Wilkes."

Chesko stood up, red-faced, and handed Annabeth a half-dozen silvery wafers. "That's all I've got for now. My boys will be back from Renton late today or tomorrow. They might have found some more."

Annabeth rattled the connectors in her palm. "This is fine. I think Uncle Ray's just being cautious. How much for all this?" she asked. Chesko added up the figures on a small chalk slate, then said, "All in, I'll give it to you for forty bucks."

"Okay, but the Holo-D's got some scratches, it might not play, and we can't really test the DVD. How about twenty?"

Chesko scratched his chin, then sighed. "Okay, I'll split the difference with you. Thirty. Good thing you're my best customer," he chuckled.

Annabeth congratulated herself on making a good bargain. Grampa would be pleased. She counted out the New Cascadian Bucks in coins on the felt mat on the counter, then stowed her purchases in her shoulder bag.

Back at the schoolground, Annabeth handed the disks and

111

connectors to Ray. He held one of the Blu-Ray disks at an angle to the sunlight, inspecting it for scratches. "It's getting harder to find decent disks. You wouldn't know, kid, but back before the war, your Mom and I practically grew up watching movies. We both thought we'd move to LA and get into the business. Of course, everything was uploaded straight to the cloud back when we were kids. I think I was about ten when the last Holo-D's went out of production. Now it's all gone, all the Academy winners for the last 30 years, after all the distribution moved online and they stopped making old disks like these."

Annabeth glanced up at the puffy white cumulus building over the mountains to the east. She still had a hard time imagining what the world was like when her Mom and Uncle were little, when movies like these were available anywhere, anytime, and everyone carried devices around with them everywhere to talk and listen and watch. She knew, vaguely, that the armies and leaders in far-off Vancouver and Seattle still used some form of these devices, but around here, it was mostly talking face to face, or sending a hand-written letter home to her Mom in the weekly mail pickup.

As dusk gathered, townfolk drifted into the school parking lot in twos and threes. The majority were middle-aged or older, sometimes accompanied by children and grandchildren. Annabeth noticed the seniors tended to dress in old-fashioned clothes, the men wearing long, buttoned jackets over pot bellies, glittering baseball caps with long brims covering bald spots, the women trailing brightly-colored ruffled skirts over tall-heeled lace up boots. Some of the fabriclight effects still worked, painting ghostly washes of color, geometric patterns or even old advertising slogans across torsos and arms. Many of the younger folk wore knee-length brown or russet tunics, belted over leggings and sturdy boots, that Annabeth found more to her liking.

As the seats filled up, Annabeth helped collect town scrip, Cascadia bucks, bottles of preserves and even bolts of homespun wool cloth in payment. The first stars appeared in the sky. Grampa, Ray and Annabeth took their jackets from the back of the camper-van. "I hope there's enough juice in those batteries, Ray," Grampa said tapping on a small LCD meter mounted in a panel on the side of the van.

"I replaced a couple of the connectors this afternoon, should have helped," replied Ray, "and I swapped out one of the old batteries for the one I reconditioned. We should be good for at least three hours."

Grampa stood upright, stretching with his hands on the small of his back. "I guess. We've managed okay on this tour so far. Marysville tomorrow, Snohomish on Thursday, then we head home for the winter. And school for you, young lady, one more year to go," he said, pinching Annabeth on her cheek.

"Ow, Grampa, I'm not a baby anymore," she cried in mock outrage, putting her hand to her cheek. "Besides, I can apprentice to Uncle Ray when I've finished school. Lot more useful than math or reading old books."

"No, it's not the same as when I was your age. The world was far more complex. We had to spend at least ten more years, and maybe a hundred thousand old American dollars, just to get enough of a basic degree to enter the workforce. Then it took years to pay off the loans. I can't tell you how many of my classmates ended up working low wage jobs despite their education, forever shackled to that debt. It was a great travesty."

Grampa shook his head. "Well, that's not going to get the show on, is it?" He turned and trotted over to the small pool of light cast by an LED lamp attached to the side of the camper-van. Annabeth could tell he was happiest when he played the showman.

"Good folks of Arlington, welcome to our humble show," he said, lifting his arms in greeting. The crowd responded with a rousing cheer. "I am glad so many of you could take time out to honor us with your attention. First, I think the Mayor wants to say a few words."

Grampa motioned for Mayor Chu to come forward. He thanked the townsfolk for their redoubled efforts getting the crops taken in this autumn, especially since the loss of twenty young men to the militia draft.

Annabeth shifted uncomfortably at the mention of the draft, scanning the faces again for Tommy. She knew Tommy was a couple of years older than her, maybe old enough for the militia to take him. She caught sight of Katie, the farrier's daughter, smiling at her. Katie gave Annabeth a little half-wave, then shrugged. Annabeth felt Katie knew what was on her mind.

Mayor Chu concluded his speech, waving to the applauding crowd as he took his seat. Annabeth moved over to the side of the red velvet curtain draped along the long side of the camper-van. Uncle Ray, standing at the open back of the van, whispered, "Three, two, one, go."

Annabeth pulled a cord hanging from the curtain rail. Dramatically, the curtain dropped aside, just as a panoramic view of distant white-capped Mount Rainier, framing the new Chancellery Building in Seattle, lit up the three meter-wide screen in brilliant color, and the Cascadian Anthem boomed from the speakers.

Most of the audience brought themselves to attention as the image of the Cascadian flag waved onscreen against a backdrop of towering mountains and rushing waterfalls.

A few of the older men remained seated, heads bowed. At the showing last spring, Grampa told Annabeth that many of the men had fought in the war, and mourned their lost comrades. Some still refused to accept the Cascadian flag, calling it a perversion of the Stars and Stripes, the old American flag. And some were just too lame from war wounds or farm accidents to stand for very long.

The crowd sat down quietly as the anthem reached its crescendo. After a moment, a familiar slap-bass guitar riff brought a cheer from the crowd. The screen lit up with an interior shot of an apartment. Kramer flung the door back and skidded into the room, yelling, "Jerry."

For the next three hours the crowd cheered and laughed to short cartoons, an episode of Barney, a highlight reel from the 2019 Super Bowl and a feature film, "Along the Rio", winner of the 2027 Oscar for Best Picture, and the last feature Brad Pitt made before succumbing to cancer.

Many of the seniors sang along with the music, some of the sprightlier ones dancing on the side. Here and there a child would tug on a parent's sleeve, asking if people really did fly through the air in jet planes, just like the ones in the movie.

Annabeth sat in a chair at the side of the screen, keeping an eye on the crowd and ready to help Uncle Ray with any technical problems. She followed the progress of a couple of local entrepreneurs walking around the edges of the seating area, selling bowls of popcorn and bottles of homemade beer.

When the beer seller reached the far end of the crowd, Annabeth noticed three men standing behind the last row of chairs, arms crossed, staring toward the screen with heads close together in conspiracy. They were the same three drifters she noticed on the bridge into Arlington the previous day. She felt a wave of revulsion as the skinny one in the green shirt caught sight of her and lifted his hat to her in salute.

As the beer vendor passed by the drifters, the tall one in the baseball cap made a grab toward the tray of bottles she had slung around her neck. A town constable quickly intervened, sending the drifters off into the dark night. Annabeth could hear them shouting curses at the crowd as they ran away into the darkness of the night.

After the show, one of the old timers hobbled up as Annabeth and Ray packed away the gear. "That's one hell of a wide screen you got there," he said, raising a gnarled hand tentatively toward the shiny black plastic of the bezel. "Where on Earth didja find it?"

Ray pulled a soft rag from his pocket and dabbed at the corner of the immaculate screen. "I found this baby in an antique shop over in Hudsonville, all wrapped in cloth at the back," Ray said. "The owner wasn't even sure if it would power up without a network connection to validate the ID code. But, I like to think of myself as one of those old-time hackers, so I fiddled a bit and bypassed the auth code. Yep, this is my pride and joy," he said, polishing the shiny black frame of the massive screen.

The old man stuffed his hands into his pockets and sighed. "Back in the day, I had a sixty-inch plasma ultra HD with Dolby QXT sound. Had to sell it, cheap, to buy gasoline for getting to work. Sure do 'preciate seeing those old shows, brings back some good memories...," he trailed off as he shuffled away into the warm night. Ray just looked at Annabeth with a shrug.

* * *

The next night, many of the same folks turned out again. Midway through an episode of "Crimewatch: Miami", a band of robed marchers trooped up the main street, thumping on drums and chanting, "Return to the Mother, give back to the Earth."

A tall man with long brown hair and a full beard lead the procession. Ray paused the show as the leader stopped at the edge of the field, raised his hands in supplication and inveighed against the sins of the past, calling on the good people of Arlington to abandon the worship of the wastefulness of the old American Way.

Three oldsters stood up and yelled at the man, "Go on, Granger, take your Gaians back to your temple, we're trying to watch a show, here." A couple of boys threw corncobs at the marchers. With a sad nod of his head, the leader turned his flock back down the road. A few of the young men in the audience trotted after the troupe. Annabeth wasn't sure whether they intended to join or harass the Gaians.

She slipped into the crowd as Uncle Ray started the show again, found Katie and crouched down beside her chair.

"Hi, it's good to see you back again," whispered Katie.

"Yeah, it's not so bad being on the road. Most of the time it's just boring." Annabeth looked around at the crowd again, then said, "um, you haven't seen Tommy around today, have you?"

Katie looked down at her fingers twisted together in her lap, then back at Annabeth. "Tommy got drafted."

Annabeth sat back on the ground. "Drafted? Why? He isn't old enough, is he?" she asked, touching the bracelet on her wrist.

Katie nodded. "They lowered the draft age to seventeen a month after his birthday. My mom saw Tommy's father a couple of weeks ago. He said Tommy's platoon was sent south, towards the Oregon boundary. They've had only one letter from him the whole six months, and he didn't say much in it."

Annabeth didn't pay much attention to the conversation after that, and wasn't much help cleaning up after the show.

* * *

The next morning, as Annabeth stacked the chairs in the school auditorium, a middle-aged woman appeared in the doorway. "Hello, are you Annabeth?" the woman asked, a worried smile creasing her face. Annabeth nodded.

"I'm Tommy's Aunt Lilly," the woman continued. Annabeth twisted the bracelet around her wrist with one hand. "Katie came around this morning, she told me about you and Tommy. He was drafted back in late May, not long after you were last here. I haven't seen him since, but I did receive a letter from him just a couple of days ago. Would you like to see it?" She held the folded sheet out to Annabeth.

Annabeth took it between two fingers, as though it might sting her. She read Tommy's neat block printing, addressed to his Aunt Lilly. In the third paragraph, he mentioned meeting Annabeth at the spring planting festival, and asked Lilly to give Annabeth his regards and regrets that he did not think he would be back in time to see her.

Annabeth's heart jumped when she read the next paragraph. "He says his cavalry troop passed through the ruins of Everett only a few days ago," she said, looking up at Lilly. "Does that mean they're coming back this way?"

Lilly nodded. "I heard a rumor at the pub, from the garrison sergeant, that the army is pulling back from Oregon for the winter. The Sixth Cavalry's already gone through to Vancouver."

Annabeth clutched the thin sheet in her hands. "Would you like to keep the letter?" asked Lilly. Annabeth carefully folded it back up along the creases, then nodded. "Thank you for coming to find me, Ma'am."

Uncle Ray pushed a trolley loaded with chairs in through the doors. "That's the last of them, Annabeth, you finish up quick in here, 'cause we want to get a good start on the road this morning."

Lilly nodded in return to Annabeth and said, "I won't keep you from your chores. But you come find me next time you're in town, alright?" Annabeth nodded again, carefully tucking the envelope into her pocket.

Once the Larkin Limo was loaded and the horses hitched up, two mounted guards from the town militia rode up alongside and escorted them out through the south gate onto the road. Annabeth and Ray began an impromptu performance of a Seinfeld episode on the railed roof of the camper-van, Annabeth's perfect imitation of Elaine's nasal whine matched by Ray's take on Jerry. The escorts roared with laughter, nearly falling off their mounts.

The escorts pulled up short as they approached a

towering tree leaning out over the road. "Folks, this is our patrol limit," said the earnest constable, tipping his cap to Grampa. "I wish we could take you along a bit farther. I don't think you'll have too much trouble from here on, see, the bandits don't bother too much between here and Marysville," he said, pointing up into the tree. A skeleton, held together only by sinews and faded rags, swung in the breeze from a rope tied to a high limb in the tree. "We make sure they get the message."

Grampa waved and slapped the reins. As the old Larkin Limo creaked and swayed up the shallow incline of the pockmarked road, Annabeth looked back toward the town until the tree disappeared from sight behind a curve in the road.

* * *

An hour further along, where towering hemlock and Douglas fir closed in a canopy over the rising crest of a hill, three bandits sauntered out from the bushes at the margin of the road, shotguns dangling from gloved hands. They planted themselves square in the middle of the cracked and buckled pavement.

Grampa hollered, "Whoa, girls." The big roan on the left hand whickered and bobbed her head as Grampa pulled back on the reins. Annabeth pushed herself upright against the cracked brown naugahyde of the passenger bucket seat.

The tall bandit standing at the fore waved the muzzle of his gun in the general direction of the Larkin Limo, spat a brown string of phlegm and announced, "this here's a lawful disposition of a bounty order 'gainst one runaway slave by the name of Lewis Carter, whom we have good cause to b'lieve you have in your possession. Release Carter into my custody and there will be no need for further disruption."

He lifted the battered ball cap from his head with the thumb and forefinger of his free hand, scratched a red spot on his balding crown with the other three fingers, then settled the cap back in place with a tug on the frayed brim. A slightly darker patch on the brow of the cap silhouetted the missing sports team logo.

"Annabeth, Get back inside with your Uncle Ray," Grandpa whispered. She crouched low behind the dashboard, her face pale with fear. "Grampa," she hissed, "I saw those guys hanging around the back of the show last night. He kept scratching his head like that every five minutes. I knew they were trouble."

As the tall one in the baseball cap advanced on the wagon, Annabeth heard the faint sound of horses clopping along the worn asphalt and men chanting in rhythm. The tip of a banner pole appeared over the crest of the hill, rising up behind the bandits. The bandit in the straw hat and green checked shirt, the one Annabeth mistook for Tommy, turned slowly toward the sound. The moment the lead rider's head appeared, he raised a horn to his lips and let out a triple blast.

The bandits whirled in confusion. Four riders broke formation into a gallop, quickly closing the gap to the bandits. The tall bandit in the baseball cap swore and brought his shotgun up at the riders. The gun thundered harmlessly into the air as a trooper's bullet caught his shoulder and spun him around. He crumpled to the ground with a scream. The other bandits dropped their weapons and fell to their knees, hands raised in surrender.

Annabeth felt the wagon lurch, leaning further and

further toward the ditch at the side of the road. The horses reared and stepped backwards, frightened by the noise and commotion. Grampa struggled to maintain control, a wail of anguish rising from his throat.

The world tipped sideways, sending Annabeth tumbling into the weeds in the ditch. A tremendous shattering sound filled the air. Grampa landed next to her, clutching his stomach and gasping for air. "Grampa, can you breathe?" shouted Annabeth. She felt warmth on her cheek. When she touched it, her fingers came away stained red with blood.

Grampa sat up with a rush of breath. "Good God, I thought we were dead," he said. "You're bleeding, dear," he said, reaching up to Annabeth.

"It's nothing, it doesn't hurt," she replied. "Where's Uncle Ray?" she said, turning anxiously to the camper-van. She climbed over the seat and pushed aside the jumbled cushions, boxes and clothing that hung from the hatchway to the back. "Ray," she yelled, "Ray, can you hear me?"

She heard a wailing from the interior of the van. Ray crawled out, clutching a jagged fragment of glossy black plastic. "The screen's busted. The batteries are split open. Acid's everywhere." He climbed out onto the verge and looked in dismay at the solar panels spilled across the ditch. "We're sunk. We can't carry on, I can't get another one of those screens for love nor money."

Annabeth swiped at the drying blood on her face. Ray helped Grampa stand up, and they went to unhitch the horses. She felt numb, oddly detached, as if she were sitting in a chair in the dark, watching her own life up on the big screen. She rested a hand against the side of the camper-van. Someone kept calling her name, but it wasn't Grampa, and it wasn't Uncle Ray.

"Annabeth, Annabeth," the voice cried. She turned slowly to one of the soldiers running across the cracked pavement toward her. How did he know her name?

He tossed his cap aside, bristly brown hair standing up in short military style. For a moment, she was confused, as he wrapped his arms around her. "Tommy," she said, "Tommy." They sank back down to the soft grass together.

For a long while they said nothing, then with a kiss she freed herself from his embrace, stood and walked over to Grampa and Uncle Ray. "I know how we can save the show."

* * *

The spring shower stopped just as the sun burst from below the cloud bank, briefly lighting the school grounds before it sank to the horizon. The audience applauded, putting aside tarps and patched umbrellas.

Up on the folding stage that Uncle Ray and Grampa had attached to the Larkin Limo over the winter, Annabeth and Ray crouched down behind an enormous white cloth screen stretched across a glossy black frame. Behind Annabeth and Ray, bright LED lamps projected the shadows of the cutout puppets that Annabeth and Ray held up behind the screen. Annabeth whined, "Well, Mister Seinfeld, I guess I'll just have to do it myself." She made the cutout Elaine march off the side of the screen, to the roaring of the audience's laughter. Ray winked at her as he jiggled the Kramer cutout at the Jerry cutout, and exclaimed, "What did I say?"

The performance continued for two hours. Annabeth, Ray and Grampa incorporated the names of local townsfolk into the improvised performance. None of the old timers seemed to mind, and a few of the more prominent townsfolk had their ribs poked by their seat mates.

Out in the audience, Tommy sat with his Aunt Lilly, beaming with pride at Annabeth's performance. Lilly leaned over and asked, "So when are you going to propose to her?"

Tommy grinned at her. "I already did, after last night's show." His grin grew wider. Aunt Lilly gave him a mock shove, then kissed him on the cheek.

Maestra y Aprendiz

By Susan Harelson

Halloween

They were pulling the coneflower today, not that much different from digging the flax, really. The petals and leaves were all fallen, leaving the seed heads. Tía Sarah broke off the seedheads and threw them a distance away, out of the oak's shade. "They still need full sun," she explained to her apprentice, "but they'll be far away from where they grew this year." She looked at Rocio to see if she understood.

"You want them to spread, so they get food from the soil there." she said. She was quick.

"And add to it. The roots are good for us, and good for the soil. They can bring minerals up from underground." She pushed the digging fork into the ground well away from the stalk of the 3 year old plant, and levered it upward, gently. They had waited and waited for a wet day so the roots would pull up easier, but the weather hadn't cooperated. They'd pulled buckets of water from the pond to pour on it, and that had helped, but it was still tough. "These plants are three years old, mostly. Some of the root will stay in the soil, and it'll come back, but not as strong. It takes a while to regrow." She looked up at the oak nearby, 150 years old. "And it doesn't get as much sun as it needs, with that tree there."

"You could chop it down?" Rocío suggested.

"Not that one."

"Why not?"

"That one's special." Tía Sarah said.

Rocio figured it had something to do with her Maestra's family, her hombre, Phillip. She told stories about them sometimes, her man, and her suegra, Phillip's mother, who had taught her the things she was now teaching Rocío. Rocío loved to hear stories about the old days. She was never sure whether they were true. People flying, trips all the way to Wyoming just for beer, hot water pouring out of pipes, enormously fat people eating at Chinese restaurants! She thought they were fabulas, cuentos de hada. Imagine— Chinese people running restaurants! Ridiculous.

They talked in a mixture of English and Spanish, neither of them really fluent in the other's mother tongue, but Rocío thought she understood most of the stories. She understood, she just didn't believe them.

"Here, you take it," Tía Sarah said, handing her the digging fork. "Step on it, the way we did with the flax, then lever it up. Palancarlo?"

Rocio shrugged, sometimes Tía used words in Spanish that she had never really heard-- she'd gotten her Spanish out of books, and Rocio often hadn't heard some of the bigger words she used. "Why didn't we scatter the flax seed?"

"Smart question. Flax seed has fat in it—it's good in winter to put it into cereal, so we separate it, some to eat, and some to plant.

The fork groaned against the soil. "I think it's coming!"

"Be careful, I've broken handles that way. Then we'll have to ask your Tío to make a new handle for me."

"Can't you do it?" She made a face. He wasn't really her uncle—he was the man of her mamá, but she called him Tío, por respeto. It was the same way with Tía Sarah—at first her mamá had wanted her to call her Doña Sarah, but she told them she preferred just Sarah at first, then let them call her Tía.

"I know how to make a handle, but he's better at it." she smiled and turned her face to the sun as it came over the roof of the house and began burning the frost off the grass.

The echinacea plant popped out of the soil, and Tía Sarah smiled, "That's good, see, " she pointed, "only a few broken roots- some left in the ground so it comes back next year to feed the bees, but if there's too much broken root, it rots before it can dry."

"And now?"

"We tie it up, and hang it in the garage." She dug in her pockets. "Can you believe…" she fished out a piece of yarn, and began untangling it, "we used to just buy balls of twine in the store. Cut it, tie things up." The piece of string she found was a length of homespun wool, cut from a sweater she'd been weaving in the ends of. There was certainly string in the store now, but who had money? She spent the little money she had on things she needed.

She tied a slip knot and looped it around the great clump of echinacea plant. After it dried, they'd chop the roots and tincture them in alcohol.

When they had first met, Rocio had been astonished at

127

how much alcohol she had bought from Tío. He was a trader, selling mostly alcohol and some marijuana and other drugs. It was a tough balance—the drugs were more profitable, but much more risky, the alcohol weighed more, and was harder to haul, but it was legal.

Then she spent time with her, and learned that Tia Sarah made medicine, and healed people with ceremonies. Tia Sarah had learned her skills from her mother-in-law, someone she called a green witch.

Once they had hung the plants from the rafters in the garage, she said, "Let's go check on your brothers, and the goats."

"Don't we need to write it down, about the roots?"

"You're right, thank you." She looked around for her notebook, "Now where did I leave it?"

"I think I saw it by the greenhouse door."

"Correcto. I wrote about the frost after I took the blankets off the tomatoes."

"They didn't freeze yet?" she moaned. The tomatoes had formed the bulk of their work the past few weeks: slicing, laying them out on the solar dryer, flipping them so they dried evenly, dipping some in boiling water to make them easier to peel, then turning the oven to follow the heat of the sun while the sauce boiled down, then stoking the rocket stove to boil the jars so the sauce would keep all winter. The lunas of her nails were brown and horrible, the acid got in her hangnails. She hated the smell of bruised leaves. "Odio jitomates."

"They'll keep your teeth from falling out this winter."

"How?"

"I don't...it's hard to explain... the vitamins..." she

shrugged, "fruits and vegetables keep you healthy."

"Mágico."

"No, not magic." Sarah grinned, she had finally found the notebook, and noted the echinacea harvest with a very short pencil. "I remember going trick or treating and some people would give out pencils instead of candy. I was always mad. I wish someone would give me a free pencil now."

She did that sometimes, said things that didn't make any sense. Rocío sometimes asked, but often the explanations were even more confusing.

"I want to thank you for helping me bring the citrus trees into the greenhouse yesterday. I had a feeling it would freeze last night, and it did."

"Magico?" she sighed, " No. Probably not."

Tia Sarah sighed too, smiling. She put her journal in the big pocket on her canvas pants, and they began walking north, to where the goats were supposed to be, if the boys were doing their job.

Rocío wanted witchcraft to be about power and knowing, but it turned out to be more about observation and practice, and writing things down; which was getting to be increasingly difficult. Pencils, paper were expensive. She could make ink, but it tended to clog her fountain pen, which had been an antique when she started using it. She had a sudden flash of memory, playing with a ballpoint pen in middle school, the tip coming out, and sticky ink going everywhere. She had gotten in trouble, not for wasting it, but because of the mess. She marveled at the things they had just thrown away back then. She wasn't even sure if the Chinese could afford ballpoint pens anymore. She hadn't seen them in the store for years.

"Magic is different—it's more about your mind, the way you think, even if you don't think you're thinking." She sighed. "Do you remember, when Sarita was born, what did we put under the bed?"

"That knife?"

"Yes. I held it up to your mother, and told her it would cut the pain in half. That was magic. She was willing to believe that the pain would be less—it wouldn't go away, but she could get through it. That was magic."

"It doesn't seem like magic."

"I know. But it is. It's the kind of magic I do." she smiled. "De todos modos, thank you for helping me with the orange trees, I couldn't have done it without you."

Groundhog Day

Today Rocío found her maestra in the greenhouse, in a woven chair, her face turned to the weak southern sun. The air was fragrant with orange blossoms. Everyone was moving slowly today—they'd stayed up late drinking cider, and playing music and singing. Rocío was hoarse. Sarah didn't turn when she felt the chill air.

"I'm glad you're here," she said. "We have to play bee today." her voice was hoarse as well. "We have to pollinate the citrus. My hands are too shaky to do it very well anymore." She took a deep breath and tried to get out of her chair, and was overcome with a coughing fit. Rocío just looked at her, unsure of what to do. Tía Sarah had gotten a cold a few weeks before, the whole family had passed it around. But she hadn't been able to shake it. Echinacea had helped a little, steam had helped a little, but the cold had settled in her lungs and set up housekeeping.

The coughing finished, Tía Sarah was pale, and spit in the soil next to the brick path. She rose, and took Rocío's arm, continuing as if nothing had happened, "We'll use a paintbrush to get pollen off each flower, and move it to the other flowers. The orange and lemon are both blooming at the same time—that's good, I think. I think it means they'll produce more fruit that way. When they bloom in the summer, the bees take care of it for us, but in here we have to do it."

"Why can't you have bees in here?"

"Oh. I…I don't know." she looked thoughtful. "I don't think the bees would like it. Did I ever tell you about when we tried to keep hives?"

She had. But Rocío didn't mind hearing the story again.

"I had done research on the internet, back when that was still up, about keeping bees and what to do, and so we built some hives. Top bar hives were supposed to be better for the bees, so we built one, and got a queen from a man over in Greeley."

Rocío began transferring the pollen from flower to flower, systematically moving around the plants, tickling all of the open flowers with the artist's brush.

"We set it up over there in the corner, where the oak tree is." She faltered a little. "That was when the neighborhood was fuller—Katherine still lived there, and the Petersons, and José and Martín." She was pointing in various directions, here a vacant house, there a cellar hole. "Phillip worried about the neighbors getting stung."

There were no neighbors anymore, not close. Rocío's family had arrived last spring—they had been on the road as long as she could remember. They had come to Loveland with a load of alcohol, some hams, some illicit items for those whom he thought he could trust. They had met Tía Sarah at the marketplace. She had been looking for chocolate, but was happy to trade for a few bottles of alcohol. They would have continued to wander, if Rocío's mother, Noemi, hadn't been tremendously pregnant.

Noemi had been 8 months along, incredibly skinny, except for a watermelon belly and swollen ankles and bags under her eyes. This was her sixth pregnancy, although only Rocío and two brothers had survived infancy. Her feet were swollen and cracked, her back ached constantly. She simply couldn't keep traveling.

Tía Sarah had given them beds in the basement, and insisted that Noemi rest and eat. She had stewed a chicken, dug some onions and garlic and carrots and fed them all.

That had been one of Rocío's early lessons in her apprenticeship: how to quickly and mercifully kill an elderly hen.

They all had chicken stew that first night, and Tía Sarah made sure Noemi got meat and vegetables and fruits every day after that, digging into her pantry and her greenhouse. Rocío and her brothers too could eat until they were full for the first time in their lives—bread and jam and goat cheese until they could barely breathe.

Tía Sarah insisted the family stay even after the baby came, saying that March blizzards could be deadly for them on the road. She had explained to Rocío later that it was a bit of magic—she had helped them change their minds, and because it wasn't completely against their will, they had stayed. She said she regretted using fear to do it, but she thought it was important to keep them safe.

They named the baby Sarita, in her honor.

Rocío was there when the goats kidded, and Tía Sarah taught her brothers, Alejandro and Trevor, how to milk them and lead them to browse.

The baby girl had been strong and healthy, although Noemi was weak. Tía Sarah gave her herb tea to help her make milk, let her sit in the sunshine and get strong.

Again, she insisted they stay, to help her with the homestead. Tío Luís found tools in the garage, and used them to trim trees and cut firewood, clean up branches knocked down by storms and prune some of the fruit trees. He used the carboys in the basement to make wine with rhubarb, then currants, all the fruit in season. He traveled only short distances now, to the communities up and down the interstate, avoiding the army trucks as much as possible, trading wine for marijuana or honey or spices, or other goods that were more portable than the wine. He kept hinting that he wanted to leave, but Noemi was healthy, their baby Sarita was strong, and the three older children dug in their heels. He mostly stopped hinting, although it was obvious he wasn't comfortable.

"Tía, I was just thinking, we've been here a year almost." She had kind of tuned out the story of the bees, just nodding when it seemed appropriate. She had pollinated all the flowers that were open, and noted the ones that would bloom in the next couple of days.

"I know—Sarita will be walking soon."

"You don't think we should move on?" she asked, looking at her out of the corner of her eye. "We don't want to be a burden, eating all of your food. And the boys, they ruined your books."

"Which books?"

"You know the yellow ones, with the pictures? They found pictures of nude girls, and they fought over them."

"Ah. National Geographic. There are plenty of those. I'll talk to them about fighting. And probably your Tío needs to talk to them about the nude girls." she laughed, and coughed a little. "No, you aren't a burden at all. You are a blessing to me, and your family is a blessing to me. I thought I would die alone." her eyes started to fill with tears. "You are welcome to be here. Always."

May Day

Rocío was worried. Tía Sarah hadn't gotten up in several days. She had helped her pee in a bucket in her room, and could tell it hurt her. Rocío had given her Echinacea tincture, and chicken broth made with plenty of garlic and ginger, but she still had a fever, and was weak.

"This infection may kill me." she said. "I've made some arrangements."

"No, you'll be fine." Rocío couldn't bear to think of her maestra's death.

"In the old days, I could have just gotten some medicine, called the doctor's office and said I had a UTI and they'd have called a prescription in to Walgreens." She sighed. She remembered the dark days when the medical system crumbled, shortages first of medicines for very ill people, like cancer or AIDS, then more everyday things, antibiotics, which grew less effective every day anyway.

Without wanting to, she went back in her memory, to this

very room that she'd shared with Phillip. The western sun coming through the window, their baby girl Lexie had woken up the night before with a fever, crying, with bright red skin. They'd tried to call the doctor's office, but phone service was spotty, when they had a signal no one picked up at the doctor's office. In their bed, she'd watched the sun go down through the window, holding the baby while she seized. Her mother-in-law kept coming with cool cloths, and teas, but nothing could have helped. By the time it was dark, she was gone.

"I've watched lots of people die. It's always hard. We all will die someday, but I can't resign myself to it." She was on the edge of crying, "I want to fight, but I'm so tired."

"Have more tea." Rocío held out the cup, her hands shaking a little.

"I know it is supposed to help, but I know it will make me pee, and it just hurts."

"I know. Drink it anyway." Suddenly, Rocío, at 14, was the adult, and Tía was the child. The tea was made with dandelion root, and ginger and garlic, all of the powerhouse herbs, and it tasted horrific. Sarah sipped some, gagged, then took a deep breath and swallowed the whole cup. It was noxious.

"My kidney is what hurts now."

"Is that worse, Maestra?" She handed her another mug, this time with tea brewed from poppy seed pods, for the pain.

"I don't know." she drank the tea—it had honey to cover the bitterness. "I think it is worse. If I can fight the infection, I'll be okay. When you make the dandelion tea next time, use lemon juice, if the lemons are ripe?" she set down the now empty mug and picked up the sock she had been working on.

"The arrangements. I've made arrangements—a will, a testamento, so you have, your family has ownership of all that's mine." She attempted to knit, but the poppy tea had made her hands clumsy even as it took away the pain. "The lawyer says it is as tight as she can make it—if they change the law, you may have to fight, but you should be able to stay here."

"But we don't have papers." Rocío objected. Land ownership wasn't legal for non-citizens.

"I paid the filing fee, for your papers. The lawyer made sure it was watertight." It had taken all the cash she'd saved, but she thought it was worth it, if she could keep her people safe. She thought of them as her people, now, even though there was no blood relation. "Your Tío will want to move. Try to get him to stay. He likes to wander, but it is safer for you to stay."

Her eyes drooped and she fought to keep them open. "The will is on file at the lawyer's office. What's mine is yours. The government might still be able to take it away, but the lawyer says she's done what she can do."

That explained who the visitor had been, a woman that Tía Sarah had introduced, and then spent several hours with in the study with the door closed.

"I'd like to be buried by the oak tree, next to Phillip." she said as she drifted off to sleep.

Empire Day

She didn't die that night, but she was weak. She had spent the rest of the spring and early summer basking in the sun, using a stick to help her balance when she walked. It was obvious her kidney still hurt her, some days more than others.

Today, she was sitting in a chair brought out to the shade, watching Rocío plant a fall crop of peas in the garden beds that surrounded the water tank. It was the same chair that a year previously had sat Noemi while she recovered from childbirth. Her tocaya, Sarita, was toddling around now. She had pulled herself up on the raised edge of the garden bed and was eating the soil. She looked like she had a beard. Noemi came over and scolded her, then put her into Tía Sarah's open arms. "Later, I'll have you do carrots, yes, carrots." she spoke in a baby voice to Sarita, but Rocío knew she was speaking to her. "What's a seed's first job?"

"Water—to take in water." Rocío recited.

"Yes! water, agua, l'eau, wasser, that's what a seed has to do first! And carrots take forever." She stood the baby up in her lap and trotted her up and down. "I got these seeds from my friend Dominic. He makes sure only one thing is flowering at a time, so he has good seeds. You have to wait so long for carrot seed anyway. The plant doesn't flower til the second year. Dominic *should* do it, he's better at it than I am. Next year, ask him for seeds. I traded some currant jelly this year. He likes the currant jelly. You know who he is?"

Rocío nodded.

"He'll help you."

She had been full of advice like this, every day, telling Rocío what she needed to know, more desperate than before, trying to share her knowledge. Sarah hadn't been strong enough to bike or walk to the market, so she requested that Rocío buy a notebook for her. She began filling it with recipes and lists of chores to be completed at different times of the year. There was a page for goats, and chickens, and medicinal herbs. There were names of neighbors and friends, go to Tyler for help with the electric system, go to Rob for help with heavy lifting, vet advice from Elizabeth and Mato. She copied it in her neatest writing, and when it was done, she had presented it to Rocío. Since then, she had been more relaxed.

Now she was playing with the baby, saying "ooooooh aaaaaah" and trying to get the baby to do it, too. "We have to practice for the fireworks tonight—oooooooh aaaaaaaaah"

"Oooooh aaah" Sarita cooed.

"We have to practice, so we can celebrate the glorious Chinese empire that we're a part of, lucky us! Lucky us!"

"Ooooh aaah" Sarita said again.

"What needs to be done next?" Rocío asked, once she had watered the rows of carrot seed.

"Mmmm. I can't think of anything. You should go to the market, maybe, and see who's there for the fiesta."

"I don't really want to."

"Why not?"

She looked away, and lifted one shoulder. "I don't know." She didn't want to say that she was worried—she didn't think Sarah should be left alone.

"You should go, enjoy the fiesta." Tia smiled, and added, "bring me back chocolate, if anyone is selling it."

In spite of her worries, Rocio went, and enjoyed the fiesta, laughing at little Sarita saying oooh and aaaah over the fireworks.

Noemi and Rocio got home late with the baby—there were still many people at the marketplace. Alejandro and Trevor stayed to run around with the other boys. Sarita had fallen asleep in Noemi's arms and they had taken turns carrying her home. Rocio felt queasy from the fried dough she'd eaten—it was drizzled with honey, and she still felt sticky.

She went to the back yard, and was surprised to see Tia Sara still in her woven chair, a candle still lit on the short table next to her. She walked over. "Tia? Wake up, let's go inside." She crouched down in front of her and took her hand. It was cold. "Tia?" she peered at her face in the flickering light, trying to see her. She half turned. "Mamá? Ven."

"Si?" Noemi called from the kitchen, and walked outside, drying her hands on a clean white towel. "What is it, mija?"

"Tia Sarah. She's gone."

"Ay, por dios." she crouched down next to them, and put her hand on Sarah's cheek. "I'm sorry, mija. I'm so sorry."

Rocio swallowed hard. She knew she shouldn't have gone to the fiesta. She could have stayed here and watched the fireworks in the garden. She probably couldn't have saved her, but at least she wouldn't have died alone.

Then a thought came to her. Mágico. Tía had sent her to the fiesta, told her not to worry. Had she known that tonight was her night, and hadn't wanted anyone to be upset? Had she wanted to die there in her garden, with the fireworks going off above her?

She sniffed loudly, and said, "We should let people know, have a service."

Her mother nodded, and they both stood. "We'll bury her here under the oak tree."

Caravan Of Hopes

By Harry J. Lerwill

I'm no good at being noble, but it doesn't take much to see that the problems of three little people don't amount to a hill of beans in this crazy world. Someday you'll understand that."

The flickering of the image cast strange shadows over the audience, who sat on hay bales and folding chairs. Dylan looked around to see who was sobbing, only to see far more wet faces than dry ones.

He turned back to the side of the barn and the large white sheet hung upon it where the film played. Compared to the movies they'd seen the previous evening, this was nothing special: not much science or technology. Earlier that evening, in a show for the younger audience, the films were far more exciting, with jet aircraft, rockets, and explosions. The only technology in this one was the old propeller planes.

A heavy hand on his shoulder snapped Dylan back to the present. George, his older brother, leaned on him as he climbed to his feet.

"You heading home?" Dylan whispered.

"Yeah, this bores me." He paused, then raised his voice as he walked away. "People used to sit around watching films while the world collapsed. I thought we'd learned from those mistakes!"

Dylan looked around to see who was staring. He was glad his blushing could not be seen in the dim light of the screen. *Again,* Dylan thought, *George creates a scene and walks away, leaving me to apologize for him.* He stood up, brushed straw off his jacket, and picked up the shopping from earlier in the day. He gave a friendly nod to Mr. Matthews and squeezed past him, out onto the road towards the church.

* * *

One week earlier, scouts for the caravan arrived to a flourish of excitement and negotiated with the village council to come trade for three days. Mr. Peterson agreed that they could set up in the field he was leaving fallow this year, next to the main road into the square. Caravans of traders usually came through once or twice a year. This one was different, though; this was a techno-caravan, rumored to buy and sell technology.

The engineers for the caravan arrived first, two riders who drove long stakes into the ground to mark out paths and placements for the stalls that would follow. Everything seemed well-organized as the first vehicles appeared on the horizon.

142

Caravan Of Hopes

Soon the field filled with more than a dozen horse-drawn wagons, painted in bright colors and decorated with strange artwork. The people were just as colorful, with each person seemingly trying to outdo everyone else for vivid appearance. Most of the vendors wore their hair tied back in tight ponytails, wrapped in ribbons of various colors.

The largest wagon pulled up parallel with Peterson's old barn. Shortly thereafter the barn had a huge white sheet hanging from it, fluttering in the breeze. The word spread like wildfire: the caravan had a mobile cinema.

By lunch time, the caravan had set up stalls, and the atmosphere began to take on a festive mood. Dylan checked out the salvage stalls, examining every piece of decades-old equipment and annoying the vendors with questions. They eventually chased him off along with the other teenagers.

"Dad, Dad!" Dylan ran into the kitchen. "One of the vendors has some nice flashlights!" He stopped short as he saw they had a visitor.

"Dylan, this is Nathaniel," his father said, smiling. "He's the chief lecky for the caravan. Nathaniel, this is my younger son I was telling you about, Dylan."

Dylan could not help ignoring the guest, staring instead at the object on the table between the two adults.

"Dylan? Dylan?" His father reached over to touch his son on the shoulder. Dylan jumped.

"Sorry, Dad. Is that really a working laptop?"

Nathaniel raised an eyebrow and asked, "Have you seen a working one before?"

Dylan dragged is eyes away from the glowing screen and looked up at Nathaniel. *He looks like a frontiersman from the old western stories,* Dylan thought. His gaze wandered over a very old leather jacket, patched many times, and in many colors of leather, giving the man a distinct caravan look. Nathaniel's long gray hair—tied back in a gold wrapping typical of the caravan style—was longer than Mum's, and his beard grayer than Granddad's was when he passed last year. Nathaniel blinked and cocked his head to one side. Dylan realized he'd been asked a question.

"No, but Dad showed me his broken one. We've tried to fix it, but we don't have the bits. Do you think a vendor might have the parts?" Dylan's heart beat faster at the idea of having a working laptop.

"Not likely," Nathaniel answered. "Most laptops get shipped back home to be fixed up and used on caravans like ours, or leased to towns and villages that have generators. Working laptops and projectors are rare and very expensive."

"Any nearby?" his father asked.

"Closest is about forty miles, up near Turlock. They have a node, some solar panels, two hand-made wind turbines, and a good battery rack. They can keep their cinema going for up to four hours between charges. The turbines are not so useful now while it's warm and calm, but provides charging in the winter when the wind is stronger."

"A node?" Dylan's father asked.

"That's what we call a remote station in our network. A radio tower, power generation, and some additional equipment, whatever the local community wants and can recover and repair. Turlock uses their extra power to charge a bunch of walkie-talkies for local communication between emergency services, plus a link to access Shasta's marketplace so they can buy and sell on the exchange. We'll pick up goods already sold on our way through Turlock and back to Shasta."

"How do you charge your batteries?" Dylan asked. "Solar? Wind? Genny-rator?"

"Generator or 'genny,'" his father corrected. "It's bad enough that people call us 'leckies' instead of electricians or electrical engineers."

"It's a good question," Nathaniel said. "We have several ways of generating power. When the wagons are rolling, there are alternators–mini jennies—that turn the rotation of the axle into power. It makes it a little harder for the horses, but when we're moving we get power. Then we have a portable water wheel that we can hang off any bridge to get a bit more power. We had solar panels, but they get old and don't travel well. As a last resort we have a hot-walker."

"Hot-walker?" Dylan asked.

"It's based on horse training equipment; they used to tie horses to hot-walkers so they could cool off from training, walking around in circles attached to a central shaft. We have a tubular frame one, and as they walk around they turn the axle to generate power. None of these methods give us a fraction of the electricity we had before The Fall, but it's more than enough for what we need."

"We need more power," Dylan insisted. "We need a node of our own!"

"More power is what everyone wanted for years," Nathaniel replied. "The pursuit of more and more energy ended up costing lots of people their lives. Making power on a huge scale does a lot of damage to the world, and besides, most of that electricity was wasted. Now we encourage people to do

145

what you do, make small amounts for what really needs it, like the cooling box your dad told me about."

Dylan beamed at the reference. "That was the first project Dad let me do on my own. I brought that cooling box home by myself. It took me ages to get it working."

Dad smiled proudly at Dylan, then asked, "What's the show tonight?"

"No idea yet. We have about four thousand hours of video with us. We're open to suggestions from people. Usually the first ones we show are for the kids, and when they go to bed we show ones the adults want."

"That's six months of constant watching!" Dylan said. "How will we watch them all in a few days?"

"That was quick," Nathaniel told him. "You're good at mathematics, aren't you? Most of the video we have on trips is not for entertainment, it's educational. We have a lot of documentaries on how to make things, history from before The Fall, travel shows from places we rarely travel to anymore—places that don't even exist since Retribution Day."

"Any films about North Africa?" Dylan asked. "I hope to see it someday. Europe, too."

"I can think of an appropriate film, but the younger kids might be bored, so maybe tomorrow night," Nathaniel replied, climbing to his feet. "I need to be getting back. Thanks for the tea."

Dylan's father stood with him and shook his hand. Nathaniel then turned and shook Dylan's with a solemn smile. "See you two later!" he promised.

* * *

"George. George!" Dylan called louder as he moved away from the barn and the audience watching the movie. George stopped but didn't turn around. His older brother stood there stiffly until Dylan caught up and then proceeded down the lane beside him.

"I know you like that technology stuff, but I don't," George said as they moved around the church, far enough from Patterson's field that their usual argument would not be overheard.

"There's no need to be an ass to everyone else about it," Dylan replied. "Besides, there was very little technology in that film. I found it boring, too."

"It's not the film that I dislike; it's the technology it represents."

"But everyone else loves it. I've not seen Mum and Dad so happy in ages. Not since I got the cooler box working. Mum wouldn't be alive if it weren't for technology," Dylan reminded him.

"That's a use of technology I can live with," George answered, treading carefully around a well-worn argument. "It's appropriate. But watching movies that glorify how things used to be? That's a waste of everyone's time. All it does is encourage people to wish they were living in the past. It's hard enough to keep up with everything today without people harping back to the good old days when everything was done at the push of a damn button."

"But it's the same technology, just used differently," Dylan said. "The same power used to keep the cooler going can be used to project the films. What's so bad about that?"

"So use it for medicine. Use it for lighting so people can work later, run classes later. Use it to pump water. But for

God's sake, stop using it for mindless entertainment. That's how people got distracted from what was important in the first place. They sat in a mindless stupor in front of films while the world collapsed around them and did nothing until it was too late. Dad said the caravan has six months of films. How many would starve this winter if everyone sat around and watched them instead of bringing in the harvest?"

"Don't be stupid. No one is going to sit around when there is work to be done; it's always quiet in the fields this time of year."

George stopped walking. He turned to look at Dylan in the faint glow cast from the eastern window of St. Margaret's church, where the sanctuary oil lamp burned every night. Dylan could see his face was redder than before.

"Well the pigs don't feed themselves, do they?" George said through gritted teeth. "Your precious technology doesn't clean out the pens. Without those pigs to trade with those thieving Blueshers for Mum's medicine, then your little cooling box would be as useful as the rest of the junk you like to salvage."

"Only a quarter of the animals go to get the medicine from them, now that we trade in bulk—because we have that cool box. You're turning into a luddie." Dylan regretted the last part even before it was out of his mouth. Luddies were colloquial for luddites, harking back to a movement centuries ago that used violence to try and stop progress.

"Why don't you listen? I don't reject technology," George said, shouting now. "I reject the worship of technology. I reject technology being at the heart of who we are and what we do. Retribution was made through technology and look what sort of world that left us."

"No one worships technology," Dylan said, and George dropped his hands to his sides in an expression of exasperation.

"Really? Did you see people at the caravans today? Did you see them fawning over salvage from before we were born? Or their faces as they watched the film? Oh wait, no, that was you fawning over the technology, selling your crap, watching the film along with the rest of them." He turned to continue walking down the lane.

"All you care about is joining that order," Dylan shouted after him, as George disappeared into the shadows.

"Joined. Not joining, joined." George emphasized the last word. "I signed the paperwork today. When the caravan leaves tomorrow, I'll be going with them."

* * *

Dylan yawned while standing in line, looking up to see what was taking so long. Last night had been very late, watching the first of two nights of films on the side of the barn. Tonight they'd get to see a part of Africa in a famous film called "Casablanca."

The first film had been a children's story, a "Disney" some parents called it. In the interlude between films, vendors wandered around selling candied fruit and jerky, and customers swamped the beer tent. The younger children, mollified by sweets and the promise of another film tomorrow, accepted the fate of an early bed. The second film was much more interesting, the story of a bunch of miners flying into space to stop a giant stone in the sky from falling on everyone.

The line moved forward a couple of steps, but it seemed to take forever to get to the front of the line. Before him, six small booths formed a horseshoe around a central caravan. They were not much more than tables with a frame covering, but they supported testing equipment of all sorts. The sign read "We buy and sell all electronics. Testing services available."

The vendor on the far right counted out some silver coins to Mr. Ellis. Dylan had not seen what he brought to trade, but it must have been good, judging by the price. Ellis shook hands with the vendor, and as he left, Dylan hurried to take his place.

"Good morning. I'm Ian. What can I do for you?" asked the young lad facing Dylan.

Dylan pulled out three small metal boxes and placed them on the table. Ian picked up the first and looked it over, checking the connectors on the end.

"Hard drives," Dylan said, wanting to be sure Ian did not think him the typical country kid who knew and cared nothing about technology, like his older brother.

"Yes, these two are from about 2004, I'd wager," Ian replied, picking up the second one. "And this one is from a few years later. Take a seat." He turned around and shouted into the caravan, "Drive tester, please!"

An arm reached out of the tent flap, offering up a bright metal case. Ian took it and flipped up the lid, revealing a laptop and some equipment Dylan did not recognize. After a few seconds of typing, "Drive Testing Suite" appeared on top of the screen.

"What does that do?" Dylan asked.

"It's a specialized machine. We can look at what's on many different drives. We pay not only for hardware but any data that is useful." As he spoke, he connected two cables to the first drive and flipped a small switch next to the biggest connector. The drive emitted a high-pitched whine, making people nearby look over.

"Not looking hopeful," commented Ian. "This one is dead. Scrap value only. Sorry. Let's try the next."

The second one made no sound at all. Ian double-checked the connections and tried again, with no effect.

"Sorry, but it's unusual to finding working drives these days. Let's try the last."

As the power came on, a low chirping sounded, and the screen lit up, displaying many lines of data. Ian pressed a few keys.

"Nice. A working terabyte drive. Let's see what's on there."

"We went looking for genny parts over near Bear Creek last year. I found these in a garage. Rats had chewed up all the wires, and my brother didn't want me bring them back. I had to sneak the drives home in my pockets," Dylan complained. "What's on there? Anything good?"

"Slow down," Ian said, laughing. "It's only got a fraction of what could be on a drive this size. I'm sorting out the files that are useful from the ones we see all the time."

Dylan fidgeted in his seat. Slow down? This is what he lived for, the thrill of finding something from the past that still worked. He glanced at the line, wonder what others had brought to sell. The column was shorter now. He could see past them into a line of simple booths opposite and was unsurprised to see George sitting at one of them, engaged in an intense debate with a young woman. She wore a plain grey robe, with an embroidered Y on the front that was drawing George's attention to a rather full bosom.

Dylan gestured over his shoulder. "How come you guys travel with Y-ists? I thought they hated technology?"

"A few Y-ists do. Most are pretty neutral to technology. After all, it wasn't the technology that broke things; it's what people did with it."

"I wish you'd tell that to my brother. He hates everything technological, even the cooler I made to keep Mum's medicine in." He glanced over at George again, finding him looking across at the salvage booths. "He wants to join them so bad. He's been corresponding with the questioneers up north for awhile. Who wants to spend their life asking people what questions they would ask God? Why not ask your own questions?"

"That's a discussion to have with a Y-ist priestess, like Emily over there. It makes sense for us to travel with them. We pool resources, and they understand hydroponics and aquaponics better than most. I've seen a couple of Y-ists stay in a village for a year and triple the food production. When they set up the apprentice node over in Sonora, they stationed an aquaponics specialist there for six months. Now I get fresh fish every time I'm home, and the caravan trades my mother's spinach dip in three villages. They've been doing good work since before The Fall." Ian waved over at the plainly robed young woman, and she smiled and waved back.

"Well I think it's a waste of—"

Dylans' opinion remained with him, however, as Ian let out a low, long whistle. "Jackpot!" Ian said.

"What is it?"

"A compressed file containing a lot of old books. They called them zip files."

"Is that good?" Dylan was confused. Books were great, but he was interested in technology.

"Better than good. Some of these books are from the late nineteenth century."

"And that's good? They didn't have computers back then."

"Neither do most of the villages we visit. Which means what's there can be used by people today. Let me get the boss." He called inside the caravan, and a young lad jumped down and ran off. Ian touched a button, and the screen went blank. "Saving power," Ian said in response to Dylan's frown.

A few minutes later the boy returned with Nathaniel in tow.

"Ian, can you go and take a look at Mr. Peterson's wind generator?" Nathaniel asked. "He's not getting much charge for the size and capacity. I'd like to get it serviced as an additional thank-you for the use of the field."

"Yessir!" Ian said. He waved at Dylan as he left.

"I understand you have a good find," Nathaniel said. "Let's take a look, shall we?"

Nathaniel sat down in the chair Ian had vacated. He brought the screen back to life, scanned down the list of files, then clicked on one with the pointer. The page of a book appeared. Nathaniel scrolled down tables of data that meant nothing to Dylan.

"What is it?" he asked.

"A lot of the information an engineer needs to make stuff. Not computers and such, but tools, blacksmithing techniques,

153

wood milling. I suspect we have a lot of them in our library already, but these are searchable on a computer, which makes them extra valuable."

"So the jackpot?" Dylan asked, eager.

"Yes. Worth an ounce I'd say."

"For the drive or for what's on it?" Dylan remembered Mr. Ellis getting a couple of one ounce silver coins – rounds as everyone called them.

"You strike a hard bargain. Ten copper for the drives."

"Great!"

"Where's your dad?"

"He's around somewhere. But it's my drive. I'm sure Dad would let me keep payment."

"I'm sure he'd want me to make sure you get home safely."

Dylan sighed. That would spoil any surprise he planned.

"Look, I need to get some material ready for the show tonight, so how about I come around later with your payment? We're not going anywhere. Shake on the deal?" Nathaniel offered his hand with the same solemn smile as the day before.

"Deal," Dylan said, taking his hand. "But—I wanted to get something nice for Mum and Dad today. And something for George, even if he doesn't deserve it."

"Tell you what; I'll pay you for the actual drives now, the data later. Will that do?"

Dylan nodded excitedly. Nathaniel handed over ten copper rounds, each stamped with an ornate letter Y.

"Thank you, sir," he said and fled with a burst of excitement. He knew exactly where to go.

* * *

"What the hell do you mean 'joined?'" Dylan demanded, running to catch his brother.

"Exactly what I said. I joined the Y-ist order." George opened the gate, then let it swing closed in front of Dylan. By the time Dylan caught up, George was up the path to the house and at the door.

"You can't talk me out of it," George said as he slipped off his shoes. "I've wanted this for a long time."

Dylan kicked off his shoes and followed his brother inside. George flicked the light switch, and LEDs lit the room with a soft glow. The indicator on the wall switch was green. Within a few hours the indicator would turn yellow, and soon after that the lights would dim. Usually, everyone was in bed long before that, though. The lack of jackets on the coat rack indicated Mum and Dad were still at the carnival. He hung up his coat and turned back to George.

"You don't mind technology when you have a need for it," Dylan taunted, indicating the lights. George ignored him and sat on the sofa. Dylan sat opposite, in Mum's reclining chair. He raised his eyebrows in expectation.

George leaned back. "Hello? Useful purpose. As I said earlier, it's not technology; it's your blindness to what harm it does that I don't get."

"So who gets to choose what's appropriate and what's not? Ian said the data that was on that drive might be valuable to lots of people. If you'd had your way, that would have been left over at Bear Creek with the rest of the technology we found. Your stubbornness almost lost people valuable information."

155

"A small price to pay to ensure we don't repeat the mistakes of the past. That's why I'm joining the Y-ists. To make sure people ask the right questions about technology, as well as other things."

"You don't care about questions, you just care about leaving. You've wanted to leave for years; you just see this as your way out."

"Of course I want to see more of the world. I want to know what others think and see how they live, and I want to bring that knowledge back home to everyone. If you screw this up for me, by God, I will make your life misery." George stared at Dylan with an intensity he hadn't seen before.

"How the hell can I screw it up?" Dylan said.

"The Y-ists require the family of a postulant to supportive their decision. They'll be coming to see us and make sure everyone is okay with my decision."

"Well, I'm *not* okay with your decision," Dylan said, folding his arms.

"You selfish little bastard. You never think of anyone but yourself, do you?" George said, rising to his feet.

"I'm selfish? You're the one who's leaving!" Dylan stood, too, fists clenched, only now realizing they were shouting.

"Worried you'll have to do all of the chores on your own?"

"I don't give a shit about the chores. You think you the only one who wants to see the world?"

Both boys jumped when someone cleared their throat by the door.

* * *

At breakfast, while Dylan struggled to keep his eyes open, Mum had mentioned seeing a stall with a nice blue dress, suitable for baptisms, weddings, and harvest festivals. She described it in detail to Dad who, as usual, pretended to be paying no attention. He talked about getting a new axe or at least getting his old one repaired.

Now Dylan looked around to see who was watching before he approached the clothing stall. All the clothes on the racks appeared to be women's, and he didn't want any of the other lads to see him looking at the merchandise. Even worse, he didn't want any of the girls giggling at him in church on Sunday. When no one was looking, he slipped inside.

"Excuse me," he said, "my mum said there was a blue dress here she really liked. She came in last night, a tall lady with blond hair?"

A plump woman looked up from her knitting. She stood, putting the knitting down in her seat. Turning to a tubular metal rack where an assortment of dresses hung, she flicked through garments and pulled out a long blue dress with white trim.

"Here you go," she said. "That's three copper."

Dylan handed over three coins. The woman insisted on wrapping the dress in thick paper and tying it with string. When she finished, Dylan peaked out around a stand of hats to be sure no one was watching, then darted across to the stall opposite, where the tools were. Buying Dad's new axe was less nerve-wracking.

* * *

Last, he visited the stall where he'd seen George talking to the young woman, Emily.

"Excuse me," he said when he found her sorting through papers on her knee. Her light brown hair was pulled back into a tight ponytail, tied with a silver and black bow. The sun on her face made her squint when she looked up. She shielded her eyes with the sheaf of papers.

"Oh, hello. You're George's brother, aren't you? What can I do for you?"

"I want to buy him something nice, maybe a book or two for his studies. I might not like him wanting to leave, but he's still my brother."

"Well, he was really interested in *First Principles of Y-ism*, *Essays on Suffering*, and I recommend *Essays on Technology*. I have copies of all three. I suspect he won't like the latter, though. Not all people are anti-technology, and over half the essays in that book are pro-technology."

"Who writes the essays?" Dylan asked.

"It varies. We ask people what questions are important to them and compile the answers into a database. Then others write essays giving their point of view about what the answer should be. We publish the best ones."

"Database?" Dylan's attention was piqued.

"Yes, back at our home centers we have databases of questions people have asked, going all the way back to before The Fall. Some of the technology collected on caravans keeps the centers going."

Dylan bought all three books and put them in the bag with the axe. He looked westwards, judging how long to sundown and the start of the movies. *Maybe I'll give everyone their presents at breakfast,* he thought to himself.

* * *

As the color drained from George's face, Dylan felt his face flush hotter. If there was one thing he knew Mum and Dad hated seeing, it was the two of them arguing. He glanced over his shoulder to see just how annoyed they were. He did not expect them to have brought home company; Nathaniel, Emily, and an older woman he did not recognize were standing behind them.

"I'm sorry about that," Mum said to the guests. "Our kids have different ideas, and we taught them to be passionate about what they believe in. Sometimes I think we did too good a job."

"No problem at all," Nathaniel said. Dad ushered George away from the sofa and gestured to the guests to sit. He pulled two chairs out from the dining table. One he left there for George while he carried the other over next to Mum's seat and sat down. Before Nathaniel sat, he introduced his companions.

"This is Maria Snell. She is responsible for the members of the caravan who collect and collate questions. This is her student, Emily. Maria, Emily, this is Peter and Kersten Burket. This is George, who we're evaluating as a potential member of your branch. And this is Dylan."

Dylan raised his hand weakly, still embarrassed at being caught shouting at George.

"Dylan, can you make everyone a cup of tea?" Mum asked. "Please?"

"Okay," Dylan said, trying to appear stoic as he headed out to the kitchen.

I'm going to be stuck here forever while George wanders off and gets to do what he wants, Dylan thought. *He'll come back every couple of months and tell everyone about how bad it is out there, how technology really did ruin it for everyone, how life would be better if we stopped trying to save the past. And everyone will look at him as the wise one, just like they look up to Mr. Peterson because he made a trip to Europe in his youth. Meanwhile, I'll be stuck here looking after the pigs and the garden, never getting to go more than a day or two away from home.*

Dylan added kindling and wood to the stove. He closed the stove door to a small crack, allowing a rush of air to fan over the coals, making them glow. A few seconds later the kindling caught and crackled.

It's just not fair. Just because George was born first should not mean he gets to be the one to see the world. There's precious little of technology left, and George will be encouraging people to abandon it. With no one else at home to help with the gardening and the pigs, he knows his leaving is trapping me here, and he doesn't give a rat's ass.

Dylan hands trembled as he filled the kettle and moved it to the stove. He lifted the heating stone for the fireless cooker to one side and placed the kettle on the hottest part of the heating plate.

While the water boiled, Dylan lingered at the door, intent on listening to the conversation in the other room. George was answering questions from all three of the guests.

"So how old are you?" Dylan heard the older woman ask.

"Seventeen, Ma'am. I've been interested in joining the Y-ists since a caravan came through here two years ago."

"Why is that?" she pressed.

"We've lost so much. I'll never see and do the things my parents did at my age, or travel like Mr. Peterson did when he

160

was young. If people had figured out what was important a long time ago, decided for themselves what the important questions were instead of letting others dictate what they talked about, things would be much better. Instead we destroyed a lot of the world in the pursuit of technology and wasteful things to do with it."

"If you think that the Y-ists are anti-technology, you are very much mistaken." Nathaniel told him. "We salvage technology and utilize it all the time."

"What we have is failing," George said. "The less we use, the longer it will last. I'd rather have light to read by and Mum's medicine cool for fifty more years than to waste it watching films for a decade."

Maybe Nathaniel will see George for the luddie he is and say no, Dylan thought, his mind racing.

"There were originally only two branches. One handled the compiling of questions, the other practical food skills like hydroponics, aquaponics, and permaculture. After The Fall, the practical food skills were in great demand, trying to supply the refugee camps."

I can't see George ever getting his hands dirty on aquaponics. All those pipes, tanks, and pumps are too technological for him.

Dylan glanced back across at the stove, where the lid on the kettle juddered. He strained to listen a bit longer.

"Since then, we have added the preservation of technology as a branch, along with a program of martial training."

"You have a military?" Dad asked.

"Some members specialize in security. We do a lot of trading. Not every community we encounter is as friendly as this one, or as isolated. You're lucky over here near the foothills. The I-5 corridor has one of the bloodiest histories since The Fall. We've had a node over in Patterson for about five years. They've been raided twice, both times by groups moving north and scavenging as they go. A third group tried to raid again last October but failed."

Preservation of technology? The techno-caravan is a Y-ist business? Oh, it gets better and freaking better. George gets to join a group that preserves technology while I get to rot on a smallholding. He'll get to travel the world preaching against technology while the people with him are trying to preserve it? Why can't they see how stupid that is?

The rattling of the lid made it clear that the kettle was not putting up with any more heat. Dylan reluctantly left off eavesdropping to make seven cups of tea, arranged on Mum's mahogany tray with a small bowl of honey and a few lemon slices. As he returned to the living room, Emily was talking.

"What impact will your leaving have on the home?" she asked.

Dylan felt himself stiffen. *I bet our arguing prompted that. Maybe she sees George for what he is.*

"Well, my brother will have the hardest time of it. He'll end up doing all of the chores that we used to split between us."

"That doesn't bother me," Dylan said, not about to let George make him sound lazy. "I do most of them anyway."

"Tell that to the animals. They run away from you like you're a stranger," George said.

Dylan ignored him and handed cups to the guests. Nathaniel gave Dylan a small cloth bag as he took his cup. From the weight of it, Dylan could tell it held a one-ounce round. George continued talking.

"I know my leaving will make it harder on everyone, Dylan and Dad particularly. At the same time, it will be one less mouth to feed. That might help, considering the harvest won't be the best this year. It's been far too dry. I just wish I could afford to buy an apprenticeship, so I could stay in touch easier."

"How much is an apprenticeship?" Dad asked. Dylan knew the family could not afford it; what extra money they made went for needles and medicine.

"Forty rounds of silver. An apprentice is a huge investment for the Order, particularly when a village has not sent any prior apprentices to join," Nathaniel said. "And we do ask for a potter's field as well. Just a small piece of land in the village. Often the community will donate something central once they realize the benefits of having a node."

"So how does it work for non-apprentices?" Mum asked.

Nathaniel sat forward and interlocked his fingers. As he talked, Dylan handed out the rest of the cups. His insides were too knotted to drink his tea. No one noticed.

Everyone is so focused on George. I might as well not be here. If he stays, will he make my life misery? In a couple of years, when I want to join, will he object if he does not go? Maybe I can buy an apprenticeship then, so he won't be able to interfere.

"It's similar to the differences between enlisted and commissioned. An apprentice has one-to-one training emphasizing leadership and excellence, with an experienced Master in the branch they are called to serve. Emily, for example, is apprenticed to Mistress Snell. Ian, whom Dylan met earlier, is my current apprentice."

That would be payback. If can salvage enough technology to buy an apprenticeship, he'll have to defer to me. So long as Mum has her medicine we'll be good. Maybe I can find some technology to make her medicine, so we won't be dependent on buying it.

"Postulants, on the other hand, are trained in classes of between six and twelve. The best postulants often go on to apprenticeships, sponsored by a master or mistress who pays their fee. All recruits go through the same basic training process for things like fitness and health, security, food production."

"What can we do to help George while he's there?" Mother asked. "Can we send letters or food parcels with caravans that go through? Books?"

"We have plenty of food," Maria said. "We've been practicing intensive natural farming methods for decades. We have quite a bit left over to trade and occasionally send relief supplies to nodes that run into problems."

Mums already acting as if George has gone. How can she let him go so easily? What if we can't produce enough to afford her medicine?

Nathan looked around. "Any more questions?"

Emily shook her head. She turned to look at Maria. Dylan kept his face a mask of stone.

"I'm not convinced."

Dylan was surprised to hear Maria voice the dissenting opinion. He looked over to see her watching him intently. He felt the rest of the family looking at him.

Great, if I don't convince her I'm okay with it, they'll blame me for shattering his dreams. Well, I have dreams, too.

"What happens to me?" Dylan asked. "I want to travel, to see the world, just as much as George does. But if he leaves, who's going to help Mum and Dad?"

"You think your brother is being selfish?"

"He's not thinking things through, like he doesn't think things through when he condemns technology that doesn't benefit him."

"You're afraid only one of you can leave home?"

"For any length of time, yes. Plants don't tend themselves, animals don't feed themselves. Mum and Dad can't do it all alone. We have to produce extra to pay for medicine and needles."

"Diabetic?" Maria looked over at Mum, who nodded.

"I'm hoping I can earn a little money on the side to send home to help with expenses," George said, looking dejected. "I'm used to raising pigs, and I'm not afraid of hard work."

Dylan glanced at George, expecting to see the look of anger that punctuated most of their arguments. He was surprised to see his older brother blinking away tears. George looked at him, then looked away. Mum and Maria were discussing medicine, how much, how often, how much they were paying for the medicine from the Blue Sheaf Traders on the Coast –Maria used their more formal name.

Oh great, that's not what I wanted. Why does everything have to be so difficult? All I want is to explore technology, see how it can make our lives easier. No one is going to waste anything, not after the last four decades, after the famines and the wars. Why can't George see that? I can make much more money from scavenging than he can tending pigs.

The conversation caught Dylan's attention.

"We do have dealings with them, but not often. They have their main operations based in the Bay Area, and we try not to venture too near," Nathaniel said.

"Why not?" Dylan asked. "I want to see the ocean one day."

"They…have different values. Their technology is excellent, far better than what we've preserved, but only the corporate council that runs things really benefits. The rest live in far worse conditions. They exploit everyone and anyone. The slightest infraction of their code, and it's years of hard labor. The Frisco Free Church runs their 'penitentiary' and sells the services of the inmates to the other corporations—they didn't read the bit in the Bible about money being the root of all evil."

"The love of money is the root of all evil," Dad corrected.

Dylan felt the blood rushing to his face. *Oh God, what an idiot I've been. Yeah, I can make more money than George. But would I destroy my own brother's dreams to get my hands on more silver? Just to buy more technology? How is that different to what George bitches about? Nathaniel must know what I'm thinking. He's probably expecting me to betray my brother with a kiss.*

Afraid to look over at George, Dylan fondled the little cloth bag in his hand. *One down, thirty nine to go.* He slipped his hand into the bag to grip his silver piece. It was far too small to be a silver round, but it weighed the right amount. A sudden realization made the hairs stand up on the back of his neck. He pulled the coin out and peeped at it between his fingers.

George wants to leave and travel more than anything. I want to work with technology more than anything. Why not?

He reached behind Mum's chair where he'd put the shopping from earlier. He pulled out the three books and handed them to George.

"I got these for you. I know we don't agree on a lot of things, but I you're my brother. I want you to be happy. If that means joining the Y-ists, then I support you." Dylan looked back at Mistress Snell. "Mum always says that actions speak louder than words. I don't want my words to hurt my brother. Please, take George as your apprentice." Dylan offered the coin to her.

A round of gasps led to stunned silence.

"Wait, wait, wait!" George interrupted. "Dylan! What are you doing?" He stared down at the tiny yellow coin in Dylan's fingers. "Where the hell did you get a gold coin?"

"My salvage earnings. But I'm not going anywhere for a few years. I'm not old enough yet to be an apprentice."

"You will be in a year or two. This could be your chance. Don't be a fool and waste it on me."

"It's not wasted. I get the bedroom to myself and besides, I get a node to play with, don't I, Mr. Nathaniel?"

"It's Mr. Morse, if we're being formal. And yes, your settlement will receive a node. If Maria accepts George, an engineering team will arrive within the month to start constructing it, before the weather gets too cold."

George looked confused. Before he could say any more, Maria took the coin, cleared her throat, and spoke with a rather formal tone. "Emily Santas."

"Yes, Mistress Snell?"

167

"In return for excellent service to the Order of the Theology of Why, I hereby promote you to journeyman, with all the rights and privileges, as well as the burdens and responsibilities commiserate with your rank."

"Thank you, Mistress."

"George Burket, do you wish to become an apprentice in the Order of the Theology of Why?"

George looked sidelong at Dylan, who nodded. "Yes, Ma'am."

"Then I accept you as my student. Proper ceremonies will be conducted when we get to Shasta. Are you prepared to leave to tomorrow?"

"Yes, Ma'am."

"You will call me Mistress Snell when we're being formal. Mistress will do at other times. I don't like being called Ma'am."

George nodded, appearing to be in shock. Dylan liked seeing his brother silenced for once.

"Ma'am?" Dylan said. "Er…Mistress Snell? My change?"

"Oh, I'm sorry, I was so caught up in the excitement. It's a rare pleasure to take on apprentices on the road these days."

Nathaniel pulled out a leather pouch and counted out the coins. "What are you going to do with them?" he asked, handing them over.

"Tools, extra medicine. Plus, there's a metal detector in one of the stalls." Dylan grinned. "George might not like the idea of scrap collecting, but that's where I think the future will be."

The Going

By Catherine McGuire

C airen moved along the rows, catching tiny weeds with the snaffle hoe, smiling to see the peas putting out tendrils. The perfume of daphne and alfalfa intermingled with woodsmoke. Everywhere, color was coming back to the fields. March had been tough; there was a week of worry when the cabbages were cut smaller and smaller, but now that the peas were up, and potatoes poking their tight whorls above the wet soil, everyone relaxed and the daily portions went back to normal. She spotted a shaggy patch of dandelions in the next field—after weeding, she'd dig them for salad and brew.

It felt good to be out; the house had felt so cramped this winter! Maybe, like Auntie Sarah said, it was because she was sixteen; the usual stories by the fire just didn't soothe her itching innards. The May Meet was almost here, and she felt a buzz thinking about the eight-town festival. Dad could swap their wintered-over turnips for extra potatoes, and get

169

the animals mated... and the plowing and roping contests would bring all the local boys. Her breath caught a little and she hoed faster, hacking clover that overran kale. She was lucky to have parents who would give her a say in her match; she remembered Arthur's large dark eyes, and Ellery's laugh, his broad shoulders. Hopefully, one of them was not already trothed. When it came down to it, she'd have the week of Meet to decide. And after so many years, she wasn't sure she wanted it to be... now.

"Cairen—come help me with this!" Her father's voice came from the front; he was working on the septic today. She wrinkled her nose, but stashed the hoe against the garage and walked around the house. The reek of sewage permeated the air; this was her least favorite task, helping to keep the wastewater flowing.

Her father was up to his waist in the hole; she could see the pipe that came out of the concrete box; he was running a snake into it, but had stopped to rest, leaning against the muddy pit. His face was shiny with sweat and pale—too pale. Cairen hurried over. "Here, Dad—let me do that!" she said.

"I'm all right. I just need you to steady the end of the snake."

"You've gotten most of it done; I'll finish it."

Not for the first time, she wished Ian hadn't been prenticed to the smith. They needed his strong back to work the fields and yard; it was no good pretending Dad was up to the task. He was trying not to draw huge breaths, trying to hide his fatigue. What good did that do? But he was stubborn; that was a family trait. Well, so was she.

"Dad, let me try it, at least. How else will I learn?"

170

The Going

That usually got him; he felt guilty, she knew, that she hadn't been prenticed away a couple years ago. As she hoped, he scrambled out of the pit and let her jump in. The mud oozed around her boots; it stank and she stooped to look at the pipe, to hide the disgust on her face. Why didn't they just dig an outhouse like the neighbors? He was so old-fashioned!

With snakey treachery, the well-named metal tube jinked and caught, and slipped. Finally, she got it punched through whatever the block was, and wedged herself as far from the pipe as possible, as noxious liquid dribbled. Working fast, she removed the snake, flung it up on the grass and re-attached the drainfield hose.

"Good job," her father said as she climbed out. He sat on the stone wall by the filbert bush, leaning his elbows on his knees. Out in the sun, she could see how sick he really looked. It might not be long now; a suddenly fear popped up, but she shoved it away—how could she get trothed at the Meet if he was dying? She busied herself with refilling the hole, went to wash off the tools and herself with plenty of sun-heated water and soap.

* * *

Later that afternoon, Trevor dropped by with his team to plow up the river field. Cairen walked with him and the horses along Mill Road, out to where the old paper mill took over the landscape. It was an odd sculptural remnant; the most useful things had been taken first; what was left curled and jutted and flapped. Rust was winning over moss in most places. The parking lots had been torn up and the fields divided; her family had the one closest to the river, by very

171

good luck. Still, her back hurt, remembering summers of bucket-toting misery when she was too young to do anything else useful. Now those chores went to Denni and Mo; and unless Mom had more children, they'd be stuck with that 'til they were prenticed. She laughed, thinking of Mo's non-subtle hints to Mom this winter. The boy was inventive, but not diplomatic. She jerked from the reverie as Trevor handed her the reins.

"Wanna lead for a while?"

"You bet!"

Guiding the horses, she stepped lightly and watched the posts they'd set as guides. Trevor didn't say much; he was a quiet young man, a year older, second cousin—she knew he was studying medicine with Rosie, but didn't know much else. For some reason, he mostly kept with the Granger girls when there was a Raising or Dinner. She glanced back, watching how he held the plow with steady arms, despite his slim build. His black hair gleamed in the sun, and shielded his neck; hatless, he was risking a burn with his fair skin. She looked ahead; the team was halfway down the second row; at this rate, they'd get the field done just before lunch.

"You have another field this afternoon?" she asked. Their other two fields wouldn't be worked until next month; the fourth was fallow this year.

"No—today is clinic."

He wasn't much for small talk, that was certain. She turned back and focused on the team—Jerry and Dude, two brown Percherons, strong and patient. He'd be helping Rosie at the Morriston clinic, then, because Springwater's wasn't on Fridays. She had a sudden thought.

The Going

"Trevor, when you stay to lunch—you are staying to lunch, right? Could you look at Dad? He was awful pale this morning."

He was silent a moment. "I don't have my certificate."

"No—not formally; just look at him, and tell me what you think. I will try to get him to go to the clinic next Tuesday but he's so stubborn…"

"I thought he was going to Charter," he stopped, and was silent.

Charter? Why would Dad go to the city for clinic? No one did that any more—too expensive, and most of the time useless. No matter what their leaflets said, Rosie was adamant that Charter's mysterious machines were "nothing but noise and bother." She glanced back again; Trevor looked uncomfortable—did he know something she didn't? She scuffed a rock aside, frowning. They said no more about it. Cairen started singing a weather rhyme and Trevor was as silent as his horses.

* * *

She suspects, but doesn't know. The thought was uncomfortable. Trevor looked down into the cabbage soup, pretending to be absorbed in eating. Cairen was so strong in many ways; would she be able to handle this? He glanced up as she pushed the tureen across the table, deliberately moving it past little Denni to offer her guest more. He smiled and shook his head; hungry though he was, he knew he could get a sandwich at Morriston—thick bread and meat, which was more than the Landley family had. He could feel Ann Landley's eyes on him, so he took a small slice of oat bread, but left the butter.

173

Backlit against the sunny window, Cairen's father was spooning soup. His pale skin and look of heavy fatigue gave away the seriousness of his diabetes. Trevor knew Rosie had done as much as she could; Jeff had a decade past what might be expected, but the last time he was at the clinic, Trevor had overhead him and Rosie arguing over Charter.

"And what do you think they'd do, Jeff? I've told you there's not even a transplant to help–"

"They've got insulin; you know they can give me a supply."

"For an outrageous price, yes—you'd be handing over Cairen's dowry—and maybe Mo's!—for another five years of life. Is that fair?"

His reply had been too low for Trevor to hear, but even that he was considering it had caused Trevor's heart to sink. Now he looked at the towhaired beauty sitting across from him. Cairen at fourteen had rocked him out of his studious daydreams; a fire seized him and he finally understood his brother's mooning over that brunette that he'd finally married. At sixteen, Cairen was the most breathtaking of all the Springwater girls; lovelier even than Cheryl, the Strawberry Queen from Josephson. She glanced over and he looked down hurriedly. She didn't know; she was dreaming of the Meet, and of the ox-strong, field-rich guys she might find there. But what if Jeff spent her dowry? The groom had a dowry, too, but starting off at half-rations meant a bigger chance of failing. And there were few chances to catch up, once you were down. Was Jeff such a throwback that he'd put his life before hers?

The Going

"Trevor, are you doing militia this season?" Ann's voice was husky and low; she sounded a lot like his mother, her first cousin.

"No, Auntie; medical training comes first, the Mayor said, so I'm excused until I'm done. Next year." He blushed a little at the childish nickname, but using her name sounded—wrong.

"Only our Ian will be starting in April, and I wondered..." she didn't finish, but he knew—his own mother worried when his brother Doug went, and him being sworn to secrecy didn't help a mother's heart at all. She shrugged; *nothing we can do*. Rising, she reached for the platters and shooed the younger boys into the kitchen. Mo came back through a moment later with an empty bucket, headed for the pump. The Landleys still used a toilet, so all washwater went to the bathroom cistern, to be used for flushing. Odd, but Jeff was over sixty; real old-fashioned in many ways. Didn't even have a pee bucket for the garden.

Trevor got up, thanking them all for the meal; Jeff told him it was barely payment for plowing. Cairen jumped up quickly, telling her father she needed to water the peas, "in this sudden heat." She followed Trevor outside, and he could see the anxiety in her eyes before she spoke.

"Do you think he'll rally again? He was sick like this two years ago, but the herbs Rosie gave him helped—he's been fine until now." The pain in her face turned the cabbage soup to stone in his gut. He hesitated.

"I wish I could say for sure. But diabetes is such a tricky illness. He could go along for a while, just like this, or—"

"Or this could be the end. Or the start of the end."

175

Lines from the Going Song flashed in his head, but he tried to smile and act reassuring. Rosie told him endlessly that much of medicking was reassuring scared patients; but that was apparently not his strong point. He patted her shoulder, wanting to hug her, fearing that his motives weren't at all clinical.

"I promise to come back and check in with him, and you, over the weekend." He felt like a traitor at the relief in her eyes. But maybe Rosie had some advice he could pass on. Suddenly, he was aware of the slant of the sun. "I need to go," he said, "I'll see you Sunday."

* * *

After Trevor left, Cairen felt oddly lethargic. There were too many things she was waiting for, or trying not to wait for. She wandered over to the south side of the house and checked the solar oven; the bread was baking quickly. She took ten minutes off the timer and went around to the shed. The sun would harden the soil soon; better get those dandelions up. She ignored the lump in her throat.

It was mid afternoon by the time she got a bucketful and had rinsed them at the pump. Nice plump roots would be roasted and ground for coffee; the greens would help the puny cabbage salad at dinner. She took a can of captured worms and beetles over to the chicken coop; the hens squabbled wildly over them. As she approached the back door, she heard their voices—Mom and Dad arguing. Was it Mo's schooling again? She wished Mom wouldn't be so hard on Dad, with him being so sick. She would never ride her husband like that—the image refused to gel, just like so many times before. Why couldn't she see herself married? She didn't want to be a Marion; she was looking forward to having children—Mom had almost agreed to her prenticing with the school. But teachers wandered where they were needed; after a long discussion, Cairen agreed she didn't want to be moving far, into uncertain territory. Better a farmer's partner.

They stopped arguing when the back door slammed; by the time she had set the bucket down and gone into the parlor, they were both knitting—Dad glanced up; by his frown, he could tell she wasn't fooled. But she only said, "The bread will be done early; this sun is working hard today."

Dad sighed and put down his needles. "Cairen—we have to talk," he started.

Mom looked almost fierce; Cairen was suddenly confused. "Is it—about the Meet?" she asked, hating the catch in her voice.

"Sort of. You see—" Dad looked over at Mom, and her expression hardened. He frowned and continued, "I have decided to try the doctors at... at Charter. They have medicines we don't have..." his voice faded; he glanced at the wall.

Cairen frowned. "So, how does that affect me—won't you be back in time for Meet? It's only once a year..." she could feel tears welling; she clamped her lips together. No crybaby stuff.

"Your father's medicine—" Mom made the word sound like poison. "—will cost pretty much the whole harvest, and probably some hirework also."

"But I'll be well enough to do it, that's the point!" Dad cut in. "Otherwise, we might as well..." his voice actually trembled.

She edged toward a chair and sat quickly. Dad was saying he wanted her dowry for medicines; he wanted...extraordinary measures. The shock erased the words she'd been starting to say, and she stuttered, "But you said...you said..."

"I know—we've told you that extraordinary measures are wrong. I know. But this isn't really...that...extraordinary. Just medicine. Not surgery, not artificial processes. Just medicine." From the look on her mother's face, this argument had been presented and failed. Her mother, at least, didn't lose the lessons in a crisis. Cairen shook her head, trying to get the bits to make sense. What did he want from her? If he was going to use the money, well—it was his, wasn't it? But then what? He would be leaving them dangerously unready for lean times. And what would the town say about—going to Charter? Images of Dinners and harvests and swaps danced around her mind, of neighbors whispering, of gradually being shunted off... No one had tried to keep themselves alive artificially since...the preacher. She was a toddler, but the story was still told sometimes—his craven theft of church funds to pay for an operation. All that, just for a year of bedridden misery. No one lives forever...it's only natural. She looked at her father, seeing the creased, leathery skin; the stubble now gray—he was watching her intently, his eyebrows hunched like fuzzy caterpillars over his chocolate brown eyes. Her heart went out to him—it was his life he wanted, that's all. But no one lives forever. Cairen looked at her mother, who spoke softly.

"Cairen, we don't want to take your dowry; we want you to start your married life with enough." She glanced at her husband.

The Going

"But if you wouldn't mind my going—just to see, just to get an idea of the costs," he said. "I would be back by May Meet. We could still go and see if there was someone—"

Somehow his words felt hollow; she knew if he went to Charter, he'd come back penniless. What did she want for him? She couldn't think.

"Give it the weekend," Mom urged. "We won't say anything more about it. Not in front of the boys, certainly." Mom sounded ashamed. Yet she stroked his hair gently as she passed by on her way to the kitchen. Cairen jumped up and ran outside. She didn't pause until she was in the back orchard, hidden from the house. Randomly, she walked between the trees, fingering the apple trunks for boring insects.

As the heart of the tree slowly hollows
As the bloom on the thorn slowly fades
I know in my heart I am going
Yet always a part of me stays.

No! She caught herself—she was singing part of the Going Song! Was she hoping he would die? No, not that... finally tears started to flow, and she sat down by her favorite cherry, watching the flouncy blossoms shake in the breeze, crying silently for the unexpected turning point in her life. Was this why she couldn't imagine herself married? Did she have intuition, like Sharla? Then why wasn't it telling her what to choose?

There's a time when the cycle is over
No honor in staying the tide

Unbidden, the Going Song kept running through her mind. All her life, she'd been taught that death was part of the natural cycle. When Dad's parents died, within two months of each other, the family had gathered and sung and spoke the words of reassurance, to ease their way into the dark. When her two sisters had died suddenly of flu, along with a third of the town, the pain was eased by the Going rituals and the knowledge of the natural cycle. Nothing lives forever. There is a time to live, and a time to die. Being in the mystery, we cannot see the whole of it. All of these things she had learned at school, and at church…and suddenly Dad had baulked, showed himself a hypocrite who said the words but didn't mean them! He was a stranger. And why couldn't she make up her mind? On the one hand, all of the lessons pointed clearly against extraordinary measures. On the other hand, how could she tell him…no?

Would it be helpful to visit Ian, and ask him for advice? Picturing her brother, broad-shouldered and intense, quick to anger and well suited to hammering hot iron, Cairen shook her head. He was traditional; he would only get angry at Dad and another fight solved nothing. But who? She suddenly thought of Trevor—he'd known! How? Could Dad have asked him? But no—mostly likely he heard Dad and Rosie, somehow. Trevor would help. At least, he would listen; he was very good at that. She felt the panic lift a little; realized she'd been sitting in the sun and would have extra freckles at the very least, and jumped up to check the bread.

* * *

The clinic was busy today—there were three new-baby checks, two healed broken limbs to un-cast and certify, a toddler with worms and Old Lady Madison who was forever scalding herself. And there were several that Rosie took aside for private chats, which could be anything from contraception to family feuds to terminal diagnoses. He got the straightforward cases: the injuries and repeat dosages, but most of the patients wanted Rosie to examine and give advice, so he spent a lot of time listening and learning. And wondering how he'd ever get good enough to distinguish the subtle symptoms and give accurate diagnoses. It was past dinner time when they wrapped up with the Tate baby—a chunky boy with a worrisome passivity—and closed the door. Rosie moved quickly to gather up the linens and gowns and bag them for Tony the washman. She was petite, plump but lively, and seemed younger than her 52 years. Her auburn hair was gray at the temples, kept back in a braid. Trevor admired her calm, practical attitude; he suspected his own quiet demeanor was part of the reason she chose him to prentice. Today he was feeling anything but calm, though. How could he ask about Jeff without admitting he'd overheard? As it turned out, when she heard he'd been plowing for the Langleys, she asked about Jeff herself.

"How was his pallor? Did he look better or worse than the last time he was in?"

That was one of the signs of a good medic—being able to remember patients in great detail. Records were brief, almost cryptic; the best doctor could list a patient's history without looking at them. Trevor closed his eyes to better recall.

"He was more pale. In fact, Cairen was worried enough to ask me—to ask me for your advice," he said finally. "She said the last time you treated him, he did get much better."

"Hmm, yes... but it's a progressive illness. And the winter rations don't always have enough vitamins." A rare frown; she was thinking of Charter, he was sure. "It may be his last year, unless—"

181

"—he goes to Charter Hospital?" Trevor finished, holding his breath. Rosie's startled expression held no suspicion. "Not a likely option, I know, but—would it help?"

Rosie frowned again. "Last I heard, they still were making insulin, so yes, it would slow the progress of the illness. But they were charging like an oil company, and it isn't, as you know, a cure."

Trevor nodded. They had a handful of diabetics in the five clinics, all following strict diets, and one child who had died at a year due to Type 1 diabetes, for which diet did nothing. Malfunctioning organs were not easily treated, since the collapse. That was the way of it. The city hospital was more like a dream or a threat than a reality. He'd never been close enough to see their region's Chartered city on the horizon, let alone enter it. Its charter status kept out most of the surrounding population; cash money had to be shown at the gates to even allow someone in. He'd heard they looked upon barter as primitive; a weird notion compared to believing some etched paper had intrinsic value.

"But if he did want to go...?" Trevor wasn't even sure of his question; he wanted to know what then? What were they as medics responsible for? What would the town say? What could be done to avoid wasting valuable produce and labor on a pipe dream?

"Jeff's a stubborn man," Rosie said grimly. "but I didn't think he was that pigheaded." She shrugged. "Let's clean up and go home." There were still yard chores to be done after dinner, and then studying the casebooks. Trevor paid for his lessons with a lot of hard physical labor, but he didn't mind. There were many worse prenticeships.

The Going

* * *

Sunday came around quickly, filled with a spring drizzle. Cairen felt the tension in her neck as she set the table for the afternoon meal. Trevor hadn't sent word, but if he dropped in around dinner time, he would be welcome as family. She had to stop herself from "accidentally" setting another place. As the aroma of ham and potato soup wafted through the house, she busied herself with cutting apart a few threadbare shirts for rags. There was knitting to do, but she was so fumble-fingered that she avoided it as a waste of good wool. She felt like her nerves were showing through her skin. Luckily, it seemed Mom and Dad were avoiding her too. Neither parent had brought up the dowry issue, but she knew they would be sitting her down later today, maybe after supper. What was keeping Trevor? The ripping of cotton broadcloth had a satisfactory growl that felt good. But soon that was done, and she jumped up to see if she could see him down the road. Maybe she could check the rain barrel—anything to work off the energy she was feeling!

From the porch, she could see a man down by the curve, walking slowly—in a little bit, she could tell it was Trevor. She let out a breath and grabbed a broom to sweep off the porch, then stopped. Where could they talk? Damn the rain, anyway! She watched him come closer, thinking furiously.

* * *

Trevor had been thinking long and hard on the walk to the Landleys. What can you say when there's nothing to say? Rosie had been sympathetic; he even wondered if she'd guessed his feelings for Cairen. But she had no miracle cure, nor any advice except to keep good diet and moderate physi-

183

cal work by watching fatigue levels—standard advice for helping the body heal, if it could. But Cairen needed more. He watched the alders that tilted along Cold Creek shivering in the rain; he could feel his steps slow, and it felt—he shook himself for being so fanciful—like he was walking through heavy mud rather than on gravel. Once or twice in the clinic he had felt this—a strong sense that he knew what he had to do, but was searching for anything else to do instead.

He saw Cairen sweeping, and pushed himself to walk a little faster. She had turned away, as if a clean porch was her only goal; he admired the strong sweeping motions, and wished he could watch the curve of her back forever. But in a moment, he was climbing the steps and she was greeting him with a wavering smile. He heard footsteps from inside, coming toward the door.

"I'm going to talk with him," he told her, before she could speak. "After supper. I'll talk with your Pa. Trust me."

She looked stunned, like it was the last thing she was expecting. But just then, Jeff opened the door.

"Hey, Trevor—good timing. You're as good as Ian in catching a meal. Come in," Jeff joked as he held the door wide. Trevor smiled at Cairen and walked inside. If he got through this afternoon, the medic test would be child's play.

The meal was leisurely as a Sunday dinner generally was, full of small talk about the town, and local news. The two young boys were oblivious to the other four, whose speech was forced, and halting. Trevor couldn't understand why Jeff and Ann would be tense, since they didn't know his "errand." But he focused on finding enough news to fill the silences.

As Cairen and the boys got up to clear, Trevor asked quickly, "Can I speak with you, Uncle?"

Jeff looked startled. "What about?"

"Um—something personal. If you wouldn't mind." Trevor could feel the boys' stares, and sensed that Ann and Cairen looked away, then herded the boys into the kitchen. Jeff shrugged, then pointed toward the living room.

There were two fat upholstered chairs by the south window, and a pair of cast-off dining chairs sitting near the small spinning wheel by the north window. That and a few end tables were all that this room contained. Jeff sat in the green corduroy armchair, so Trevor took the brown vinyl one opposite him.

"Is this about Cairen?" Jeff asked. Trevor braced himself; how he wished it was about Cairen!

"No, I just wanted to speak to you—partly as medic, partly as family. It's about your idea to go to Charter."

Jeff paled; a complex of emotions shifted across his face in a moment—Trevor wondered if Rosie could get in trouble for this intervention. Jeff leaned back in the chair; his frown grew deeper.

"Trevor, I know you don't understand—"

"No, I don't," Trevor interrupted. "Excuse me, Uncle—no, I don't. And please don't think Rosie told me—I happened to overhear you two talking. I know you've thought about this a while. But—hear me out—I wonder if you have really thought this through. You spend all the money once, quickly, and then—what? Have you pictured coming back home with the insulin, knowing that everyone knows what you're doing? And they will know. And never mind that the insulin would have to be kept cold through the summer. Never mind that—think about working, every day, alongside your neighbors—and they know. Think about the Dinners and Raisings—because once you find out that you hate living with their eyes watching you, it will be too late. You'll have already spent that money. I can't make your decision for you, but I just want you to really picture the next couple years— day in and day out—once you've made that choice."

"They don't have the right to judge me!" The old man half-lifted himself from the armchair, then sank down. "They don't have the right." His right hand clenched and un- clenched, spasmodically.

"I know—but they will anyway. It's human nature, and you can't change them. They will be looking, and they will be whispering—and your family will have to live through that too. And, like I say, once you've spent the money is too late to realize that it won't be much of a life. Remember Preacher Kane." Trevor hated to bring that up.

Jeff's face flushed, whether anger or shame, and he bent to pick something from the floor by the chair. Trevor waited, watching the tremble of the man's arm, the tight movements. How to keep the thread of the conversation going where it needed to? The gift of knowing when to be silent and when to speak—how does one get that? He held his breath, giving Jeff some time to think, but not enough to evade, trying to pace it as Rosie did, when she was delivering bad news.

"Uncle—think about what we all know. We are part of nature's cycle; no different than the plants, the animals. We don't know our span, but it's limited. There's always an end."

"You're a child!" Jeff blurted, staring at him with red- dened eyes. "You think you have your whole life ahead—so you don't care! Wait 'til you get to my age... wait—see how scared... how scared—"

Rosie never really spoke about how hard it was to watch someone grapple with death. Trevor wondered if he were cut out to be a medic. No songs or rituals had been made for this moment, that he knew. He hesitated, then gripped Jeff's hand.

"No, I know that I don't know. Each of us pauses on our own Gateway, alone. The town can only hold you in our hearts, and help you with the everyday things. It's your Gate, your journey. There's a time when the cycle is over, No honor in staying the tide; I'm a drop that is flowing beyond, now; to find out what's on the other side."

As he softly sang a bit of the Going song, Trevor noticed Jeff nodding; some of the anger quenched. Trevor sat back. Tears began to roll down the man's cheek; he didn't try to hide them now. Tears were the rain that allows acceptance to bloom, Rosie always said, so Trevor let him cry for several minutes, in silence. Then, steeling himself, he asked softly, "What will be different five years from now? What will allow you to let go then? Or will you bankrupt your family before you go?"

"No—not that. I wouldn't do that," Jeff said, squirming a bit in the chair. "It's just... I don't know. It's a good question." He was silent, then, looking down at his knees. He started to speak, then stopped; nodded again. "I will think about it. I will, Trevor. Promise." He grinned and leaned forward to pat Trevor's hand. "I appreciate your coming to talk with me. Tell Rosie that."

"She didn't send me—"

"I know that. But she should know she's got a good student." Jeff got up and moved slowly toward the hall door, wiping his face. He paused at the door, then turned back.

187

"Thanks, again, Trevor." Then he left. Trevor felt dismissed, and unwilling to wander the house looking for Cairen, so he plodded down the hall and out the front door, hoping he hadn't made things worse.

Cairen was waiting by the edge of the property, out of view of the house. A giddy kind of courage filled Trevor, like the one time he'd tasted carbonated wine. As long as everything was up in the air—

"Trevor, what did he say? What did you tell him??" Cairen's oilcloth poncho was dripping; her face was slick with rain. "You didn't tell him I sent you?"

"No—I told him I was speaking both as a medic and family member. I told him I'd overheard him and Rosie—and that's true—and we... talked." He was suddenly aware of the split—medic and family. He really shouldn't tell her anything. "Honestly, I don't know if it helped. But I tried... just tried to get him to see... what he already knows." She frowned; it surely wasn't what she wanted to hear. He rushed ahead.

"And as long as we're talking about...futures...I—doubt you noticed, but I'm very interested... in making a future with you—" his words sounded crazy even to himself. "I—know you are going to Meet next month, but—if you would consider—could we at least talk about—" Her jaw had dropped, and that silenced him. Okay, well—he could always become a medic over in the east county. They were always short in that harsh country. No need to stay here and watch her raise someone else's kids.

"I—okay, to be honest, no—I didn't notice," she said. "You're kind of quiet, you know."

"Yes, I know that."

188

"Not that that's bad," she hurried on, "Just—I always see you with the Granger girls…"

"Nice girls; always been like sisters. I didn't have to worry about what I said."

She nodded; her serious look told him little. "Yes. I can see that. Okay—let me get my bearings. I was so wrapped up in Dad."

"You don't have to say anything. Really—"

"No, no—I do. And I want to." She smiled; why did that choke him up? "It's not—I guess I'm willing to consider, to get to know you more. I realize…I don't know that much about you, cousin."

"And I know they allow dispensations—"

"You're thorough—you would have checked." Her smiled broadened; she didn't look unhappy. Suddenly it all felt more hopeful—and dangerous. He clamped his lips shut to avoid saying something stupid.

"Well—I'll ask Dad and Mom to give us some time off; I assume Rosie will let you out?"

He nodded. She repeated the motion.

"So—let's give this the month, anyway… and see where we get. And I might not have a dowry—"

"Doesn't matter!"

"—but all those details come later. Right?"

"Right." He breathed out again; realizing he'd been choking back tears since the parlor. He was so grateful, at that moment, for the rain soaking them both. No real chance of a hug; that was for another day. "I—thanks—I… I have to get back and get to my lessons. I'll—I'll see about staying in town after the clinic Tuesday, okay?"

"Okay. Now I've got to go in—they're waiting to talk to me about my dowry." She winced, then smiled. "I'll see you Tuesday evening."

Trevor walked back to Rosie's, wanting to break into a jog at every step.

* * *

Cairen paused inside the back door shaking off the rain, before putting her poncho on a mudroom hook. So cousin Trevor was sweet on her? It was still new enough she didn't know what to think. He was cute; maybe not as boisterous as the farm boys. But medics were valued, and less chance of him becoming injured and unable to work. Love was only a piece of things these days; her married friends told her friendship lasted longer. She leaned against the door to the kitchen; it felt like one of those spring squalls where the yard was swirled and upended. And Dad—what had they talked about? What were the plans now, she wondered? Trying to think ahead to summer, she found a gap, like a missing bridge—no way of knowing how the next two months would play out. But it proved that you couldn't count on things staying the same. Her mother's voice called her name faintly. With a suddenly tight chest, and an odd giddy feeling, she walked into the house.

The Going Song

As the heart of the tree slowly hollows
As the bloom on the thorn slowly fades
I know in my heart I am going
Yet always a part of me stays.

Chorus:
Oh, you will have me forever –
I'm in song, and in smiles, and in sighs
It's just this one branch that's going
Remember the roots never die.

Though I tremble like aspen in autumn
Though I rest like a snake in the sun
I can feel some new tendril curling
Round a thread that is leading me on.

Plant me where I can take root as
The grass and the herbs and the 'shrooms
Plant a sapling above – call it my name
I'll be there giving strength to the bloom.

There's a time when the cycle is over
No honor in staying the tide
I'm a drop that is flowing beyond, now
To find out what's on the other side.

Think Like A Tinkerer

By Thijs Goverde

I. Bud

It was in one of the dust-coloured villages near the edge of the wasteland, where a man is counted rich if he owns more than five goats. There lived a man there named Jon who had eleven goats and a mule and a well no one else could claim a drop of water from by right. That meant he was rich enough to have the village named after him; rich enough to feed a slave or two but not quite rich enough, alas, to buy them.

One June evening, when the honeysuckle was heavy in the air because the rains that occasionally changed the village colours from dust to mud had only just subsided and the air was still damp, Jon came to the tarp in front of Mik's house and sat down at one of the three tables there.

The men of the village greeted him respectfully, half hoping for a round of beer. It would have been the first round he

193

ever stood yet they watched with a certain eagerness as he waved Mik over.

"What'll it be, Jon?"

"Pint of your best, Mik."

The men, disappointed, slumped back in their seats.

Mik brought Jon his pint and started to retreat inside, but Jon unexpectedly asked: "How're your boys doing, Mik?"

A sly look entered Mik's broad, mastiff-like face. He sat down. "They're fine," he said. "Just fine. Especially Jak. He's my second one, you know?"

Jon nodded. He knew Jak was the second one; knew it now, anyway.

"Seventeen years old now," Mik went on. "Light of my life, that one. Broad-shouldered, keen-eyed, eager... very eager to learn a respectable trade. Very eager."

"You're a lucky man, to have a son like that! One you don't need to worry about, I mean. I mean he sounds like the kind of boy who'll make a way for himself, no matter what."

Mik cursed inwardly. He'd been overdoing it. Jon wouldn't take Jak now that he knew how badly Mik wanted the boy off his hands.

"So," Jon went on, "what about your youngest? What's his name again?"

"Bud. He's even broader-shouldered, and keener-eyed, and..." It was a lame attempt and Mik knew it.

Jon beamed generously. "Well, if he's such a fine lad, I'd like to take him on as an apprentice. If he's looking for a position, that is."

Mik cursed again, in silence. What to do? Bud *was* a fine lad and Mik loved to have him around, but he was also another mouth to feed.

"I'll ask him," he sighed. "Send him around tomorrow. See if the two of you can reach an agreement."

That was all there was to it, apart from the fact that a few small coins changed hands around the tables: there'd been bets on the question what Jon would do first, marry or take an apprentice.

The next morning Bud came to Jon's house.

"My dad says you're looking for an apprentice," he said sullenly.

Jon eyed him suspiciously. "What's your name, boy?"

"Bud."

"You're sure it's not Jak, now?"

"I think I know my name, thank you."

"Just checking." Jon felt a little uneasy. Had Mik outsmarted him, after all? The boy looked strong and able, but he was pretty. Very pretty, with thick black curls, a fairly complete set of straight, white teeth and the blue eyes that you never encounter in real life – only in the old stories, where everybody seems to have them somehow.

Bud had a face that girls would swoon over and since he was at an age where all you want is to have girls swoon over you, he probably felt that it was natural for him to get all he wanted. Which is a dangerous feeling in an apprentice.

Bud confirmed Jon's suspicions by saying: "Look, I'm not going to be your slave or nothing."

"Of course not, boy. You'll be an apprentice. Completely different thing. You don't get paid, of course, but you'll get board and lodging, and Sundays off."

"Right. And I'm a free man. I can leave whenever I want, no ifs, ands or buts."

"Of course."

"And no whipping. Ever. Or I'm off."

"Of course."

So there was no whipping, ever, and after six years Bud sneaked off in the dead of night, which was his right as a free man. He never returned.

So after six long years Mik finally got Jak off his hands, who was lazy and overly fond of beer but he wasn't pretty and he wasn't prone to running off and he didn't much mind the occasional whipping. Those are the qualities you look for, in an apprentice.

II. Jennifer

It was the Ides of March and Jennifer decreed there should be a bonfire.

"A what?"

A bonfire. A big roaring fire in the middle of the square. To celebrate the coming of spring, or more specifically, the coming of the new greens, the new food, the end of the lean winter-time.

The people of Jonsboro scratched their heads. They were glad the new growing-season was beginning, but they really didn't see how that meant you had to waste a load of fire-wood. The winter hadn't been very cold, no, not very cold at all really, but the rains might start soon, so...

"Come on, folks! Today is the Ides of March, that festival was already celebrated by the very Romans."

"The who?"

Think Like A Tinkerer

Jennifer sighed. These people! They had no culture, no past, no awareness of their place in history *at all*. Other than a dim knowledge of the passing of the Yesterday, of course.

"Come to the square tonight. Bring food and drink and firewood. I'll tell you about the Romans, and many other things, and we'll sing songs till daybreak. A grand time. You'll see."

Jim, easily the oldest man in Jonsboro, cleared his throat. Jim had chest problems; the sight and sound of him clearing his throat was not something for the weak of stomach. "Wasn't there a book in the Bible called Romans?" he asked.

"Epistle to the Romans, yes. Two of them."

"So... were they Christians?"

"In the end, yes. As a matter of fact, the..." She faltered. She'd been about to bring up the Roman Catholic Church, but that was probably a bad idea. These bumpkins wouldn't know a Roman if Julius Caesar himself were raised from the grave to stand up and say hello, but they were very, very aware of the age-old sectarian hatreds.

"So this Ides... is it a Christian thing? Like Easter?"

"Yes, yes! It's the Roman name for Easter." She shot a look at Godfrey, to see if he could keep a straight face if he heard his wife tell such a blatant lie.

He could. In fact, he nodded thoughtfully.

Several of the village men looked at him. "So... basically... your wife means that today is Easter?"

"Yes," he said. "That's what she means."

The village had no priest to calculate the date of Easter for them. They knew it had to be calculated and they couldn't do it themselves; Jennifer and Godfrey were people of cul-

197

ture so there was no telling what they mightn't know. Maybe even the date of Easter.

"I thought Easter was where you had the eggs?" Mik ventured.

Jennifer nodded. "Eggs and bonfires. Very old Christian traditions."

So there was a bonfire that night. There were eggs, too. The people of Jonsboro ate the eggs while Jennifer told them the story of Easter as they'd never heard it before.

No one in Jonsboro could read, so their knowledge of the Bible was somewhat sketchy. They knew by heart all the verses pertaining to, for instance, the doctrine of predestination—but uncontested points like the resurrection were not kept alive in the debate.

They knew about Judas' betrayal, but were quite shocked by Peter's trifold denial.

They were disappointed that one of their favorite bits was left out completely. (The bit about the bunny who burrowed into the Holy Sepulcher, saw things no bunny was meant to see, and came out laying eggs like a demented chicken, forever and ever, as a punishment.)

After the story, Jennifer sang songs of the Yesterday.

She started with the Yesterday song itself, that bemoans the loss of mankind's splendor like one grieves for a love lost. Then the World Is Green Song, which does it the other way around.

Sad songs both, so to change the mood she sang the Forty-two Song. A camp-fire classic, for sure. She was worried if these hicks knew the joke; if they didn't, the mood would go down even further.

She sang mournfully:

Think Like A Tinkerer

How many roads must a man walk down
before you can call him a man?

To her relief, the audience duly responded: "FORTY-
TWO!" They didn't really understand the joke—even Jennifer didn't—but they knew it was for laughing. After that
she could sing more upbeat, nonsensical songs like the Blue
Sweet Shoes Song, the Yellow Brick Road Song and many,
many others.

Then another story.

Jennifer looked at her audience. She had them in the palm
of her hand now; she could almost love them. They were ignorant, crude, living lives of hardship and poverty even by
Today's standards, but they were her people now. Hers by
marriage and conquest.

The marriage was that of her idiot daughter Emily, who'd
been lured here by the local grandee, Jon, with his tales of
wealth and an "unlimited supply of Tinkering materials" that
had turned out to consist of one (1) old steam-engine.

The conquest was her own. She had won them by her art,
and now she would win them some more.

"In the evening of the Yesterday," she began, "there lived
a man named Agostino. He was a wise man; wise enough to
see that it was, indeed, evening and that night would soon
follow. He saw it because his father was in the dream-trade,
and what do you do in the evening? You go to bed, right?
That's right, and what do you go to bed *for*? To dream, yes,
exactly. So when Agostino saw his father get richer and richer, because more and more people needed to dream, he knew
that it was, indeed, evening.

This worried him. He spoke to his father, but his father was "a practical man", which meant he was only interested in buying and selling.

Now the dreams he sold were of a low quality, because you can't really sell dreams, can you? Only counterfeit garbage.

And do you know what happens when you don't dream enough? Yes, you go crazy in the head. Medical fact. You can ask my husband if you want. He's sitting right over there. Fully qualified Medicin. Ask him later.

The same thing happens if you dream only the low-quality garbage. You go crazy in the head.

So the dream-trade was full of crazy, violent people.

This worried Agostino, also. But his father would not listen. Instead, he gave Agostino an insane amount of money to open up a new line in the dream-trade.

Agostino did not do that. He did something else.

He used the money to build a city. A very small city, by the standards of Yesterday, but a city nonetheless. It was hidden deep in the desert and very cleverly built.

Agostino gathered many people there, people of great knowledge and wisdom, and he gathered books there that preserved all the knowledge of man.

The people of the city possessed the powers of Yesterday, of course: the power Elektrick and the power Combusting. They had all the machines that built the high age of man, when we could look back through the mists of time, make islands rise out of the sea, reach beyond the stars. They had machines for doing everything they didn't want to do themselves: from hauling loads to washing clothes. They even had one of the flying-machines, the Aeroplanes that rode the sky in those days.

Their very houses were machines, for with their shining roofs they produced the power Elektrick. The entire city was covered in the shiny Elektrick-stuff, and therefore its people called it the Shining City.

It was so cleverly designed that it could live on if the Yesterday would end, and man fall from his high estate, as Agostino had seen they surely must.

When the Shining City was ready, Agostino went back to his father. "Oh my father," he said, "I have taken thy money and used it not for dream-stuff and craziness. I have built a city with it, a city that will endure after all the other cities have fallen."

His father waxed angry and replied: "Oh my son, thou hast doomed us all, for the money was not thine to spend as thou sawst fit. It was not even mine. It belonged to the Dreamtraders Guild we are part of, and they will surely deal roughly with us. They are not kind men."

"I know this, father. That is why my city is well-hidden. Let us go there, and live in peace, if not in our accustomed comfort."

"Begone from my sight," said the father, "and hideaway like a girly-boy, if that is thy pleasure. I am a Dream-Lord and I shall not live as anything less." Then Agostino's father and his brothers gathered all the weapons they could find, and they fought a bloody battle with their enemies, and when they were defeated their bodies were handled in a most gruesome manner. For those were crazy, violent times and the men of the Dreamtraders Guilds were the craziest and most violent of all.

201

But they never found Agostino, and when the Yesterday ended his Shining City still stood.

It still stands today.

Yes, it stands, and I have seen its shiny roofs from afar. I have heard the rumble of their glorious machines, but I have not seen them, because no one may enter that place. Which is sad, because they have the complete knowledge of the Yesterday, and they have even added to it. Their Medecins are so skilled that no one dies before the age of sixty, their Agricolers grow all the food you can imagine, let alone eat, and because they have their machines, they do not work but spend their days creating beauty and joy.

It is sad, my friends, that we may not go there. But isn't it a glorious thing, to know that the Yesterday still lives? That the splendor of mankind may never be destroyed?

Jennifer looked at the faces around the embers of bonfire. They were staring, lost in the visions of food and health and leisure.

"Let's all go to sleep," she said quietly. "Busy day tomorrow. Planting and so on."

To sleep they went and every single one of them dreamt of the Shining City, of the wonderful knowledge and art of the Yesterday.

This suited Jennifer well, because Medecins, Storysingers and Tinkerers trace their arts back to those times, so she and her family shared a bit of the glory of the Shining City.

Jonsboro might be a god-forsaken hellhole and its people ignorant louts, but we all want respect and we take it wherever we can find it. Even if we must seek it in Jonsboro.

III. Max

Grandma was squashing bugs in the potato patch and Max was helping her. He liked squashing bugs. If you squeezed them just right, the red stuff inside them squirted over distances of two meters or more.

Grandma was muttering to herself, as usual: "This is disgusting. This is *so* disgusting. We shouldn't need to do this. We're people of culture, we have family papers. We're well-respected, we possess valuable skills, we don't need to stinking well *do* this. Oh listen to me, splitting an infinitive, and me a Storysinger, there's what happens to your standards once you start squashing bugs. To your culture. Family papers, we have. This is absolutely disgusting..."

Behind the goatshed, someone was whistling the first three notes of the Yesterday Song.

"...your grandfather wants to talk to you, we shouldn't ever have come here, squashing bugs, I ask you, what kind of work is that? Eeeurgh! Right in my eye!"

Max would have found the face she made very comical, but he would also have rushed to help her wipe the red goo from her eye. He loved his grandmother dearly.

However he was already behind the shed, getting instructions from Grandpa. "Do you know the house of the widow Eev? Good. I want you to bring her this. Tell her to rub it in three times a day. And to stay in her chair. And to eat all the fruit she can get her hands on. Get someone to look after her. Tell them I sent you, if that's what it takes, but make sure your dad doesn't find out about it."

"Why not, grandpa?"

"It's a grown-up thing. There's grown-up reasons. Understand?"

Max nodded cheerfully. This sounded like a very thorough explanation to his six-year-old ears. A more thorough explanation than his dad ever gave him for anything, anyway.

He darted through the rustling, dry-brown weeds. There was a sort of path there, if you knew where to look, that went straight to the Jonsboro square, worn out by the many secret missions Grandpa had sent him on.

He passed by the meadow where Jak and dad were making hay. Or rather, Jak was making hay and Jon was struggling with the old mule. The animal seemed to have a very strong opinion as to where all the hay should go; Jon had an equally strong opinion, but an altogether different one. They were more or less deadlocked.

Fifteen minutes later, Max was at the widow Eev's house. The door was open. Inside there hung the rank smell of pus. It easily overpowered the smell of the herbs that hung to dry behind the stove. The widow Eev was in her comfy chair in the middle of the kitchen. Her left leg rested on a little stool, the skirts hitched up to allow the sores to breathe.

Max didn't flinch at the sight. He'd been running errands for his grandfather for over a year now. He'd seen a thing or two.

"Is that you, Max? How sweet of you to come by! Did you bring my ointment? Ah, wonderful! Your grandfather is a saint, I swear he is. And your grandmother has the voice of an angel. Really, what they're still doing over at Jon's place, I can't imagine..."

Now it is a universal law of nature that six-year-old kids are always just a little bit smarter than we give them credit for and they hear *everything* we say.

So Max asked: "Why? What's wrong with our house? It's the biggest house in the whole village!"

"Oh, there's nothing wrong with it," the widow hastened to say, "nothing wrong, as such. But your grandparents, they... well, they're people of culture, aren't they? They'd be more appreciated in the world at large. I've even heard it said," almost whispering now, "they have family papers." Her quintessential widowness got the better of her; she got nosy. "Do they? Eh? Do they have 'em? Family papers?"

Max just stood there, shifting his weight and hoping she would stop asking him questions he did not understand. After a while he realized that the widow would keep up her questioning until she got an answer out of him, so he mumbled "Dunno." He had to repeat it five or six times before she gave up.

"Oh well," said Eev, "thanks for the ointment, anyway. You're a good boy. Do you want a biscuit?" She started to rise from her chair to get him a biscuit. Max had to invoke the authority of his grandfather to get her to stay in the seat. This meant foregoing the biscuit, so Max felt like a proper, tragic hero, causing his own grief by doing the right thing.

All aglow with his self-sacrifice he set out to find Eev's sister Soo, in the hope that she would take responsibility for the widow. Maybe give him a biscuit for his troubles after all. Or even two biscuits, to reward him for the nobility of his spirit.

"Grandpa Godfrey says you have to look after Eev, she can't leave her chair he says, she tried to give me a biscuit but I said you can't leave your chair so I didn't get it but I didn't mind."

He ran along as Soo went to Eev's house in long, angry strides—there was little love lost between the sisters. "I mean I would have liked the biscuit, I love biscuits but Grandpa said she mustn't get up and I figured that was more important," Max panted. After a while it dawned on him that Soo hadn't taken in a single word he'd said. She was far too busy cursing the day that landed her with a sister whom she did not like and whom she must now care for or risk the displeasure of the only Medecin within a two days' walk.

He might as well go home. On his way he passed Mik's house; under the tarp was his father, who had apparently given up on the hay and was now explaining his woes to all who would listen: "I told him, no more curing people for free, okay? I mean he grows his herbs on my land, using water from my well, and then he mixes 'em with my honey, he even makes alcohol in my still, that my useless wife tinkered for me even though I need a still like I need a hole in my head. So the very least he can do is pay me for the materials, am I right? But no, he took an oath to help people for free. If I catch him at it again I'll break his face. These people of culture—completely useless, every one of 'em. The Dark Lord take them and their precious family papers..." Then he saw his son. "What are you doing here?" he demanded angrily.

The men under the tarp hid their smiles; Jon was the only person in the village who didn't know what Max was doing there.

"Nothing," said Max.

"Why aren't you in the field?"

"Finished." He looked at the ground.

"If I find even one bug in that field tonight, I'll make you eat it. Understand?"

Max nodded and ran to the field with the speed of a swallow.

Grandma was still there: "...squashing bugs, I studied for years and years, I know hundreds of stories, thousands of songs, I've got family papers and I know them by heart, why should I need to squash bugs? I'm a woman of..."

"Grandma?"

"Yes, dear?"

"What are family papers?"

There was an intense relief in her smile as she said: "I thought you'd never ask."

IV. The Family Papers

In the attic there were two large, iron-bound suitcases. Grandpa Godfrey opened them carefully and showed Max what was inside. A motley collection of books, manila folders, letters, diaries and loose sheets of paper—some with just a few remarks jotted down on them, some tightly scribbled, some with diagrams or pictures.

"What are they?" asked Max.

"They are knowledge," his grandmother said. "All the little black marks are letters. Together they make words, and the words tell many things. The history of our family, but more importantly the things our family has learned. There are many books about the way to keep, or make, your body healthy, and your grandfather has studied them. Which makes him a Medecin."

"There's a bit more to it than that," Grandpa said mildly.

"I know, dear, but I can only explain so much at any one time, can't I? Anyway, there are also books about making, or repairing, machines and your mother studied them so she became a Tinkerer."

"And there are also books of stories and songs?"

"Clever boy!" Grandma Jennifer beamed. "There are, yes, and they made me a Storysinger. There are other things a person of culture may become. An Agricoler, for instance. That's someone who knows how to grow plants and animals."

"You mean a farmer? Like dad?"

"*Not* like your father, no. He is, regrettably, not a man of culture. An Agricoler would grow a lot more and better food than he does, quite possibly on less land. But Agricolers don't spend their time growing food; they mainly teach others. People of culture use their knowledge to help others, you see. They don't keep things to themselves. There are a few exceptions, of course. There are bad apples in every basket. Can't be helped."

"But why doesn't dad want to be a man of culture?"

"He never had the choice," Grandpa Godfrey said. "His ancestors never had the foresight to store the knowledge when it was freely available. Ours did, and the papers have passed from parent to child ever since. They're called "family papers" for a reason, you know. And now, it is too late for him. You have to begin learning at a young age. Even you are almost too old, already."

Max was startled to hear it. He was quite used to hearing he was too young for this, that and the other. Being too old for something was a new experience; he didn't like it. "Why didn't you tell me this before?"

"Don't get angry, dear," said Grandma. "We couldn't offer it to you; your dad would not like it. He resents it, you see. Our family. Our culture. People of culture are quite well-respected. *Quite* well-respected. Better than a farmer from the wastelands, even a relatively rich one. If we offered you our family papers he'd feel as if we were stealing you away from him. From his kind of life. We had to wait until you came to us."

"But now," said Grandpa, "we can begin."

So they began. Every day, after work, they taught him how to read. They taught it from a book; a very old book, that had pictures to help you understand the words but very few of the pictures meant anything to Max so they didn't help much.

Grandma never muttered anymore when they were working in the fields. Instead, she sang.

She sang the Four Last Songs, The Yesterday Song, the Blue Sweet Shoes song and many others. Max sang along as he worked until he knew them word for word.

She tried to teach him stories too, after work, but he didn't have the patience to listen to them. He wanted to learn Tinkering. He spent hours looking at the things his mother had tinkered. Grandpa's still, the treadle thresher, the washing machine and the dehydrator.

"Why isn't there more?" he asked.

"Well," said Grandma Jennifer, "to be able to tinker, you need to have things to tinker *with*. Machine parts and the like. That sort of stuff is hard to come by, out here."

"Tinkering is the least of the arts, anyway," said Grandpa.

Later, when the boy had gone off to look at the still again, Grandma gave her husband an earful about that last remark.

"How could you say that? The least of the arts? Don't you understand why he wants to tinker?"

"Oh, well, boys will be boys, right? Shiny machinery has a powerful..."

"Oh, you old fool! How can you possibly misunderstand your own grandson so badly? He wants to feel closer to his mother, what did you think?"

The old man blushed. "I see. You may be right. Yes. I... I'm sorry, I... do you think we should tell him that she—"

"Certainly not!"

A few months after that, he came to them with a book in his hand. He tried to act indifferently, but his feverishly excited eyes belied him. "I found the book," he blurted.

"What book?" Godfrey asked.

"The book with the still in it. The design my mother used. For your still."

"Oh. Well, that's clever of you!"

"There's a note in it that I can't read. Do you think she wrote it?"

"Let me see..." Jennifer took the book from his hands and found the note, a lighter yellow between the almost ochre pages of the book. Tears filled her eyes when she saw her daughter's messy handwriting. "Vwsj Esp," she read, "ax qgm sjw jwsvafy lzak..."

"Yes," she whispered, "yes, that's your mother's hand..."

"What does it say? Is it in another language?"

"No," said Grandma. "None that I know of."

Max was nine years old at the time. He was too young to see that his grandmother wasn't telling him all she knew.

He spent whole days staring at the note, willing himself to understand it, but that is not how the world works. In the end he gave up. He didn't only give up trying to understand, he gave up the whole subject of Tinkering and took up Medecin, to his grandfather's great joy.

They studied books together, they grew herbs together, made salves, pills and potions together, they visited patients together; it was the happiest time of the old man's entire life until the day they were called to the widow Eev's house. Her sister Soo had been standing on a rickety chair, trying to reach a high shelf. She'd fallen off. The Medecin and his pupil were called for, but they could do nothing except close her eyes.

They were walking back home through the darkening streets of Jonsboro when Max asked his grandfather: "What did she die of?"

Godfrey was slightly taken aback. "Well, her head hit the stove with some force, causing a large fracture of the skull, severe blood loss and a dislocation of the atlas vertebra which led to a lesion of the medulla. Any of these might have done the trick, but if you—"

"Not Soo," Max said impatiently. "My mother. What did she die of? I mean she died giving birth to me, but how could that happen? She was right under your nose! And you are very good at that sort of thing, I've seen you! Everyone says you've never lost a baby or a mother and I say 'except my mom' and they go oh yeah, your mom, as if she didn't really matter!" *What happened*?

It was only then that Godfrey realized why Max had been studying Medecin. For him it was merely a way to learn more about his mother. All the information anyone had ever given him was that she was dead. She had been a Tinkerer and now she was dead. So Max had studied Tinkering first, and then

he had studied Death. It had been called Medecin, but to him
it had meant only Death and Death had meant only his mother.

Godfrey made up some plausible cause of death, knowing
that he would lose the boy.

And sure enough, two days later Max came down for
breakfast and sullenly said: "I don't think I want to be a
Medecin."

Everyone else was already seated at the table. Jon laid his
spoon down, beaming with happiness, and said: "You're
right, son. You're right. What's the use of Medecin, eh?
What's the use? You can't make a living by it, 'cause you're
not allowed to accept money for your services, so what's the
use?"

Godfrey couldn't let that one pass unchallenged. "A
Medecin doesn't need to make a living," he said haughtily.
"No one would ever deny us food and lodging. In fact most
villages would be so happy to have a Medecin, that they
would freely provide us with the best house they could find."

"And the same goes for Storysingers," his wife added.
"Story-singing is the highest art, you know. Tinkerers know
how machines work, and Medecins know how the human
body works. But Storysingers, now... we know how the human mind works. And that is the highest knowledge of all."

"That may be true, dear, but there's no bread in it.
Storysingers wander the roads, trading gossip for scraps, telling stories in return for a night in the hayloft, and only getting the grand treatment when there's a festival."

"I was offered a house wherever I went," Grandma Jennifer snapped.

"That's because you're married to a Medecin, dear."

Jon gave a deep, rumbling laugh. "Will you listen to them, son? Arguing who is better treated by the common man, the peasant, the farmer! Well—if these high and mighty cultured folks vie for the love of us farmers, then what is the grandest profession of all? Eh? I'm glad you're not going to be a Medecin, boy. Stick with me, stick to the farm. People will always need us, because they'll always need food. Eh? Haha! This calls for a little celebration, I think. Jak! Run to your father's and get four jugs of his very best beer. The very best, do you hear me?"

Jak ambled out of the kitchen in his slow, oxen way. As soon as he was gone, Jon leaned over the table and whispered: "I have a plan, my boy. I happen to know that Jak is sweet on a girl from the village. Plain-looking, dull-witted thing called Jil. She seems to love him back, for some reason. He has no property, of course, and neither has she. Now here's the plan. I ask her as an apprentice. She'll say yes, because she wants to be with Jak. So with a little luck, there'll be babies in less than a year. And then we have them! We have them forever! They can't support a family on their own – they have to either stay on the farm or split up. Now no family wants to be split up, so they'll stay on the farm. For life! Whatever we'll make them do—they won't leave. We'll virtually have slaves, without even paying for them! Now that's a plan, eh? Eh? I may not be a man of culture but I'm pretty smart all the same, eh?"

Godfrey and Jennifer looked at him with open disgust, but Jon either didn't notice or didn't care. He was far too pleased with the course of events. He seemed positively invigorated by what he saw as the return of his son. Within a week he had taken on Jil as an apprentice and started clearing a new field, with the help of Jak and the mule. It was a bit late in the season for that, but with a little luck they could get some fast-growing crops in before the fall.

Jon took his son everywhere. He made a big deal of treating the boy as an equal, as a business partner. It was always "*We* have room for a new apprentice", "What shall *we* plant in our new field" and "Are *we* tired yet? Eh, boy? Thought not. Being tired is something for the likes of Jak, here, but not for *us*, eh? Not for men of property!"

In short, now it was Jon's turn to have one of the happiest times of his life. Godfrey and Jennifer seemed to have faded into the background; Max's cultural education ground to a standstill. Jon had his boy all to himself.

For a while, anyway.

Grandma Jennifer wasn't much interested in giving up. One night, when Max was in bed and his father had gone to sit under Mik's tarp, she slipped into Max's bedroom and woke him up.

"Grandma? What's the matter?"

"Nothing, dear. I just want to give you something."

It was a piece of paper, of course.

It was the yellowed note in his mother's handwriting.

V. Emily's Note

"I don't want it, Grandma."

"Hush. I'll tell you a little secret; *then* you can tell me whether you want it or not. A secret about this note."

"What?"

"It's a letter. A letter to you, left where you might find it. Do you think Emily would have written it if she didn't think you could figure it out?"

The boy didn't reply; unless you count a mute, starry-eyed gaze as a reply of sorts.

"Read it, my dear. Figure it out and read it. And remember: your mother was a Tinkerer. To read it, you must think like a Tinkerer."

Max was eleven years old now. He had seen his father dealing with men from the village; he had seen his grandfather talking to patients. He knew enough now to realize that Grandma Jennifer was holding something back. He even knew enough to understand that he would never coax it out of her. "Think like a Tinkerer" was the only hint he would get.

So he set to work, staring at the note again.

Instinctively, he hid it from his father. It wasn't a letter for Jon; it was a letter for Max.

Think like a Tinkerer, he kept telling himself, you'd better stinking well think like a Tinkerer.

Easier said than done.

There was nothing tinkerish about the note. Tinkerers used machines, not words. Words belonged to Storysingers. Maybe there was some sort of machinery hidden in the paper? Now that was a dumb idea – there wasn't room. Maybe there was a hidden ink?

He sprinkled the paper with every sort of substance he could think of – alcohol from Grandpa's still, vinegar, water, sugar (honey, really), milk, salt, molten butter...

All this only had the rather predictable effect of making the words completely illegible.

215

In a last desperate attempt, he burned the note.

This left him with a very small heap of ashes.

So. No hidden devices in the note.

Maybe it had to do with the words themselves? He knew them by heart now and he pondered them night and day. While working in the field with dad, while eating, while lying in his bed in the attic, looking at the silent, time-blackened beams of the roof...

Think like a Tinkerer, think like a Tinkerer!

It finally came when he was thinking about something else. When he was, in fact, thinking like a Tinkerer.

He was carrying two buckets of dung to the newly-cleared field, thinking: I wish I had a wheelbarrow. Jon had a mule-cart, but that wasn't used for dung; it was used for either hay, or for riding around looking grand. You can look tolerably grand in a cart smelling of hay, but not in one smelling of dung. So for dung, the buckets were used.

If I had a wheel, I could make a wheelbarrow, Max thought. Maybe I can cut the bottoms of the buckets, nail them together, put some sort of axle in there...

He knew he wasn't actually going to do it, but he liked the idea. Take apart one machine, made for carrying things, to build another machine for carrying.

I am thinking like a Tinkerer, he thought. Who but a Tinkerer would think of a bucket as a machine?

To a Tinkerer, *everything* is a machine.

Then it struck him: even a word is a machine. A tiny machine for carrying meaning like a bucket carries dung.

He stood as still as a stone, mouth wide open with astonishment. He knew he'd solved the riddle; the rest was easy. Because words, like any machine, had parts you could take to build another machine with. The letters were the parts and what you made with them was a new word. You could substitute a bucket-bottom for a wheel, so why could you not substitute an A for a D, for instance?

His mother's letter to him had started with: "Vwsj Esp". If it was a letter to him, wouldn't that mean "Dear Max"? Of course it would! The capitals were in the right places, and in both the places where there would be an A, there were now S-es.

From there on, it was easy. Within half an hour, he had the message in his head:

Dear Max,
If you are reading this you have the mind of a Tinkerer unless my mother has told you of the Caesar cipher, in which case I shall never talk to her again.

If you have the mind of a Tinkerer, instead of a stinking goat, you are more my child than your father's. In that case, I and Uncle Bud would love to see you, and be with you, and teach you the art of Tinkering.

Yes, be with you. I know they will tell you that I am dead. I am not. I am leaving your worthless father and going to live somewhere else with Bud. I can't take you with me.

I wish I could! You grandparents will stay in Jonsboro to look after you. I know they will. I will tell Jennifer where you can find us. Do not ask Godfrey; he won't know.

Please come, my child! I long to look upon you, and call you my own.

217

Love,
Your devoted mother
Emily

The cloudless sky was already darkening, but it was still warm. An oppressive heat; you could feel the power Elektrick building up in the sky. That was very good: the dry earth thirsted for a thunderstorm. But it would be a while yet.

Jon was away, getting drunk under Mik's tarp. Godfrey was away, looking after a patient. Jak and Jil were asleep, or at least in bed.

A small figure quietly moved out of the farmhouse and made for the dry, rustling weeds. It carried a heavy backpack and an iron-bound suitcase.

"Did you read the letter?" Grandma asked from the shadows.

Max nodded.

"You didn't come to me. How could you find your mother if I didn't tell you where she..." but the look in his eyes stopped her dead.

"You're not going to look for her?" she gasped.

"Who," Max asked coldly, "is Bud?"

Jennifer was quiet for a while. Then she took a deep breath, as if she had made some sort of decision. "Bud is Jak's brother. He may also be your father, for all I know."

"Was he an apprentice, like Jak?"

"Yes."

"And my mother loved him?"

"Yes. He was very pretty. Very pretty. Easy to fall in love with."

"And he loved her?"

"I hope so, but I am not sure. She was... well, *I* think she was lovely, but few men did. Jon mostly wanted her to show how well-off he was. To show he could afford to marry a woman unsuited for farm work. A "useless" woman, as he called her." Tears ran down her face. To hear her sweet, clever Emily called useless! "And Bud, well... to him she may have meant a way out of Jonsboro, and little more." She sobbed a few times.

Max smiled bitterly. "You were all thinking like Tinkerers, eh? She was a machine. A status machine. A money-and-travel machine."

"Yes," Jennifer sighed, "It seems poor Emily was the only one who didn't think like a Tinkerer. Ironic, really."

"Yes she did! You all did!" His anger lashed out like a whip. "*I* was your machine! She saw me as a getting-in-the-way-between-her-and-Bud machine, and she only wants me back if I turn out to be a Tinkering machine! And you, and Jon, and Godfrey, you all want me to be a following-in-your-footsteps machine. Well I won't."

"I don't... I didn't..." but she knew he wasn't as wrong as she liked to think.

"You were the worst," he hissed. "To you, I'm a proving-Jon-wrong machine and a getting-back-together-with-Emily machine."

She suddenly noticed she was on her knees, crying her despair at the sullen, suffocating sky. "Not fair," she wept. "I love you, I love you so much!" but he had already disappeared down the secret path between the weeds.

"Come back," she shouted. "Come back, I can guide you! I know where it is!" She knew where he wanted to go; it is man's fate always to follow the most impossible dream his mind will hold.

Her offer brought him back.

"You do? I thought that was just a Storysinger's boast."

She was ready to claim anything: "No, no, I really have seen it. Let me pack my things, and I'll go with you. I'll do anything for you. I'll make up, I swear I will make up for all the lies and the... I'll lead you there. I'll take you to the Shining City."

So they set off, Grandma the guide-machine and her dear Max, who had finally learned how to think like a Tinkerer.

Winter's Tales

By John Michael Greer

1. Christmas Eve 2050

Jane tucked the pie into the oven, wound the timer, and found herself blinking back tears. It was going to be a good Christmas this year, for the first time in too long. For once they'd been able to get a Christmas ham, and though they'd had to hoard ration coupons all year to do it, she didn't regret all those dinners of squash and beans from the garden out back. There were presents for the children, candles for the table, more than enough food for everybody: just like old times.

It wasn't just Christmas, either: life was good, better than it had been since before the war. She and Joe both had good jobs at the metal recycling plant down the street; she did bookkeeping, and he'd just been promoted to shift foreman. Nothing the plant used was likely to hubbert any time soon, too, so their jobs would be around for a while. Inflation was

221

low enough you hardly noticed it, not much more than thirty per cent a year since the latest currency reform. Food still cost too much, but you could count on getting it, and electricity was cheaper now that the new solar plant was online most of the time.

"Honey?" Joe's voice, calling from the living room. "Everybody's ready."

"I'm on my way," She took off the oven mitts and went out of the kitchen to where Joe and the children were waiting.

Memories from childhood jarred against the cramped little living room, the one bare light bulb hanging from the middle of the ceiling, the radio playing tinny holiday music in one corner. Back then, Christmas meant snow, colored lights, the balsam scent of a Christmas tree, crowds of relatives from all over, TV and internet entertainment blaring in the background. All of that was long gone. Snow hadn't fallen once since the big methane spike in '24 sent the climate reeling. Electricity cost too much to waste, and nobody cut down trees these days, though it wasn't a labor camp offense any more, the way it was when fuel ran short during the war. Traveling across country was for soldiers, prisoners, government officials, and the very rich; TVs were too expensive for most people, and the government and the army hoarded what was left of the internet after e-warfare and electricity shortages got through with it. Still, there were cards and decorations on the Christmas shelf, and stockings to hang beneath.

They always opened one special present each on Christmas eve, but stockings had to go up first, and that brought a sad moment. She and Joe hung theirs, then stepped aside for Joe Jr. He had three stockings in his hands: one for himself and two for the children they'd lost. With all the solemnity a twelve-year-old could muster, he put the stockings on their hooks: one for him; one for Cathy, who died age three from drug-resistant pneumonia; one for Brett, who died age seven when the hemorrhagic fever came through in '45. Then he stepped aside, too, and turned to look at the fourth person there.

Molly wasn't Jane's daughter, though it was hard for both of them to remember that sometimes. She was the child of their friends Bill and Erica. Bill was a derivatives salesman who got caught cooking his books in the crash of '41, went to labor camp, and died there. A very pregnant Erica moved in with Jane and Joe, gave birth to Molly, and lived with them until the same epidemic that killed Brett took her too. So Molly had three stockings of her own to hang. She was small for her eight years, and had to stretch to get the stockings on their hooks.

Once all the stockings were in place, Joe crossed the room to his armchair, sat down with a grin, and took four small packages from under the end table with the air of a magician pulling a rabbit out of a hat. Each one was wrapped in a bright scrap of cloth. Jane recalled wrapping paper from her own childhood, used once and thrown away, and wondered why anyone even in those days put up with such waste. Didn't people have anything better to do with all the money they used to have? Jane was more sensible; once the family's presents were unwrapped, the cloth wrappings went back to the quilt drawer where they came from.

Joe Jr. got his present unwrapped first. "Sweet," he said in awed tones. "Look at it." The slide rule sparkled as numbers slid smoothly past one another. He had a gift for math, so his teachers said, and he'd won a cheap slide rule in a contest when the government launched a Sustainability Initiative two years back. The government was always launching Sustainability Initiatives, but this one actually made some sense: pocket calculators cost close to a month's wages these days, and word on the street was that some of the minerals needed for the chips were about to hubbert, so Jane and Joe worked extra hours to afford a professional model. Joe Jr. would need tech skills and an exempt job to stay out of the army; even with the war over, going into the army meant coming home maimed or dead too often to take any chances.

The wrappings of Molly's present came open a moment later to reveal two books with bright flimsy covers. Jane caught the flicker of disappointment before the child put on a bright smile. Molly hadn't tested high enough to get into charter school, and since the war, that meant no school at all unless she could get her scores up next year. She was bright enough, and good at math, but reading was a challenge. One of the old women who kept themselves fed tending and teaching the local children guessed that Molly had dyslexia, but what exactly that meant and what could be done about it, Jane had never been able to learn. She gave Molly a hug, hoping she would understand.

She and Joe opened their presents, knowing that each contained something they already owned – one of Joe's ties and a pair of Jane's earrings, wrapped up late at night so the children wouldn't know. After the slide rule, Molly's books, and the ham, there wasn't money for more luxuries. The rest of the presents, the ones that would wait for morning, were clothes and other necessities. They always were; it would take much better times to change that.

A chime from the kitchen caught everyone's attention. "That's the pie," she said. "First one in to help set the table gets an extra slice." The slice was for Molly, of course, though Joe Jr. made a game of it, racing her into the kitchen and losing on purpose. Jane and Joe followed at a less hectic pace. The four of them had the table set in minutes: ham and applesauce, sweet potatoes, cabbage, mashed carrots, a plate of homemade Christmas candies, and the squash pie steaming over on the counter: more food in one place than Jane ever thought she'd see again during the worst years of the war, enough for everyone to get gloriously overfull for a change. The plates and silver were Bill and Erica's, real 20th century stuff.

They mumbled their way through grace, an old habit not yet quite put away. Jane and Joe had belonged to one of the Christian churches years back, but drifted away around the time the last traces of religion got shouldered aside in favor of political propaganda for one of the prewar parties, she didn't remember which. These days, you saw a lot of churches lying empty or converted to something else. Most of the really religious people Jane knew belonged to some other faith, Buddhist, Gaian, Seven Powers, or what have you. She'd thought more than once recently about visiting the Gaian church up the street. The Gaians took care of their own, and that appealed to her a good deal.

She loaded her plate with food, glanced at the window. Warm December rain spattered against it, blurred the windows of the apartment building across the street into vague yellow rectangles and turned the unlit street into pure darkness. Joe Jr. chattered about the slide rule and his hopes of getting an apprenticeship with an engineer someday. Jane glanced across the table at Molly, then, and saw past the taut smile to the too familiar look of disappointment in her eyes.

Somehow that was the thing that brought the memories surging back up: memories of Christmases from Jane's childhood, when her family lived in a sprawling suburban house with its own big yard and the world still seemed to work. She remembered snowmen in the yard and sled tracks down the street; the big Christmas tree in the corner of a living room bigger than their apartment was now, sparkling with lights and decorations; dinners where even the leftovers made a bigger meal than anyone could eat; driving—in a car, like rich people!—to a bright sprawling space called a shopping mall, where anything you could think of could be bought for money you didn't even have yet; gifts that didn't have to have any use in the world except the delight they brought to some child's eyes; all the extravagant graces of a world that didn't exist any more.

Tears welled up again, but they were tears of anger. *Why, goddammit?* She flung the question at the memories, the bright clean well-fed faces of her childhood. *Why did you have to waste so much and leave so little?*

Joe saw the tears, but misread them. "Beautiful, isn't it? Just like old times."

She kept her smile in place with an effort. "Yes. Yes, of course."

2. Solstice 2100

Bits of windblown rubbish clattered down the street as Molly reached for the doorlatch. She'd been at church most of the day helping get everything ready for the solstice ritual, and had come home now only because the boy would be back from school soon and would need some getting ready himself. For that matter, she had a few preparations of her own to make, and one more than anything else. She opened the door, closed it quick behind her to keep dust out.

Once inside she took off coat and dust scarf, shook out hair the color of old iron, brushed dust off her hands: no water to spare for washing them, not since autumn rains failed this year. Still, the little two-room shack was as clean as dry rags and a meticulous eye could make it. The few furnishings she had—table and two chairs, cooking stove, cupboard, washboard and washtub—glinted in the vague light from the four small windows; not a spot of rust on any of them, and not because the blacksmith who made them used some fancy metal, either. Good plain salvaged iron kept if you took care of it, and it didn't put a burden on Earth Mother or stray into the extravagance that got Old Time people in so much trouble with Her.

Knowing the boy would be home soon, she went into the bedroom right away, stepped past the two iron bedsteads to the room's far end and unlocked one of the trunks there. Homespun was good enough for everyday but holidays called for better. She considered, chose a dress the color of Earth Mother's own good green, set it on her bed. That would do. A small box inside the trunk gave up a pair of earrings with bright stones—her mother's, worn only on special days. Then, from the bottom of the trunk, she pulled a package wrapped in coarse brown cloth. Her hands shook a bit as she set it on the bed next to the dress.

A few minutes later, dressed for holiday, she came out of

227

the bedroom and put the package on the table. Clatter of the latch told her she was just in time. The door flew open, letting in a cloud of dust and a boy, brown-haired and barefoot, in clothes that had seen many better days.

"Earth's sake, Joe, shut the door!" she chided. "You'll let all the dust off the street in with you."

"Yes'm." Abashed, the boy pulled the door shut, submitted to a thorough dusting with the cleanest of the rags. "There," Molly said. "How was school today?"

That got her a sullen look. "I don't want to go any more."

She said nothing, pursed her lips. "I don't," the boy repeated. Then, in a rush of words: "Pacho doesn't have to go to school any more. He works for his brother the savager."

"Salvager," she corrected.

"Everybody says it 'savager'."

"You can say it however you want with your friends, but at home we speak good English."

Joe gave her an angry look. "*Sal*-vager. That's what his brother does, stripping metal in the towers, and Pacho helps him. He says his mom's happy 'cause he's bringing money home."

"Because."

Another look, angry and ashamed at the same time. "Because he's bringing money home. I bet I could make as much as he does, 'stead—" He caught himself, glared at her. "Instead of sitting in old man Wu's house and learning stuff that doesn't matter any more anyway."

So, Molly thought, it's come to this already. "It matters more now than it used to, back in Old Time. You look at Pacho now, and you think he's got a trade, he makes money, and that's the end of it. But all he'll ever be is a salvager. You deserve better."

He said nothing, met her gaze with a hard flat look. That angered her more than anything he could have said. "You think school doesn't matter," she snapped. "You don't know how many times I cried because I didn't get to go to school, or how many times I did without because the jobs I could get without schooling paid barely enough to live on. And I promised your mother—" She hadn't meant to bring up Linny, now of all times, but no point in trying to unsay it. "I promised your mother you'd get an education and I'm not going to break that promise."

Joe looked away, his face reddening, and Molly berated herself inwardly for mentioning his parents. That had to sting, though Earth Mother knew there were plenty of families in the same case these days, young and old with no blood relation living together under one roof after plague and famine and two civil wars finished with the people they called family beforehand. At least she'd known Jeff and Linny back when Joe was born, had changed his diapers and fed him goat milk from a bottle often enough to feel like some sort of family.

Only one way to mend things, she decided. She'd meant to wait until after church, but that couldn't be helped. She went to the table. "Come over here. I want to show you something."

He came after a moment, still looking away, trying to hide the wetness on his cheeks. Molly unwrapped the package, revealing an old book and a long thin shape in a case of cracked black plastic. "What's that?" Joe asked.

"Take a look."

He picked the case up, gave her a wary glance, opened it.

229

The slide rule caught the light as he took it out, black and red numbers still crisp on the white body. "Hoo! Where'd you savage this?"

She let it pass. "I didn't. That belonged to my brother Joe. When he died in the war, the army tried to send his things to my mother. We were in the refugee camp by then, but one of the families who stayed behind in our neighborhood kept the package for us until the fighting was over and we came back. And this—" She pointed to the book. "This was just about the only thing that didn't get looted from our apartment. It's one of Joe's schoolbooks, and it teaches how to use a slide rule like this one. You need to stay in school so you can learn to read it."

"I can read better than anybody in my class."

"You can't read this." Meeting his angry look calmly: "Try it."

That was a gamble—she couldn't read more than a few words out of the boy's schoolbooks, for that matter—but as he flipped through the pages and his shoulders hunched further and further up, she knew she'd won it. "Tom Wu says you're a better reader than anyone in your class, too. That's why it's important for you to stay in school, so you can learn to read this and books like it. Do you know what my brother was going to do with his slide rule? He wanted to be an engineer, before they drafted him. He wanted to make solar engines."

"Like the old rusty ones by the mill?"

"Yes. Nobody knows how to build them any more, or even how to make the old ones work. Maybe you could figure that out. People would be glad to get electricity again, you know."

She watched his face, waited for the right moment, as dreams collided somewhere back behind his eyes, Joe-the-salvager against Joe-the-engine-maker, Joe-the-bringer-of-electricity. "That's why," she said, "I decided to give these to you." That got a sudden look, wide-eyed, no trace of the sullen anger left. "But," Molly went on, holding up one finger, "only if you promise me you'll stay in school. They would be wasted on a salvager. They should go to someone who'll learn how to do something with them."

Joe opened his mouth, closed it, swallowed. "Okay," he forced out.

"You promise you'll stay in school? All the way through?"

"I promise."

Molly allowed a smile, indicated the book. "Then they're yours. You can keep them in your trunk until you know what to do with them." He picked up the book and the wrapping cloth, gave her an uncertain look, as though half expecting her to take them back. "While you're putting them there," she said then, "you should get something nicer to wear, too, and quickly. We shouldn't be late for church, especially not on solstice day."

"Yes'm." He started toward the bedroom, stopped halfway there. "Didn't people use to give each other presents on solstice day?"

Memories jabbed at Molly: the apartment she'd grown up in, full of soft furniture and the glow of electric light, scent of a big holiday dinner wafting from the kitchen, new clothes every year and Christmas stockings with real candy in them, and the look on her brother's face when he got the slide rule that Christmas when she was eight. People had so much back

231

then! "Yes," she told the boy. "Yes, we did."

His face grew troubled. "But wasn't that wicked?"

"No." Was it? She pushed the thought away. "There was plenty of wickedness in Old Time, all that extravagance, and next to nobody sparing so much as a thought for Mother Earth that gave them life. But I don't think it was wicked for my mother and father to give Joe a slide rule."

Joe took that in. "Then this'll be my solstice present," he announced, and took it into the bedroom.

3. Nawida 2150

"Mes Joe? She kee."

The old man looked up from his book, saw the boy's smiling brown face at the door. "Da Manda Gaia?"

"Ayah, en da gran house. Habby Nawida!" He grinned and scampered off. Joe closed the book and rose slowly to his feet, wincing at the familiar pain, as the habits of a lifetime picked at the boy's words. Nawida, that was from old Spanish "Navidad." Ironic that the name remained, when the faith it came from was no more than a memory now. Half the words in Alengo were like that, tenanted with the ghosts of old meanings like some haunted building in the old ruins.

He got his cane and a bundle wrapped in cloth, looked out the open door to make sure the rain would hold off a little longer. Out past the palms and mango trees, dark clouds billowed against the southern sky. Those promised another round of monsoon within a day or so, but overhead the sky was clear and blue all the way to space. He nodded, left the little thatched house and started down the broad dirt path that passed for the little village's main street.

Ghosts, he said to himself as a pig trotted across the way, heading off into the rich green of the fields and the jungle beyond them. Alengo itself—that had been "our lingo" back when it was a makeshift pidgin born on the streets of a half-ruined city. Half Spanish, half English, half Mama Gaia knew what, that was the old joke, but the drought years turned it into a language of its own. These days people spoke Alengo all along the coast from Tenisi west to the plains, and only a few old fools like Joe kept English alive so that somebody could still read the old books.

He wondered what old Molly would have thought of that. She'd spent most of his childhood bribing and browbeating him into learning as much as she thought he could, and went to Mama Gaia convinced she hadn't done enough. He hadn't expected to step into old Tom Wu's footsteps as the village schoolteacher, either, but somehow things turned out that way. Ghosts, he said to himself again. It wasn't just the language that they haunted.

Off to the left a stream that didn't exist at all in the drought years splashed its way between jagged lumps of concrete and young trees. There stood the grandest and saddest ghost of all, the little brick building they'd raised for the waterwheel-driven generator. What a project that was! Dan the blacksmith, ten years in the earth now, did all the ironwork just for the fun of it, and a dozen others helped put up the building, craft the waterwheel, and wind the coils. Even the village kids helped, scrounging wire from the old ruins.

They got it working, too, turning out twelve volts DC as steady as you please. That was when reality started whittling away at the dream of bringing back Old Time technology, because they didn't have a thing they could do with that current. Light bulbs were out of reach—Joe worked out the design for a vacuum pump, but nobody could craft metal to those tolerances any more, never mind trying to find tungsten for filaments or gases for a fluorescent bulb—and though he got an electric motor built and running after a lot more savaging, everything anyone could think of to do with it could be done just as well or better by skilled hands with simpler tools.

Then someone savaged an Old Time refrigerator with coolant still in the coils. For close on twenty years, that was the generator's job, keeping one battered refrigerator running so that everyone in the village had cold drinks in hot weather and milk that didn't sour. That refrigerator accomplished one thing more, though, before it finally broke down for good—it taught Joe the difference between a single machine and a viable technology. It hurt to admit it, but without an industrial system backed with cheap energy to churn out devices it could run, twelve volts of electricity wasn't worth much.

When the refrigerator rattled its last, then, Joe bartered the copper from the wire—worth plenty in trade by then—for books for the village school. He'd done well by it, too, and brought home two big dictionaries and a matched set of books from Old Time called the Harvard Classics, written by authors nobody in the village had ever heard of. His students got plenty of good English prose to wrestle with, and the priestess borrowed and copied out one volume from the set because it was by one of the minor Gaian saints, a man named Darwin, and no one else had ever seen a copy. Still, he'd kept one loop of wire from the generator as a keepsake, and left another on Molly's grave.

234

A voice broke into his thoughts: "Ey, Mes Joe!" A young man came past him, wearing nothing but the loincloth most men wore these days. Eddie, Joe remembered after a moment, Eddie sunna Sue—hardly anybody used family names any more, just the simple mother-name with a bit of rounded English in front. "Tu needa han?" Eddie said. Before Joe could say anything, he grinned and repeated his words in English: "Do you need any help?"

That got a ghost of a smile. "No, I'm fine. And glad to see you didn't forget everything I taught you. How's Emmie?"

"Doing fine. You know we got a baby on the way? I don't know if you got anything in your books about keeping a mother safe."

"Sharon should have everything I do. Still, I'll take a look." Sharon was the village healer and midwife, and all three of her medical books came by way of Joe's school library, but the reassurance couldn't hurt. Emmie was Eddie's second wife; the first, Maria, died in childbirth. That happened less often than it used to—Sharon knew about germs and sanitation, and used raw alcohol as an antiseptic no matter how people yelped about how it stung—but it still happened.

"Thanks! I be sure they save you a beer." Eddie grinned again and trotted down the street.

Joe followed at his own slower pace. The street went a little further and then widened into a plaza of sorts, with the covered marketplace on one side, the Gaian church on another, and the village hall—the gran house, everyone called it—on a third. Beyond the gran house, the ground tumbled down an uneven slope to the white sand of the beach and the sea reaching south to the horizon. A few crags of concrete rose out of the water here and there, the last traces of neighborhoods that had been just that little bit too low when the seas rose. Every year the waves pounded those a bit lower; they'd be gone soon, like so many of the legacies of Old Time.

Another irony, he thought, that what brought disaster to so many had been the salvation of his village and the six others that huddled in the ruins of the old city. It took the birth of a new sea to break the drought that once had the whole middle of the continent in its grip. Another ghost hovered up there in the great thunder-gray billows to the south—the day the monsoon clouds first came rolling up over the sea and dumped rain on the parched and dusty land. He'd been out in the plaza with everyone else, staring up at the clouds, smelling the almost-forgotten scent of rain on the wind, dancing and whooping as the rain came crashing down at last.

There had been some challenging times after that, of course. The dryland corn they grew in the drought years wouldn't handle so much moisture, and they had to barter for new seed and learn the way rice paddies worked and tropical fruit grew. Too, the monsoons hadn't been so predictable those first few years as they became later: Mama Gaia testing them, the priestess said, making sure they didn't get greedy and stupid the way people were in Old Time. Joe wasn't sure the biosphere had any such thing in mind—by then he'd read enough Old Time books that the simple faith Molly taught him had dissolved into wry uncertainties—but that time, at least, he kept his mouth shut. People in Old Time *had* been greedy and stupid, even the old books admitted that, and if it

236

took religion to keep that from happening again, that's what it took.

He crossed the little plaza, went into the gran house. The solemn part of Nawida was over, the prayers said to Mama Gaia and all the saints, and the bonfire at midnight to mark the kindling of the new year; what remained was feasting and fun. Inside, drums, flutes and fiddles pounded out a dance tune; young women bare to the waist danced and flirted with young men, while their elders sat on the sides of the hall, sipping rice beer and talking; children scampered around underfoot, bare as the day they were born. People waved greetings to Joe as he blinked, looked around the big open room, sighted the one he needed to find.

He crossed the room slowly, circling around the outer edge of the dancing, nodding to the people who greeted him. The one he'd come to meet saw him coming, got to her feet: a young woman, black-haired, wearing the plain brown robe of the Manda Gaia. Hermandad de Gaia, that had been, and likely still was west along the coast where Alengo gave way to something closer to old Spanish; Fellowship of Gaia was what they said up north where something like English was still spoken. The Manda Gaia was a new thing, at least to the Gaian faith, though Joe knew enough about history to recognize monasticism when he saw it.

"You must be the schoolteacher," the woman said in flawless English, and held out a hand in the Old Time courtesy. "I'm Juli darra Ellen."

"Joe sunna Molly." He took her hand, shook it. "Yes. Thank you for agreeing to come."

"For three years now we've talked of sending someone here to see you, since we first got word, so your letter was very welcome." She motioned him to a seat on the bench along the wall. "Please. You look tired."

He allowed a smile, tried to keep his face from showing the sudden stab of pain as he sat. "A little. Enough that I should probably come straight to the point." He held out the cloth-wrapped bundle. "This is a gift of sorts, for the Manda Gaia."

The cloth opened, revealing a battered book and a narrow black case. She glanced at the spine of the book, then opened the case and pulled out the old slide rule.

"Do you know what it is?" Joe asked her.

"Yes." Carefully, using two fingers, she moved the middle section back and forth. "I've read about them, but I've never seen one. Where did you find it?"

"It's been in my family for around a hundred years." That was true in Alengo, at least, where "mi famli" meant the people you grew up with, and "mi mama" the woman who took care of you in childhood; like everyone else, he'd long since given up using Old Time terms of relationship. "The book explains how it's used. I can't claim to be an expert, but I've done some respectably complex math on it."

"This thing is precious," she said. "I'll take it to our mother house in Denva, have it copied by our craftspeople there, and bring it back to you."

"That won't be necessary. I don't think it'll be possible, either." He met her gaze. "Cancer of the bowels," he said then. "Not the way I would have chosen to go, but there it is. It's been close to three years now, and by the time you get to Denva and back I'll most likely be settling down comfortably in the earth."

"Mama Gaia will take you to Her heart." Seeing his

smile: "You don't believe that."

"I think the biosphere has better things to worry about than one old man."

"Well, I won't argue theology."

That got another smile. "Pity." Then: "I have one other thing to ask, though. I hear quite a bit about the Manda Gaia these days. They say you have schools in some places, schools for children. For the last twenty years all my best pupils have gone into the church, and there's nobody here to replace me. I'd like to see someone from your order take over the school when this thing gets the better of me. I wish I could say that's a long way off."

She nodded. "I can send a letter today."

"Thank you. You've made a cynical old man happy, and that's not a small feat." The dance music paused, and in the momentary hush he fancied he could hear another, deeper stillness gathering not far off. He thought about the generator again, and the concrete crags battered by the waves, and wondered how many more relics of Old Time would be sold for scrap or washed away before the world finished coming back into balance.

Contributors

John Michael Greer is the author of more than thirty books, including four books on peak oil and one science fiction novel, *The Fires of Shalsha*, as well as the weekly peak oil blog *The Archdruid Report*. A native of the Pacific Northwest, he now lives in an old red brick mill town in the north central Appalachians with his wife Sara.

David Trammel is a moderator at the GreenWizard.Org website, where he helps people learn how to make the changes in their life to survive and prosper in the coming Post Peak world. Stop by and join the community.

Kieran O'Neill is a South African studying towards his PhD in bioinformatics in Vancouver, Canada. When not writing about or contemplating the future as our civilization bumps into hard ecological limits, he brews gluten free beer, grows organic vegetables in a back-alley container garden, and volunteers with the local bike co-op.

Susan Harelson lives on the front range of Colorado with her husband and two children. She works at a middle school where she continually has her hope for the future renewed.

E. A. Freeman lives with his family somewhere between North Carolina's Triangle and the Triad regions, on a three-sided property, and is himself something of a square. When he's not paying the bills working in Information Technology, he pursues idyllic notions about being a writer, a small farmer, and a loving husband and father, with occasional success.

Catherine McGuire is a writer and artist with a deep interest in philosophy and ecology. Her poetry chapbook, *Palimpsests*, was published by Uttered Chaos in 2011, and two children's science fiction novels were published by TSR in 1984 & 1985. She lives in Sweet Home, Oregon on a mini-homestead, with chickens.

Harry J. Lerwill was raised in a poor mining village in the South Wales Valleys, where family values, the joys of home-grown and home-cooked meals, and a deep community spirit far outweighed the bleak prospects of life with collapsed fossil fuel industry: coal mining. Three decades later, he is an I.T. Manager in California, choosing to walk, rather than fall, down the far side of Hubbert's peak, and looking forward to those same benefits as we rediscover the joys of a slower lifestyle.

Avery Morrow was ordained an Archdruid at Carleton College. He is currently studying alternative history and traditionalism in Japan, under the premise of teaching English.

Randall S. Ellis is sixty-one year old reader of books and a first-grade teacher.

Thjis Goverde was born in the Dutch town of Nijmegen and lives there to this day, with his girlfriend and their two kids. Having attained a Masters degree in philosophy, he makes a living as an author of childrens books, doing some stand-up comedy on the side. This is the first time he has published in English.

Philip Steiner is a proud father of two, a software developer and a budding science fiction author who lives in Richmond, British Columbia, Canada. This story marks his first professional publication. When he isn't hacking code or worrying about all the ways civilization might end, he reluctantly submits to his wife's penchant for poetry slams and outings to the beach. He won't admit it, but he actually does enjoy getting away from the keyboard.

J.D. Smith's third collection of poetry, *Labor Day at Venice Beach*, was published in August 2012, and his first humor collection, *Notes of a Tourist on Planet Earth*, is forthcoming. His other books include the essay collection *Dowsing and Science* (2011) and the children's picture book *The Best Mariachi in the World* (2008). He lives and writes in Washington, DC.

Printed in Great Britain
by Amazon.co.uk, Ltd.,
Marston Gate.